The COLOR
of
FOREVER

D1558647

By
Julianne MacLean

Text copyright © 2016 Julianne MacLean
All rights reserved.

ISBN: 1927675340
ISBN-13: 9781927675342

Ah! what pleasant visions haunt me
As I gaze upon the sea!
All the old romantic legends,
All my dreams, come back to me.
　　　　—Henry Wadsworth Longfellow, "The Secret of the Sea"

Katelyn

CHAPTER

One

❦

I've often heard that a close brush with death can cause your life to flash before your eyes in an instant. There was a time I didn't believe it, because how could all the experiences of a person's life possibly replay in his or her mind in such a short interval? Wouldn't your brain be occupied by the task of finding a way to save yourself?

Some say that such a flashback is brought on by a rush of adrenaline, which causes the brain to function at hyper speed. Have you ever been in a situation of shock and panic, where the disaster appears to occur in slow motion before your eyes, yet you can do nothing about it? When your body simply cannot keep up with the velocity of your perceptions?

In other situations, people have been known to take action with incredible strength and speed—lifting a car, for instance, to save a crushed child. How can that possibly occur? Is adrenaline truly that powerful?

Others theorize that the purpose is to help the person to access all his memories in order to find a way to save himself, or someone else. This seems logical to me, but who knows the true origins of such miracles?

All I can tell you is that I believe it is true. Life *can* flash before your eyes at the moment of impending death. I know it because I am one of those people who—while skirting death by a narrow margin—experienced a rush of adrenaline so potent that I glimpsed my entire lifetime, like slides flashing rapidly before my eyes. So who am I to doubt such a phenomenon?

What I fail to understand, however, is why I saw a life that was completely different from my own.

Oddly, the life I viewed in those fleeting seconds before the accident was not someone else's. The memories were all mine. I was the so-called protagonist in the show, confused as to why I felt such a deep, emotional connection to the people in my mind's eye, who were complete strangers to me. I felt a love and a longing for them, with as much emotion and clarity as any other momentous experience, yet little that was revealed matched the existence I'd known.

In reality, on that day I peddled up the mountain with my cycling club, I was a thirty-two-year-old, childless divorcee. I wish I could say I was emotionally secure, happy to be a single, independent woman, and optimistic about starting a new chapter in my life. But on that particular day—like most days recently—I had woken up feeling desperately alone, with a knot in my belly the size of a football. And more so, because my ex-husband had just remarried after receiving a fantastic promotion. All I wanted to do was get into my car, drive to his office, ride the elevator up fourteen floors and rant to his boss about what a louse he was.

Did they not understand that he was unreliable, dishonorable and self-absorbed? How could they promote him to a partner in their firm when he was a philandering cheater who couldn't be faithful to his first wife?

It boggled my mind that Mark always won. No matter who he stepped on, or who paid the price in tears, he always got what he wanted, then slept like a baby each night after enjoying the fruits of his labors—the luxury home, the trips to Barbados, the Mercedes and the beautiful wife who lay beside him in bed— probably wearing Victoria's Secret lingerie.

At one time, I was that privileged, beautiful wife—and oh, how he adored me in those early years. I was an up-and-coming celebrity television journalist in Seattle with a good chance of eventually becoming anchor on the evening news. While still in my twenties, I covered major political events and attended charity dinners with the mayor. Meanwhile, Mark was an ambitious criminal lawyer who loved showing me off at every opportunity, because I shone a bright light on us as a stylish Seattle couple.

I hesitate to use the word perfect—because nothing is ever perfect, right?—but that's how it felt, and that's certainly how others perceived us. At least until everything came crashing down like a jet spinning out of the sky.

I remember, precisely, the day the turbulence began, and it's rather unnerving that I can pinpoint the exact moment.

Mark and I had gone out for dinner with a few friends, and after they said goodnight and got into a cab, I stepped to the curb to flag down the next one, but Mark grabbed my arm and pulled me back.

"What are you doing?" he asked, glancing down the street. "It's barely midnight. Let's stay out."

My heart sank because it had been a busy week at work and I was ready for bed. Looking back on it, I'm sure I could have convinced him to head home by slipping my arms around his waist, smiling coquettishly and promising some fun and games in the bedroom, but as I mentioned, it had been a long week and I was spent. I wasn't in the mood for "sexy talk," so I said the absolute wrong thing with a tired sigh.

"Come on, Mark. We're not in college anymore. I'm done for the night. Besides, it's time to grow up. Let's leave the after-hours' partying to the twenty-somethings."

His head drew back and his eyebrows lifted. It was as if I had suggested we retire, downsize and move to Florida.

"You just want to go home? It's Friday night."

"I know..." I felt suddenly intimidated, inadequate. *Dull.* So I backpedaled and struggled to explain myself. "I'm sorry, but you know how stressful my week was. That story about the alcoholic bus driver really took its toll on me. I'm not up for more socializing. I just want to curl up on the sofa and watch TV."

Frustrated, he inhaled deeply and held his breath for a few seconds, then looked away, down the street again. "We watch TV every night, Katelyn. It's *Friday.* Don't you want to be a social butterfly?"

Maybe I was a tad irritable because it was late. Moreover, I loathed the fact that he wanted me to fake it and play a role, when I'd just explained how tired I was. I wished he felt the same way—that the idea of curling up on the sofa with me held at least *some* appeal.

I realized in that moment that for him, it was the worst kind of torture—to stay at home, just the two of us. Sure, there had been a time when I loved going out every weekend, but I was starting to grow away from that lifestyle. I preferred an early evening that didn't result in a pounding headache the next morning.

"Who are you hoping to see?" I asked. "The guys from work? Because I'm quite sure the partners are all at home with their wives and children. Isn't that what you aspire to? To take some time away from the rat race?"

He frowned. "What are you trying to say, Katelyn?"

I knew, by the challenging tone of his voice, that he knew exactly what I was trying to say. I'd been dropping hints for two years.

"Don't you think it's time we slowed down a little? I just turned thirty. You know I want to have kids, and if we're ever going to be parents, we can't be out partying till four in the morning every weekend."

He glanced around at the people walking past us on the sidewalk and lowered his voice. "I've told you, I'm not ready for that."

"So you've said. Many times."

I spoke loudly, heatedly, without concern for who might take notice, which was dangerous because, as I said earlier, we were recognizable in Seattle. Anyone could whip out a cell phone and start recording our argument. It could show up on YouTube within the hour.

Mark grabbed me by the arm and dragged me into the recessed doorway of a flower shop.

"I've been patient," I continued, roughly shaking his hand off my arm, "waiting for you to be ready, but I'm not getting any younger and neither are you. If we don't start trying soon, I'm going to be popping out my first kid when I'm forty."

His eyes widened with horror. "*Forty!*"

I laughed at him, bitterly. "What…? You think we'll never be forty? We *will* be, eventually, Mark, and that day's not that far off.

And guess what. We're going to be fifty some day, too. I'd like for our kids to at least be in middle school by then. Wouldn't you?"

He stared at me in disbelief for a moment, then raised his hand to stop me from saying anything more. "I don't want to talk about this right now."

"When *will* you want to talk about it?" I replied. "Because you always put it off. You change the subject. And for the record, I hate it when you put your hand in my face like that."

He turned away and strode to the curb. "Go home if you want, Katelyn. I'm staying out."

I scoffed resentfully, and followed him. He raised his arm to flag down a cab for me.

"Do you want this one?" he asked as it approached.

"Yes," I firmly replied. "I'm going home. Where are you going?"

He shrugged a shoulder and reached into his pocket for his phone. "I don't know yet. I need to see where people are." He searched through his texts.

I exhaled with defeat as the cab stopped in front of us. Suddenly, I wished the night weren't ending like this. We'd had such a great time at dinner, and Mark had been his most charming self. He sat next to me with his arm across the back of my chair, listening attentively as I talked about the bus driver story. And he was so impossibly handsome in that gray sweater I'd bought for him at Bergdorf Goodman, in New York. It matched his gray-blue eyes and made me remember why I'd fallen in love with him. *Was I crazy, leaving him like this, downtown at midnight on a Friday night?*

The cab driver waited until I opened the back door, but I hesitated before getting in. "Mark," I said more gently. "Why don't you come home with me? We can talk about this some more. Figure things out."

His eyes lifted briefly. "I told you, I don't want to talk about it tonight. Go home. Get in your pajamas. I'll see you later."

He returned his attention to his phone and began texting.

"Fine. Bye," I tersely said as I slid into the back seat and shut the cab door.

I watched him, still texting on the sidewalk as we drove off, but he never looked up. I wonder now if he had texted Mariah, the sexy, young articling clerk at his firm. I hadn't suspected anything at the time, but if I had known about her—known what she looked like and how all the men at the firm were drooling over her like schoolboys—might I have mustered the energy to stay out a few extra hours and suffer the headache the following morning?

Probably.

—⁂—

Much later that night, Mark slipped quietly into bed, working hard not to wake me. I lay with my back to him and pretended to be asleep, though I was fully aware that it was past 3:00 a.m. and he smelled like cigarette smoke. I wondered where he had been, but didn't want to start another fight, so I decided to wait until the morning to ask about his night.

When I woke, he was gone. At least he'd left me a note on the kitchen table to let me know he'd risen early to hit the gym. It wasn't unusual for him to work out on Saturday mornings— even with a hangover—so I simply let it go. I didn't bring up our argument again.

Three weeks later, I would come to regret that decision.

"I don't understand," I said as I followed Mark to the door where his suitcase was packed and waiting. "Maybe we hit a few rough patches lately, but I thought everything was fine. How can you just pack up and leave like this? Don't you even want to *try* to work things out?"

"Trust me. It's better this way," he replied as he reached hurriedly for his coat in the front hall closet. "There's no point dragging this out over months or even years."

"But…" I watched him slip his arms into the sleeves and check his pockets for his gloves. "You haven't even given me a chance to process this. I'm in shock, Mark. I come home from work and find you sitting on the sofa with your bags packed. Surely you're not serious. You're not going to leave right now."

"I am."

The chill in his tone made my stomach turn over with a sickening ball of dread. "How long have you been feeling this way?"

"A while," he replied, without hesitation, which came as a total shock to me.

"Wait…" I reached out to touch his arm, wanting to hold on to him. He was my husband and I loved him. We were supposed to be building a life together. I thought he was going to be the father of my children. "I know you weren't keen on the idea of having a baby," I said, "but we can talk about that. Maybe I've been pushing too hard lately. But I still don't understand how you suddenly decided, at the drop of a hat, to throw our entire marriage out the window."

"It's not at the drop of a hat," he replied irritably as he wrapped his Ralph Lauren scarf around his neck and bent to pick up his travel-sized suitcase. "I told you, I've been thinking about this for a while."

"But you never said anything." My heart began to thump heavily in my chest and perspiration beaded on my brow. *Was this really happening?* "I thought we were happy."

He rolled his eyes and shook his head, which caused a sudden rush of anger to thrash in my blood. I gritted my teeth, grabbed him roughly by the arm and forced him to look directly at me. "How long have you felt this way?"

He paused. "You and I both know it's gotten stale lately. A year maybe," he conceded at last.

I blinked a few times and spoke with rancor. "A year? And you think we're *stale*? What the hell does that mean?"

"It means we're not in love like we used to be. The spark's gone. Come on, Katelyn, there's no passion and you know it."

I let out a breath of shock. "No, I don't. I'm your wife and I was ready to have a baby with you. Now I find out that you're *not that into me*?"

This news was like a knife in my gut, because I'd always worked so hard to make Mark happy—to do all the things he enjoyed, like tennis and water skiing. I showed interest in his work and I was always supportive of what he wanted. I was never a nag and I never "let myself go," as far as appearances were concerned. I hadn't gained a single pound since the day we married, nor had I succumbed to the temptation of sweatpants, or wearing no makeup, or pulling my hair back in a ponytail on the weekends. I'd avoided all of that, for him.

"There's really no point in discussing this," he said, raising his hand in my face and turning away, moving toward the door. "It's over, Katelyn. There's nothing you can do to change it. It's better to make a clean, swift break, because I just don't want to be married anymore."

He opened the door and walked out, leaving me speechless and gasping in the front hall, unable to do anything but rush to the open doorway and stare as he drove away.

What I didn't know at the time was that he had driven straight to Mariah's apartment, where he'd already begun the paperwork for a legal separation. I received the documents not long after that.

"I can't believe it," I said to my best friend, Bailey, the moment she walked through my front door. "How could I *not* have known? Was I that oblivious to what was going on around me? Am I really that stupid? Or self-absorbed?"

I had called Bailey earlier to tell her what I'd just learned—that Mark had been unhappy in our marriage for over a year, and was having an affair with Mariah, the young clerk at his office.

Bailey had been my best friend since kindergarten, and there was no one in the world I trusted more than her. It came as no surprise when she immediately hopped in the car and drove over.

"I'm a cliché," I continued as I ushered her in and closed the door behind her. "He called a few times a week to say he had to work late, and I always believed him. I never questioned or suspected a thing. But every time he went to the gym, he was really working out with *her*. No wonder he spent so many hours there."

"You're not stupid or self-absorbed," Bailey replied as she removed her jacket and tossed it onto the upholstered bench next to the stairs. She walked with me to the kitchen where I'd already opened a bottle of wine. "He's just a really good liar."

I poured Bailey a glass and handed it to her. We regarded each other intensely for a moment before raising our glasses and clinking them together.

"To your freedom from a total jerk," Bailey said, then took the first sip.

I let out a heavy sigh and covered my eyes with a hand. Normally, I wasn't the crying type, but I felt like I'd been hit by a truck. Blindsided. My whole world was collapsing around me, but worst of all, the man I trusted had betrayed me, and he didn't love me anymore. He felt no desire for me, nor did he care about my feelings. It didn't matter to him that I was emotionally devastated and crying myself to sleep every night in our empty king-sized bed. I meant nothing to him.

I let out a small hiccup as I tried to suppress my tears. Bailey set down her glass and wrapped her arms around me.

"It's going to take some time," she gently said, "but you'll soon realize that you're better off without him. He wasn't the one for you."

"But he was so perfect," I replied, recalling the early years of our relationship, when we were head over heels in love. "At least I thought he was. He was everything a woman could ever want. He was unbelievably handsome and devoted—at first—not to mention that he made buckets of money. He was charming and funny and he drove a great car."

"He did look pretty good on paper," Bailey replied, stepping back and picking up her wine again.

"When we first started dating," I said, "I remember ticking off all those little boxes on the Great Husband Material List and believing I'd hit the jackpot, but now everything feels so superficial. What does all of that matter if you don't really know somebody?

If you're not truly connected—*in here*—like you should be?" I held my fist over my heart.

"He wasn't the one for you," she said, a second time.

"But is there really such a thing as *the one*?" I argued. "God, the world's such a big place. How do you ever find that one person, and how do you know they're it? I thought Mark was the one for me, but most of the time, I had no idea what was going on inside his head, and he didn't know what was going on inside of mine. I thought that was normal, because no one's a mind reader, right? You live together, you get to know each other pretty well, but you're still two separate people."

We moved into the living room and sat down on the sofa, facing each other from opposite ends.

"But the whole time," I continued, "it was like we were playing house, pretending to be each other's one and only, but we weren't really connected at all. We couldn't have been, or I would have known he wasn't happy." I sat forward and set my wineglass on the coffee table.

"Is that what all marriages are like?" I asked Bailey, thoughtfully. "Is it just a big act for everyone? After the initial passion wears off, do most people just pretend to be happy and in love as the years go by? Do they stay together for appearances, or because they signed a piece of paper that said 'until death do us part,' and feel as if they have no other choice?"

Bailey considered that for a moment. "I wish I had the answers, but I don't because I'm still single. All I have to go on is my parents, and they seem pretty happy—*genuinely* happy. I can tell by the way they look at each other sometimes. They share intimate, knowing looks and they still make each other laugh after all these years. I'm pretty sure it's the real thing."

"You're lucky," I replied. "My parents got on each other's nerves constantly and divorced when I was fourteen, so I don't really have much of an example to go by."

Bailey sipped her wine. "For what it's worth, I do think it's possible to find your soulmate and be happy together, forever."

I let out a sigh. "Maybe, in rare cases. And to tell you the truth, I would have been perfectly happy growing old with Mark if he'd been willing to stick it out and start a family. I'm sure he would have been a wonderful father. He would have taken our kids to the playground and taught our son how to throw a baseball. And he had such a great sense of humor. The family dinner table would have been lots of fun."

Bailey's eyebrows pulled together with a look of sympathy. "But he cheated on you, Katelyn, and he lied to you, so I think you need to stop idealizing him as your dream husband. That's just a fantasy because he probably wouldn't even have made it home for dinner most nights. He would have called to say he was going to be late."

I lowered my gaze and nodded. "You're right. I'm dreaming. He saw something shinier and younger and he broke our marriage vows to go after it. And I hate him for that—honestly, I do—and feeling that way is killing me because I did love him. Maybe I'm crazy, but in a way, I still do and part of me wants him back. I loved our life together. If only he could have loved me as much as I loved him, and wanted the same things."

I paused a moment and felt my throat close up again.

"But was it Mark that you loved?" Bailey asked. "Or was it the idea of married life?"

I buried my face in my hands and groaned with frustration. "I don't know, but either way, my heart is broken. He's ruined me for anyone else, because how will I ever trust someone not to do this to me again?"

"I'm so sorry," Bailey said with compassion. "I wish there was something I could say to make it better. To take the pain away."

"I wish there was, too," I replied, "but there's nothing anyone can say." I fought to collect myself. "I'm just going to have to get through this somehow and hope that in time, I'll get over him and find a way to move on."

We sat in silence for a long moment.

"Why can't people just *resist* the desire to cheat?" I asked heatedly, lifting my gaze. "I understand feeling attracted to someone different—that can happen—but why not just wait for it to pass? Exercise some self-discipline, for pity's sake. Go home and make love to your wife."

"I agree wholeheartedly," Bailey said with a nod. "You're absolutely right."

"And honestly, what marriage, after seven years, is still as passionate as it was in the first two? No relationship can sustain that kind of madness for an entire lifetime. But if you're committed to a life together, and you enjoy each other's company, shouldn't that be enough?"

"Absolutely."

My shoulders slumped with resignation. "I just wish Mark had been more willing to have a baby sooner. It might have given him something else to focus on besides himself." I lowered my eyes and shook my head. "Poor Mariah," I said, regarding Bailey in the warm lamplight. "I hope she knows what she's getting into. Because you know what they say: Once a cheater, always a cheater."

Bailey sighed with resignation. "I wonder if that will be true in his case."

"Only time will tell."

CHAPTER

Five

ᵕᶜᷜᐪᐪ

The thing I remember most about the crash—besides the strange, unfamiliar life that flashed before my eyes—was the sound of the cyclist's wheel a few lengths in front of me, clipping the wheel of another cyclist beside him. My awareness of the impact sent my blood racing through my veins with white-hot terror because we were traveling at a tremendous speed downhill, coasting around a bend with nothing but a guardrail to keep us from flying over the edge, into the ravine below.

Both riders' bikes began to wobble, and my heart exploded like a fireball in my chest.

Time stood still as the rider in front of me became tangled in a jungle of spokes and wheels and went flying over his handlebars.

In a panic, I squeezed my brakes and tried to swerve around the pileup, but everything was happening so fast, it was impossible to avoid it. Another rider went down in front of me and suddenly I was catapulted through the air, over a sea of carnage and mangled bicycles and spinning wheels.

In that instant, everything went silent and still as I flew toward the guardrail and steep cliff beyond. My husband's face appeared in my mind, but strangely, it wasn't Mark's face I saw. It was another man I didn't recognize, and yet I knew him intimately. He was a good man, a faithful man, the father of my child, who loved our son as deeply as I did. Our boy's name was Logan, and he was the most beautiful baby imaginable. After a long, hard labor, I held him in my arms and wept tears of joy and love, while my husband kissed the top of my head and told me how much he loved me.

Moments flashed by like shooting stars—incredible moments that filled me with exhilaration, euphoria and hope. Our son took his first steps at eleven months; my husband put together the swing set in the backyard; I said good-bye to Logan on the first day of preschool, went home and cried over the loss of his sweet presence in the house during school hours.

We spent summers in Maine, where Logan played on the beach and caught hermit crabs with his cousins.

My husband—*his name was Chris*—gave me diamond earrings for our fifth anniversary.

I was hesitant to have another child. A part of me was still searching, longingly…for something. I felt lonely but I didn't know why.

There was another man named Joe.

Chris was angry with me. He shouted and made threats on the phone.

My son seemed more tired than usual. *Was he coming down with something?*

Constant hospital visits…needles…blood work…medications…

Suddenly I saw myself here in this very place, flying over the guardrail into the ravine below and waking in intensive care the next day, confused and in pain. My back was broken. I was paralyzed from the waist down, concerned about how I would care for my sick child.

No….it can't happen like that. I have to be there for him. For Logan.

Somehow, with unfathomable strength and agility, I twisted my body downward and collided with the guardrail, which sent pain shooting into my skull but that shift in direction prevented me from tumbling down the steep rock face into the wooded ravine below.

When I opened my eyes, I was staring up at a rescue worker.

"Can you hear me?" he asked, shining a penlight in my eye. "Do you know your name? Do you know what day it is?"

While others writhed in agony on the road beside me, I managed to speak a few words. "Am I dead?"

He grinned with relief and sat back on his heels. "No, ma'am, you're just a little banged up. You fell off your bike and hit the guardrail. Your star must have been shining this morning, because you just missed going over the edge." He leaned forward again. "Now, can you tell me your name? And what day it is?"

"It's Friday," I said. "And my name is Katelyn Roberts."

"Good. Where do you live?"

I gave him my current address in Seattle—the house Mark had left to me in the divorce—then wondered suddenly if that was indeed my house, because all the images I'd seen as I was flying through the air had me living in a different house entirely. With a son named Logan and a husband named Chris. I could still see their faces vividly in my imagination.

"I must have blacked out," I said, trying to sit up and get my bearings, but the paramedic urged me to remain on my back.

"You sure did," he said. "You were unconscious for about fifteen minutes."

"I was dreaming, then." I glanced around at all the mangled bicycles and riders lying on the side of the road with cuts and bruises, then pressed the heel of my hand to my forehead. "Am I okay?"

"You're better than you were five minutes ago," he replied, "but you'll need to get checked out at the hospital. Another ambulance is on its way and we'll have a stretcher here in a minute or two. Just stay put, okay?"

Dazed, I blinked up at the sky. A part of me feared I might have broken my back, not because I was in pain, but because I remembered my wheelchair from the flashback—the black leather seat, the texture of the rubber wheels in my hands as I insisted upon rolling myself down the long hospital corridor in the recovery unit, rather than have someone push me.

Had that been a premonition?

"I need to call my mother," I said shakily, "and my friend Bailey." I felt desperate to speak to them and make sure I was the person I thought I was—a single, divorced television reporter who had been emotionally ravaged by her husband's affair and the divorce that followed.

Because the life that had flashed before my eyes as I faced death had been something else entirely.

Bailey was first to arrive at the hospital, while my mother had to travel all the way from Port Orchard. The paramedics had just brought me into the ER when Bailey hurried through the sliding glass doors and found me on a gurney with a neck collar and backboard.

"Oh, my gosh, Katelyn," she said, rushing to my side. "Are you okay?"

"I don't know," I replied. "I'm waiting to get checked out. The paramedic said the neck collar is just a precaution, but I'm really scared. What if it's bad? What if I can't walk?"

She gripped my hand and squeezed it. "Is there anything I can do? Have you called your parents yet?"

"Mom's on her way."

"Are you in any pain?"

"I'm achy from the fall and I have a few bad scrapes, but it could be worse. I'm just afraid that my back's broken or something."

She glanced around with concern. "Do you want me to get someone?"

"No, the paramedics are here to keep an eye on me. We just have to wait until a doctor can see me."

For a moment, neither of us knew what to say.

"What happened?" Bailey finally asked. "Did a car hit you or something?"

I explained what caused the crash—that a cyclist had accidentally clipped the wheel of another. Then I described how I went flying over my handlebars. "That's the weirdest part," I said. "You know how they say your life flashes before your eyes in the moment of death?"

"Yes."

"Well, that's exactly what happened, except that I saw a totally different life. I was still me, but…" I paused and swallowed uneasily while a pregnant woman walked past us. "Nothing was the same."

She frowned with bewilderment. "What do you mean, nothing was the same?"

I took a moment to shift slightly on the gurney and gather my thoughts. "I saw myself living a different life," I explained, "where I was married to a man named Chris and we had a son, Logan, who got leukemia. When I woke up, I thought maybe I'd dreamed the whole thing because I'd been unconscious, but now I can't stop thinking about that little boy—*my son*. Honestly, Bailey, I know it sounds crazy, but I think he exists. I can't explain it, but I can't get rid of this feeling, this awful melancholy—like he was my son and we were together, but now we're apart. I feel like he's waiting for me."

Bailey regarded me with concern and glanced over her shoulder again. "I think you need to see someone. You hit your head pretty hard. It must have been a hallucination."

"Maybe," I replied, fully aware that I wasn't entirely rational at that moment. "But it felt so real. There were so many details I can't even comprehend. Things I find really upsetting. "

"Like what?"

I squeezed my eyes shut and tried to find a way to admit what I didn't want to admit. "After what happened with Mark, I can't believe I would have done that."

"Done *what*?" she pressed.

"The man I was married to..." I paused and took a breath. "I cheated on him. I had an affair, and then I asked him to move out so I could be with that other man. I broke up our family." By then my stomach was churning with guilt and remorse. "How could I have done that, after what Mark put me through? I vowed I would never do anything like that to another person. That I would never be a cheater. You know I hate cheaters."

Bailey laid a hand on my shoulder. "It wasn't real, Katelyn. It never happened. It was just a dream."

A nurse arrived just then and asked the paramedics to wheel me into one of the examination bays.

"I'll be right here in the waiting room," Bailey said with concern as they took me away.

CHAPTER

Seven

cᴄ⁓ꜱꜱ

Thankfully, the CT-scan showed no evidence of a spinal cord injury or damage to my brain—which caused a profound flood of relief in me. This meant I was not paralyzed, and the life that had flashed before my eyes was not a premonition of things to come. There would be no wheelchair in my immediate future.

My relief, however, was tainted by sorrow, for this also meant that the son I'd envisioned and loved in that apparent alternate reality did not exist. He was nothing but a fantasy.

At least I had never cheated on my husband.

As for my prognosis, the doctor informed me that I'd suffered a serious concussion from the accident, having lost consciousness for such a lengthy duration. On the upside, my cuts and bruises were minor. I required no stitches, just a few bandages. The doctor warned me that I would be stiff and sore for a few days. He recommended I take some time off work to recover.

When I was given the option to be discharged, it came with a condition that someone would be available to escort me home and remain with me for the next twenty-four hours. I was to be awakened every two hours throughout the night to ensure my speech wasn't slurred or I wasn't suffering any pounding headaches, in which case we were to return to the hospital immediately. Naturally, my mother volunteered for the task.

‎ ❧

I fell asleep that night working hard to convince myself that the images of Chris and Logan on the sandy beaches of Maine were simply aspirations. It was the life I wished I'd lived, with the family I'd always longed for.

As far as the cheating was concerned, I decided that I'd dreamed about that as a reminder to never, *ever* do such a thing to someone I loved.

But this caused an uncomfortable turmoil in me—for I felt suddenly lost and displaced, as if I were spinning around in an unfamiliar world—searching for something, like an astronaut, hurtling through space without a tether. I longed for home, which seemed hopelessly distant. I longed for my loved ones. *Where were they? Was I really this lost? This far from true happiness?*

‎ ❧

I woke to the jarring sensation of my mother's hands on my shoulders, shaking me hard. She shouted at me from the edge of the bed.

"Wake up, Katelyn! Wake up!"

My eyes fluttered open and I stared up at the overhead light. Heart racing, I leaned up on my elbows. "What's going on?"

"It's five in the morning," Mom said. "I was supposed to wake you every two hours, but I fell asleep. Are you okay? Does your head hurt?"

I rubbed my eyes. "Yes, but only because you were shouting at me and shaking me like a martini mixer." I flopped back down on my pillows.

"Do you know what day it is?" she asked, bending forward to gape at me, as if I were a peculiar alien from another planet.

"It's Saturday morning."

"Do you know who I am?"

Wanting to fall back to sleep, I groaned. "Of course. You're my mother."

She rose to her feet and blew out a breath. "Thank *God*. I was worried when you wouldn't open your eyes."

"I was sound asleep, Mom," I replied. Flinging my arm across my forehead, I lay in silence for a moment or two while my mother stood over my bed. Finally, unable to go back to sleep, I tossed the covers aside and sat up.

"You were talking in your sleep," Mom said apprehensively. "Were you dreaming?"

I tried to remember, but couldn't. The past few hours of sleep felt like a black hole. "I don't know. What was I saying?"

I hadn't told her about the alternate life that had flashed before my eyes on the mountainside. I'd only told Bailey, because I knew I could trust her to keep a secret. My mother, however… not so much.

"You kept saying 'I'm sorry, I'm sorry.' Over and over."

Though I remembered nothing from any dream just now, I suspected I was apologizing for my imaginary affair.

I began to wonder if I should return to the hospital and tell someone about all of this. A head injury wasn't something to mess around with.

"I don't remember," I replied, wishing Bailey were here instead, because I knew she would listen with understanding.

She wouldn't panic like my mother would if she thought I was delusional.

Rising to my feet, I reached for my bathrobe. "I just realized I didn't eat any supper. I think I'll make some toast."

Mom followed me into the kitchen, insisting that I sit down and wait at the table while she took care of it.

Five days later, after my mother returned home to Port Orchard and I returned to work, I found myself feeling increasingly stressed and anxious. I wondered if I should see a psychiatrist or something, because I still couldn't purge, from my mind, the life I had relived on the mountain, as I flew like a human projectile over the handlebars of my bike.

Thoughts of that other life began to consume me like some sort of teenage obsession, and I couldn't let go of the desire to reach it somehow. I felt a frustration like nothing I'd ever known. Night after night, I went to sleep praying that I would escape back to that world again, if only in my dreams, to be with the son who needed me.

I felt it deep in my gut—that Logan was waiting for me to be his mother again.

During the day, I wrestled with feelings of longing that led to feelings of hopelessness, which I feared might eventually lead to something darker—perhaps a serious depression that would swallow me up.

After a week of this torture—which I tried to convince myself was not rational—I decided that I needed to understand what, exactly, had happened to me on that mountain, so that I could move on and live the current life I had been given.

I googled "life flashing before your eyes" on the Internet and read all sorts of accounts from people who'd had near-death experiences, but no one described anything that came close to mine. They all, in their brief brush with death, revisited their own lives, which only left me more confused and uneasy.

I was about to call my doctor and make an appointment for an assessment of some kind, when I stumbled across a conspicuous link within the text of someone's personal account: *Memories of Past Lives.*

Naturally, I clicked on it.

Eight

❦

I must have sat in front of the computer for three hours, reading scientific and theological theories about reincarnation, accompanied by actual case studies. From what I read, it appeared that the scientific community placed more value on the reports from young children than adults, for children were less likely to be influenced by what they had seen or learned during their lives.

One case described a child who, at the age of two, told his parents they were not his real parents, and he named the people who were, along with details about where they lived and the names of his brothers and sisters. The boy's name was Paul, but he insisted it was Derek.

Paul's mother, understandably disturbed and upset by her son's emotional state and his insistence that he belonged to someone else, began an investigation and uncovered evidence that there was indeed a family by that name living in the town Paul described. Further investigation revealed that the family's twenty-three-year-old son had died tragically in a motorcycle accident. The death had occurred shortly before Paul's birth.

The mother arranged for her and Paul to visit the family, who lived on the opposite side of the country. When the family was introduced to Paul, who was now four, they believed wholeheartedly that he was the reincarnation of their late son, Derek.

Later in life, when Paul reached adulthood, he bore a shocking physical resemblance to Derek. Black-and-white photographs of the two men, both aged twenty-three, were displayed side-by-side on the web page, and they could have been twin brothers. The sight of it sent an unexpected shot of fear and foreboding to my core, for this—at least to me—represented substantive evidence that they could indeed be the same person, living two decades apart.

But was it truly reincarnation? Or some other strange phenomenon no one had yet understood? Or was their report a hoax?

The radiator shuddered in my living room and the heat came on, causing me to jump with alarm. Laying a hand over my heart—now pounding like a drum—I gazed around and realized it was pitch dark everywhere in my house except the corner in the living room where my desk was located. I must have switched on the lamp at dusk, but I didn't remember doing it.

I checked the time. It was 10:30 p.m. and the house seemed eerily quiet, though the wind was gusting outside and rattling the windowpanes. Shivering a little, I pulled my sweater tighter about myself, feeling rather creeped out by everything I had just read on the Internet. I hadn't felt that way since I watched *The Exorcist* on television with Mark, a year before we were married. He went home afterward and left me alone in my apartment. I didn't sleep a wink that night.

Rising from my chair, I crossed to the kitchen and switched on the overhead light, then went room to room and turned on lights everywhere, as well as the TV, and that was much better. I didn't feel quite so alone with the reassuring laughter of the audience on *The Big Bang Theory*.

I then decided to call my mom and check in with her. I asked about her day and she asked about mine, and eventually I made the mistake of letting it slip that I'd had a vision during the accident and hadn't been able to stop thinking about it. She asked me about a few details and then I told her about what I'd just read on the reincarnation website.

"Oh, Katelyn. Surely you don't believe in any of that mumbo jumbo," she scoffed. "You were unconscious and had a dream. That's all it was, and you had it because of your divorce and because you still want to be married and have children. That's a goal you should be focusing on. You shouldn't be reading about reincarnation and past lives on the Internet. You should be surfing around a dating site. What about that eHarmony place I always see advertised on television? I'm sure you could meet a wonderful man if you just put yourself out there. The clock's ticking, you know."

I held the phone away from my ear, because I didn't want to listen to what she was saying. I wished I'd called Bailey instead.

Later, after I promised not to waste any more precious time reading about reincarnation—only so she'd stop pressuring me about finding a husband—we hung up, but I still couldn't get all the unsettling ideas out of my head. And still, I had no real understanding about what happened to me.

I'd heard of people undergoing past life regressions through hypnotism, but did I really want to venture into such a New Age world? Most people I knew would think I'd lost my marbles if I told them I thought I was reincarnated. And there were so many quacks and scam artists out there—trying to take advantage of people like me.

No, Katelyn. This is ridiculous. There's no such thing as reincarnation and you didn't have a vision of a past life. It was just a very vivid dream.

Besides, what good would it do to know about a past life? This was my life today—I was Katelyn Roberts, recently divorced television reporter—and if I had been someone else, in another time or parallel universe, what difference would it make to know about that? Wasn't it more important to live for today and the future, not the past?

In the end, I resolved to do what any sane person would do. I forced myself to stop thinking about that vision on the steep tract of the mountain, focus on the here and now, and investigate eHarmony.com.

One Year Later

"I think you should go for it," Bailey said as we sat down at the crowded bar and ordered two glasses of white wine while we waited for our table. "It's CNN."

"Yeah, I know," I replied, without much enthusiasm.

Bailey touched my hand and spoke compassionately. "I'm sorry. I know you were hoping to get that anchor position at the station, and it sucks that they brought in someone else. So maybe this is your cue that it's time for a change. This could be your dream job, or it might lead to something else that's new and different. On top of that, you'd be working in New York City at the Time Warner Center, and I could come and visit you. We could shop and go to shows."

I shifted my purse on my lap. "It's on the other side of the country. You know I'm a West Coast girl, born and raised. My parents are here, you're here, all my friends. And rental prices in New York…" I whistled. "I'd probably have to live in a closet."

"I'd bet you'd get an adorable apartment," Bailey replied. "Or you could commute from Brooklyn or—"

"Become a Jersey girl," I finished for her, more enthusiastically, as the bartender poured our wine and slid both glasses closer.

"Not that there's anything wrong with that." Bailey picked up her glass and raised it for a toast. "*Cake Boss* is in New Jersey.

His bakery is in a town called Hackensack, which is where John Travolta grew up."

"Wow." I raised my glass as well. "You are a lovely and cascading fountain of information."

We clinked glasses and sipped our wine, then she set hers down on the bar. For a moment, she fingered the stem of her glass, watching me intently, then she raised an eyebrow. "There's something else on your mind. I can tell."

"What do you think that is?" I asked. "Because I'm not exactly sure myself."

"Don't be coy," Bailey replied. "I know for a fact that you've been biting your tongue these past few months, not wanting to sound like a broken record by bringing up your...What should we call it? Your *biking vision*. I know you too well, Katelyn. You haven't stopped thinking about those summers in Maine with your handsome, golden-haired husband and the son you had together. None of the men you've gone out with have interested you in the least, though I give you props for trying. Now you have a chance to get a job on the East Coast and I suspect you want to go—just so you can search for Chris and Logan. Because a part of you still thinks they're real."

I leaned back on the bar stool and crossed one leg over the other. "That's *not* why I want to go there," I told her, even though I was lying through my teeth, mostly to myself. "I'm over that and we shouldn't even be talking about it."

I didn't want to slide back into anxiousness, like I was in the weeks following my accident when all I'd wanted to do was escape from this life and live another one.

"Why not?" she asked, leaning forward. "You've just spent the past year forcing yourself to go out on dates while trying to convince yourself that it was just a dream. Maybe it was a dream, maybe it wasn't, but either way, something is pulling you there, and because of that, you have no interest in meeting anyone else around *here*."

I stared at the ceiling for a few seconds and shook my head at myself before turning my attention back to Bailey. "If you must know, I'm starting to wonder if it wasn't a past life that I saw that day, but a premonition of things to come. Maybe that's where my future is—out east."

"Exactly," she said. "And I think you should follow your gut."

I thought about that for a moment and frowned. "Do you think Chris actually exists? I don't even know his last name. That part was never revealed to me."

"Maybe," she said, sipping her wine again. "Or maybe not. Maybe they're just images and representations of the sort of life you want to live."

"*Hmm.*" I sat forward, considering that. "Maybe that's what it was. I don't know." I threw up my hands. "All I want is to feel as if I'm fulfilling my true destiny, whatever that might be, and I certainly don't feel that way here and now—especially after losing the anchor job to the reporter they brought in from a different station. I feel like I'm in limbo, waiting for something to happen, and I want to feel fulfilled, like I'm on the right path."

"I think we all feel like we're in limbo until we find our true calling."

I drew in a deep breath and let it out, taking notice of the lights dimming for dinner in the restaurant and the increasing volume of the mellow jazz playing on the sound system. "Have *you* found your true calling, Bailey? Or do you still feel like there's something more out there, just over the horizon?"

She inclined her head with a smile. "I can't imagine living life with the belief that there's *not* something more over the horizon.

At least not at our age. We still have so much living to do. I just hope that when I come to the end of the road, I'll feel like I had a great life and I did all the things I wanted to do. I'd like to feel… *satisfied*." She picked up her wine again.

"That sounds very Zenlike, but you still haven't answered my question. Do you know what your true calling is?"

She glanced down at her hand that rested on the base of her wineglass. "Honestly? No. And maybe that's the biggest challenge—figuring it out." Her eyes lifted. "At least I like my job. I have no desire to change careers—only to keep climbing in the current one—but maybe that's the problem. I'm too content. I haven't had a glimpse of something else. I'm not really on a quest like you are, searching for something different. Yet, I don't want to give up the idea that there might be something more out there that will make my life truly complete."

I leaned forward, intrigued. "Like what?"

She shrugged a shoulder. "I don't know. That's the missing piece of the puzzle. Maybe it's a husband and kids, but I'd hate to be the sort of woman who needs a man to feel complete."

"Trust me," I said, gazing about the restaurant, "a man doesn't always make you feel complete. He can suck the life right out of you if he's the wrong sort."

The waitress arrived just then and led us to our table.

"Do you think you'll ever forgive Mark for what he did?" Bailey asked as we sat down.

"I'm not sure," I replied, "but at least I no longer feel like I want him back as my husband. I haven't felt that I wanted him that way since the accident. If anything, that vision made me realize that it's exactly like you said: He wasn't the one for me. We weren't meant to be together, and maybe one day I'll look back on this and realize he did me a favor."

"I'm sure you will."

I glanced down at my menu and decided once and for all that it was time I said good-bye to the comfort zone of this familiar life and made a change—because it was entirely possible that my true destiny was waiting for me in New York.

CHAPTER

Ten

❧

Something felt different the following morning when I woke up later than usual—at 10:30 a.m. Maybe it was the sparrow singing a cheerful melody outside my bedroom window, or it could have been because of the firm decision I'd made the night before—to pursue the job at CNN and move to New York City if I was offered it.

There's something rejuvenating about new beginnings, and when I rose from bed, feeling inspired for the first time in ages, I realized I had been coasting along on the same dreary road for too long. Suddenly, the idea of living in a new city and making new friends sent a burst of energy into my veins, so I did it. I boogied to the kitchen to make a healthy shake for breakfast and then drove down to the station to put together a submission portfolio of my best interviews and news stories.

When I arrived, I found Gerry, one of the weekend producers, sitting at his desk eating a mess of Mr. Noodles from a Styrofoam tub. Gerry was about my age with a face as perfect as Brad Pitt's. Even so, he was a computer geek at heart, and he dressed like a slob and lived at home in his mother's basement.

"Hey," I said, dropping my oversized purse onto the floor and flopping down on the swivel chair beside him. "I don't suppose you'd do me a favor."

"Sure, what do you need?" He leaned back in his chair and raised his feet onto his desk, which was littered with an empty chip bag and a half bottle of Coca-Cola.

Wheeling my chair closer, I leaned forward with my elbows on my knees and spoke conspiratorially. "Can you keep a secret?"

He gave me a devious look. "Always."

I paused and checked over my shoulder. Thankfully, because it was Saturday morning, the newsroom was quiet. "I need to create a portfolio of some of my stories and interviews, so I have to get into the archives and pull something together. Would you be able to help me with that?"

"Are you applying for another job?" he asked in a hushed tone, leaning forward as well.

I glanced over my shoulder. "I haven't told anyone yet, and I don't want to spread it around unless there's a good chance I'll get it, and I have to apply first. Do you have some time this morning?"

"This feels very secret agent-ish," he replied. "I'm in." He lifted his feet off the desk, reached for his mouse and pulled up a new screen. "Do you know the dates of the stories you want?"

"Only roughly. I'd like to grab that interview I did with the mayor about his embezzling staffer. That happened in February."

"I remember," he said. "I should be able to find that, no problem." Within a few seconds, Gerry had located it and copied it to a flash drive.

"And the hostage situation in 2010," I said. "There was no cameraman, but I was nearby and the first reporter on the scene. Remember? Bob had me cover it from my cell phone until the rest of the team got there."

He gave me an appreciative, sideways glance. "Of course I remember. You were amazing that day."

I grinned at Gerry before he returned his attention to the screen and resumed scrolling through lists of files.

"This might be it." He clicked on a link, but it brought up one of the follow-up stories.

"It could be the one right before that." I pointed.

"Got it." He opened the file and found the right piece. We watched the whole thing together, then he copied it onto the flash drive as well. "Any others you want?"

"Yes, if you have a bit more time. Do you mind?"

"Not at all. Shoot."

I wracked my brain, thinking back to all the stories I'd done over the years, and the ones I was most proud of. "I'm not sure about the exact date," I said, "but do you remember when that Physics professor at UW was arrested for drug trafficking? I did that in-depth interview with the president of the university after the prof was arrested."

"Wasn't that 2007 or 2008?" Gerry asked, with a furrowed brow.

I chewed on my lower lip. "I'm not sure. It was a couple of years after I first started here, which was 2004. Can you do a search for the University of Washington?"

His fingers flew across the keys. Then he laid his hand on the mouse while we waited for a directory to pop up.

"What about that one?" I said, pointing again. "It has my name on it."

Gerry called up the file and pressed the play button. A wide shot of the university appeared, along with the sound of my voice, introducing the piece. I began to talk about the challenges and odds of getting accepted into some of the grad programs, and realized this wasn't the story I was searching for.

"I don't think this is it," Gerry said. He reached for his mouse and was about to click the stop button, when a shock wave—like a buzzing electric current—surged through me.

"Wait! Don't stop it!" I grabbed Gerry's arm and his mouse went flying off the desk.

"Why? What is it?"

I couldn't seem to make my mouth work. All I could do was stare with wide eyes and a racing heart at the face on the screen—the golden-haired young man who was spellbindingly familiar. I knew those eyes. I'd seen laughter in them, sadness, anger, heartbreak. Even his voice filled me with a bewildering sense of intimacy.

Gerry rolled his chair backwards to pick up the mouse from the floor behind him.

"I know that guy," I said, rather breathlessly as I read the caption at the bottom of the screen.

Chris Jenson
First Year Student, UW School of Dentistry

"Of course you do. You interviewed him."

"No, I mean…I know him from somewhere else."

Gerry wheeled his chair back to the desk, replaced the mouse on the pad, and watched me intently. "From where?"

I exhaled heavily, struggling with how to reply, because I couldn't possibly reveal the truth. "I don't know, I can't put my finger on it. But I'm sure I know him."

"It'll probably come to you later." Gerry gripped the mouse and moved the cursor around on the screen, as if he wanted to click on something. "Do you want this saved on the flash drive, too? Or should we keep looking for the other interview?"

"First, let me watch the rest of it, then we'll keep looking. But yes, I *definitely* want this on my flash drive."

"No prob." Gerry stared at me with questioning eyes.

A short while later, I walked out of the newsroom in a mystified state with the flash drive in my hand. As soon as I stepped off the elevator, I called Bailey.

"I'm so glad you answered," I said. "I know his last name. It's Jenson. And I interviewed him in 2004."

"Interviewed *who*?" Bailey asked on the other end of the line as I walked briskly to my car.

"Chris—the guy I was married to in my vision. It was him. I know it was. There's no doubt whatsoever. I recognized him, Bailey. He was a lot younger on the tape, but I knew him. I mean…now I know, I *really* knew him."

"Okay, slow down and back up a few steps. I don't know what you're talking about."

I explained that I had gone downtown that morning to visit the station and retrieve some old video clips to attach to my CNN resume. "And there he was!" I continued. "It was the weirdest coincidence that Gerry clicked on that file."

"Why did you interview him?" Bailey sounded genuinely interested.

"I was doing a piece about how hard it was for students to get accepted into graduate programs like dentistry and medicine at UW. It was one of the first pieces I did after I started working here. I interviewed a couple of other students, too, but he was the one who had the most intelligent things to say."

Bailey was quiet for a few seconds. "So what are you going to do?"

I arrived at my silver Elantra, pressed the keyless remote, unlocked the door, and got in. "Track him down, of course. He was in the dentistry program. He must be out working by now. I want to get home so I can watch this video again and then google him."

I turned the key in the ignition, set up my phone on Bluetooth to continue the conversation, and checked my rearview mirror before pulling out.

"This is crazy," Bailey said, still on the line. "Are you sure it was him?"

"One hundred percent."

There was another pause on the line while I backed out of my parking space. When I shifted into first gear and started driving toward the lights, I glanced down at my dashboard display. "Are you still there?"

"Yes," she replied, hesitantly.

"What's wrong?" I asked. "You think I'm crazy, don't you."

"Of course not."

"Yes, you do. You think, while I was unconscious, I had a desperate-spinster dream about some good-looking guy I met once, years ago. You think I was storing him up in my memory banks, and it was all a big fat fantasy."

Bailey went quiet again. "Maybe. Seriously, Katelyn, what else could it be? You never married this guy or had a son with him. I'm not sure what you're hoping to find if you go searching for him."

"I don't know either," I replied, feeling suddenly uneasy. "And I'm not convinced it wasn't the future I saw. I'm not even sure he'll remember me. Please don't think I'm nuts."

"I don't think that."

I came to a stop sign and paused momentarily, then hit the gas—and drove straight into the path of an oncoming car. My stomach exploded with panic as I slammed on the breaks. My tires screeched to a halt as the other driver swerved wildly into the center of the intersection, barely missing my front bumper. He honked his horn noisily and shook his fist at me.

"Geez," I said to Bailey as I put my hands on my head and squeezed big clumps of my hair. "I nearly hit someone."

"Are you okay?"

"I'm fine," I replied, checking left and right with extra care before pressing the gas and crossing the intersection. "But I'm way too distracted to be driving."

"Why don't you hang up and call me when you get home," she suggested. "Or do you want me to come over?"

"Maybe that would be best," I replied. "You can keep me from doing anything stupid, because obviously I'm flying off the rails here."

"I'll see you shortly."

Bailey was already parked in front of my house when I arrived, hit the garage door opener, and pulled inside. I got out, slung my purse over my shoulder, and waited for her to walk up my paved driveway.

"Thanks for coming over," I said, moving to the front door. "I can't believe how wound up I am. It took every ounce of my self-control not to google him from my phone while I was at a stoplight."

"That could have been disastrous. After what just happened, you should know better than to text and drive."

"Which is why I didn't do it," I replied, holding the door open for her. "But I'm dying to get to my computer."

We walked into my mudroom, kicked off our shoes and dropped our purses onto the bench.

"I'll show you the video of him first, so you can see what he looks like. He looks exactly like he did in my flashback."

"It wasn't a flashback," she reminded me.

"I know, I know, but I hate calling it a dream or a vision, because it still feels like a memory. Especially the stuff that involved Logan."

A rush of anticipation moved through me at the notion of finding the boy I'd envisioned as my son—although rationally,

I knew it couldn't possibly be true. Because if I'd had an actual biological son, I would most certainly know about it.

"Maybe this is all a big conspiracy," I said, "like in *Total Recall* where Schwarzenegger had his memories erased and they planted him in another fake life where he was married to Sharon Stone, who turned out to be his enemy. Maybe Mark was my Sharon Stone."

Bailey followed me. "Congratulations. Now you're sounding *totally* crazy."

We went straight to my computer desk in the family room and turned on the power. I inserted the flash drive into the USB port and within seconds, the video piece about the UW grad schools came up.

"That's him," I said, pointing. "Does he look familiar to you?"

Bailey, who stood behind my chair, leaned closer over my shoulder, studied his face, and shook her head. "Not at all. He's cute, though."

"That was just over ten years ago," I told her. "So I don't know what he might look like now. Let's find out."

I opened another window and searched for the name *Chris Jenson, dentist in Seattle*. Thousands of web pages appeared, but there were no dentists in the city by that name.

"He might have moved somewhere else," Bailey said. "Or never graduated. Maybe he hated putting his hands in other people's mouths and is doing something else now."

I let out a breath and sat back in my chair, staring at the computer screen intently.

Where are you?

With a sudden tingling sensation in my fingertips, I sat forward again.

"This is probably a long shot, but let's search for *Dentists in Maine—Chris Jenson*."

I typed the words quickly and hit Enter. The little circle spun around and around while I waited with bated breath, bouncing my foot repeatedly on the floor.

At last, a new listing of web pages loaded onto my screen, and the one at the top sent ripples of goose bumps across my entire body. I had pins and needles everywhere.

Hastily, I clicked on it.

"Are you serious?" Bailey said, bending forward to stare.

I covered my mouth with my hand as the website's homepage loaded.

"This is nuts." I looked up at her. "So what do we do now?"

A fter making a pot of coffee, I returned to the computer desk and sat down. "Should I just call his office and ask to speak to him?"

I probably shouldn't have bothered with the coffee, because I was already wired. I couldn't keep still.

"And say what?" Bailey replied. "He doesn't know you. He'll think you're insane if you tell him you had a dream about him—where you were married and had a son together, where you spent summers on the beach in Maine."

"That's true. I have no idea what I would say. Part of me just wants to tell him the truth and ask if *he* ever had any near-death visions like that."

Bailey thought about that. "He'll still think you're a nutcase. Besides, what else do you know about him? He could be married with a family of his own and his wife might think you're a husband stealer. Or maybe he's a cocaine addict, or some kind of weird freak."

I heard what Bailey was saying, but her words seemed to float over my head without really sinking in.

"I've never been to Maine," I said contemplatively.

Bailey gave me a look. "I know what you're thinking. You want to go there."

"Why not? I could just…" I thought about it for a few seconds. "I could make an appointment to have my teeth cleaned."

"Careful. You're starting to sound like a stalker."

"Well, I have to do *something*." I leaned forward in my chair and placed my hands over the keyboard. "Let's just find out if he's single. It's an important fact to know, don't you think? It will affect how I handle this." I typed in his name again, and another link popped up. As soon as I saw the image, my stomach exploded with fascination.

"Oh." Bailey laid a hand on the back of my chair. "I suppose we shouldn't be surprised—a good-looking guy like that, and a dentist to boot. He's a great catch. She's a lucky woman. Wow, gorgeous."

I stared, transfixed, at the photo for a long moment, taking in the bride's simple, classic wedding gown and white flower arrangement. Her blond hair was pulled into a loose knot at her nape and spiraled tendrils framed her face. She had a sparkling, joyful smile.

Chris also smiled as they walked down the church aisle, surrounded by family and friends.

"Look at the date," Bailey said. "They were married just last February. They're newlyweds." She squeezed my shoulder. "Sorry, Katelyn."

"It's okay," I replied with surprising resilience, glancing up at Bailey. "Really, I'm not devastated, even though I thought he might be my future husband. This is so weird. I think a part of me expected this, and it doesn't change anything. I still want to talk to him. And her."

"But why?" Bailey asked.

I sat forward and began to type again. "I just need to know why I saw what I saw."

Bailey went to the kitchen and helped herself to a cup of coffee, then returned to the computer and leaned on the edge of the desk, facing me. "You're still thinking about the boy."

Trying to ignore the note of concern in her voice, I scanned the computer screen, searching everywhere on the web. "Now I'm wondering if Chris has any kids, maybe from a previous marriage."

Nothing popped up to suggest he had children. The lack of an answer frustrated me.

I let out a breath and propped my elbows on the desk, cupped my forehead in my hand. "Lord, maybe I *am* going crazy. I don't know what's happening to me. You should have me committed."

Bailey gave no reply. She simply watched me, waiting to see what I would do next.

I sat back and drummed my fingers on the mousepad, then stood up and went to the kitchen to look at my calendar, which was tacked to the wall next to the refrigerator.

Bailey followed me and set her water glass down on the island's countertop. "I can see the wheels turning," she said. "I'm afraid to ask. But what are your intentions, Katelyn?"

I turned to face her. "I want to visit Maine. I have a bunch of vacation days owed to me, and my boss has been encouraging me to take them. I could probably get some time off this week. I could even go tonight if I can get on a flight."

Bailey's mouth fell open in disbelief. "Part of me *does* think you're crazy, but another part of me admires your determination and sense of adventure."

"You should come with me," I suggested. "We could make a vacation of it and lie on the beach, drink lots of wine and eat lobster. We could stay in some quaint little Victorian bed and breakfast with a view of the Atlantic. Wouldn't that be great? Besides, I could really use a friend, just in case I really *am* losing my mind. Could you take a few days off?"

Bailey inclined her head as she thought about it. "I'm the boss. I can take time off whenever I like."

We regarded each other for a long moment, our thoughts percolating....

"Do you feel like checking out some flights?" I asked.

"I'm on it." Bailey whipped out her phone and wagged her finger at my computer. "You go and look for a nice hotel. Where are we going, exactly? Portland?"

"Yes, that's where Chris's dental practice is. I'll see if there's anything nearby, on the water."

While she searched for flights on her phone, I sat down at the computer. Without looking up, she mentioned, "I'm only coming along to keep you out of trouble."

"Of course, I appreciate that, but don't pretend you're not loving this. I know how much you enjoy a good mystery. And you've always wanted to see the Atlantic. We'll visit some light-houses. You know...I used to be obsessed with lighthouses when I was a kid." I keyed in a search for hotel accommodations around Portland, and scrolled through a number of options before my eyes zeroed in on a magnificent white Palladian-style mansion that caused my whole body to quiver. *Please, let it be on the water.*

I clicked on the link, saw a view of the Atlantic at sunrise beyond a rocky beach at the edge of the lawn, and knew, without a doubt, that it would be the perfect place for us.

"How about this?" I glanced over my shoulder. Bailey moved closer to check it out. "It's just outside Portland, in a coastal community called Cape Elizabeth."

"It looks beautiful," she said. "Can we each have our own room?"

I picked up my phone. "I'll check on that right now."

While Bailey continued to search for flights, I waited for the innkeeper to answer the phone. I clicked through the picture gallery, admiring the mansion's massive front veranda with Georgian-style columns and high portico. Inside, the house maintained a historical style with antique beds and a spectacular dining room with gilt-framed family portraits on the walls.

At last, someone answered. "Fraser House Inn. Could you hold for a moment, please? I'll be right with you."

I waited with high hopes that there would be two rooms available.

"That's the strangest thing," the woman said to me on the phone. "I had to put you on hold because I was handling a cancellation for two rooms just now. Otherwise, we were fully booked. So yes, I can most certainly accommodate you tonight. How long will you be staying?"

"Let me check." I glanced over my shoulder at Bailey and spoke quietly. "They have two rooms available. How long will we stay? A week?"

"Yes, that sounds good. And I found a flight. It's at 5:10 p.m. Flying time is under six hours, so we should get there around midnight. But we'll have to pack in a hurry. Might have to skip lunch and grab something at the airport later."

"No problem." I spoke into the phone again. "We'll be staying a week, checking out next Saturday. Will that work?"

The clerk paused while confirming it. "Yes, that will work out fine. And if you're arriving at midnight, I'll unlock the front door for you. Just come in and I'll get you settled."

"Thank you so much." I gave her our names and our credit card information, then hung up.

Turning to face Bailey, who was still working on our flights, I said, "I can't believe we're doing this. It's so impetuous."

She nodded, somewhat distracted. "I can definitely use a getaway."

Ten minutes later, after the flights were booked and paid for, Bailey left to go home and pack, while I ran upstairs to do the same.

Maine

Fourteen

ℭℌℭ

I t was past midnight when our cab turned off Cape Elizabeth's main road and pulled onto a narrow, wooded lane.

"I've never been inside the Fraser House Inn before," our driver said, leaning forward over the steering wheel as he drove slowly through the fog. The beams of his headlights barely penetrated the dense wall of mist. "I think it's a good thing that someone is finally making good use of it."

"What do you mean?" I asked.

"Well, it's a historic landmark, of course," he said, as if he shouldn't have to state the obvious. "But it was empty for a number of years after the wealthy, New York widow who owned it, passed away. Actually, it was empty for quite a while before that because she hadn't set foot in the place after her son and husband died there—on the same night. It was a terrible thing."

"What happened?" I asked, glancing at Bailey who raised her eyebrows at me.

"Oh…let me see…" He tapped his thumb on the steering wheel. "As I recall, the father had a fight with the teenage son and he got a bit rough with him. He pushed him into the fireplace and the kid cracked his skull right open and died. Then the father, upset with himself, no doubt, went upstairs and did himself in."

"That's horrible," I said. "When did that happen?"

"Not that long ago," the driver explained. "Less than twenty years, I would guess. Time seems to fly by so fast these days. I can't keep track anymore. Ah, here we are."

Bailey gave me a look and shook her head with disbelief, as if to say, *Why in the world would he tell us that?*

All I could do was shrug my shoulders.

We emerged at last from the tree-lined lane, and the brightly lit house appeared before us, like a giant sailing ship, out of the mist.

"It's bigger than I expected," Bailey said.

I sat forward on the seat, craning my neck for a better view while the cab's tires crunched over the white-gravel parking lot, until the car came to a halt at the foot of the wide, painted staircase.

As our driver got out and retrieved our luggage from the trunk, I slid out of the back seat, set my feet on the ground and stood up to breathe in the delectable, briny scent of the sea, while working hard to purge that tragic story from my mind. I closed my eyes, inhaled deeply and held my breath for as long as I could before letting it out.

When I re-opened my eyes, I wished I could see the water, but there was nothing but blackness and fog surrounding me, cloaking the thunderous roar of the surf crashing onto the rocks beyond the edge of the lawn.

"The surf's not usually that loud," our driver informed us, "but we had a few days of high winds. It should calm down for you by tomorrow. It's supposed to be a clear, windless day. The ocean will be quieter."

"That's good to hear," I replied as I accepted my large red suitcase and paid him his fee, plus a tip. "It's kind of frightening. It doesn't make me want to go for a walk in that direction."

He inclined his head. "Me neither."

Bailey, standing beside me and looking up at the steep staircase, extended the pull bar on her suitcase. "This should be a challenge. As usual, I packed way too many shoes and books."

"Two of my favorite things," I said with a grin as our cab drove off. I lifted my bag and led the way up the stairs to the front door.

⌁

"Welcome to Fraser House," the innkeeper said, crossing the spacious entrance hall from a room at the back. She was a slim, attractive older lady with upswept hair and rimless glasses. "I'm Angela."

Standing on the welcome mat, I allowed my gaze to sweep across the dark wood wainscoting, antique portraits, and the large crystal chandelier over our heads. The staircase boasted an ornately carved, oak newel post topped with a brass statue of a woman, like a Greek goddess, holding a lighted globe in her hand. Everything felt very familiar, from the pictures I'd seen online.

I set down my suitcase. "What a beautiful home," I said as Angela reached us.

"Thank you. I'm sure you'll enjoy your stay here. But you must be exhausted after your long flight. Would you like to come this way? I'll get you your keys."

We followed Angela into a parlor to the left where the reception desk was located, along with a number of inviting-looking sofas and oversized upholstered chairs in front of a massive white marble fireplace.

I nudged Bailey and gestured toward it, wondering if that was where the son cracked his skull open.

No doubt this house held a number of secrets in its past. Wouldn't it be interesting to learn them all?

A few minutes later, Angela showed us to our rooms on the second floor. She kept her voice low as we climbed the elegant staircase, so as not to wake the other guests.

"Breakfast is included," she informed us, unlocking Bailey's door first. "We serve it in the dining room from 7:00 until 10:00. You each have your own private bathrooms, and you should find everything you need in there." She showed Bailey inside while I waited in the corridor, peeking over Angela's shoulder to sneak a look at the room. I spotted a four-poster canopy bed with a floral quilt, and a braided rug on the floor.

Next, Angela took me to my room at the end of the hall and unlocked the door for me. I followed her inside and marveled at the canopy bed of my own with a clean white comforter and pillows. "Does the fireplace work?" I asked, strolling across the rug to the window, though I could see nothing but my own reflection in the glass.

"Yes, it does. There's kindling in the box right there. You can use it whenever you like, or if you'd like some help getting it started, just let me know. Can I get you anything else before I retire? A glass of brandy perhaps?"

"No, this is wonderful. Thank you, Angela. I'll see you in the morning."

She left me alone and closed the door gently behind her.

I stood in silence for a moment or two, feeling dazed as I stared at the empty grate in the fireplace. When I lifted my eyes I beheld a portrait of a young Victorian woman over the mantle. She was very beautiful, with red hair and penetrating eyes that seemed to stare right through me.

A soft knock sounded at the door just then. Knowing it was Bailey, I broke myself out of my reverie to answer it.

"I just wanted to see your room," she quietly said as I invited her in. "Oh, this is gorgeous. What do you think?"

"I love it," I replied. "Look at that picture."

She stared up at it. "Wow. She's beautiful." Bailey moved to the window. "I wonder what the view is like."

"I don't know. You can't see anything right now, through the fog. But listen to the ocean. I can't believe how loud it is, even with the window closed."

"No kidding."

"And I can't wait to wake up tomorrow and see what the day brings."

"Me too," she replied. "Now let's get some sleep. I'm pooped."

She walked out and left me alone to get undressed and slip into bed, where I continued to listen to the sound of the waves exploding onto the rocks at the base of the lawn.

For the longest time, the constant roar kept me awake, but I was mesmerized by it, and half-tempted to walk down to the shoreline to see what the waves looked like. But I knew better than that because I could only imagine how massive they must be and how dark it would be outside. Instead, I put my earplugs in and forced myself to turn over and go to sleep.

"Let's not forget," I said to Bailey the following morning as we stood in the car rental office, waiting for our vehicle to be brought around, "that the entire reason I'm here is to try and meet Chris and see if he'll be willing to talk to me. Once that's done, we can relax on the beach for the rest of the week. Although I do need to get my resume sent off to CNN. Don't let me forget to do that."

We stepped out the front door as our rental car pulled up.

"This is great," Bailey said, striding closer to the shiny white SUV and running her hand over the hood.

We looked it over with the attendant for any scratches or dents, then I signed on the dotted line. We both got in, shut the doors, and drove off the lot.

"I was thinking about everything when I woke up this morning," I said, pulling onto the street and trusting the GPS on Bailey's phone to lead us to downtown Portland. "I think it would be best to simply call Chris's practice and ask to speak with him. I don't want to pretend to be calling about anything else, other than what I'm actually calling about. I'll tell him who I am, mention that I interviewed him ten years ago at UW, and say that I'm in town and have some follow-up questions about the past ten years since we last spoke. I'll ask if he wouldn't mind meeting me for lunch or coffee. Today, preferably."

Bailey nodded with approval. "That sounds surprisingly reasonable, considering how bizarre this is."

"Unfortunately, there's no getting around that. If he asks specifically what it's about, I'll say it's complicated, and that I'd prefer to meet in person. I want to see his face when I tell him about my flashback. I want to know if there's anything there. Maybe he has a nephew named Logan, or a son, or God knows what. Or maybe he's had a similar experience."

We drove into town, straight to Temple Street Dental, and pulled over to the curb, out front.

"This is so weird." I dug out my phone from the depths of my oversized purse. "If you only knew how freaked out I am right now, knowing that he's in there—the guy I remember being married to." I held up a hand. "And you don't need to say a word. I know it's not real."

"Thank God."

I found the website for the dental office and called the number. It rang twice before the receptionist answered.

"Temple Street Dental," she greeted cheerfully. "Cassie speaking. How may I help you?"

"Good morning. Dr. Jenson please."

"I'm sorry, he's with a patient right now. Who may I ask is calling?"

I gazed uncertainly at Bailey, hesitant about giving my name, but it would seem odd if I didn't. "It's Katelyn Roberts. I'm a television reporter from Seattle. I interviewed Dr. Jenson a number of years ago and I'm doing a follow-up piece. Could you have him return my call as soon as possible? I'm only in Portland for a few days."

"Certainly. He should be available in about fifteen minutes. Can I get your number?"

"Sure." I gave Cassie my cell number and hung up.

"So what's happening?" Bailey asked expectantly.

"He's going to call me back in about fifteen minutes." I gripped the steering wheel and lightly tapped my forehead against it a few times. "This is nuts. My stomach is churning."

Bailey watched me for a few seconds. "It's a beautiful day. Let's go window shop. Take our minds off it."

"Impossible," I replied.

Nevertheless, I got out of the car and followed her to a shoe store.

At the fifteen-minute mark, we were climbing back into the leather seats of the SUV, waiting for my cell phone to ring. Five minutes went by, then another five minutes. Then at last, my phone rang.

My heart flew into a frenzy. I took a deep breath before swiping the screen with my finger. "Hello?"

"Hi, is this Katelyn Roberts?"

The quiet sound of Chris's voice surged through me like a lightning bolt.

"Yes, it is. Hi, Dr. Jenson. Thanks so much for returning my call. I'm not sure if you remember me, but—"

"I remember you," he coolly replied, cutting me off. "You interviewed me for a news segment in Seattle, about ten years ago."

My blood began to race as my heart rate accelerated. I swallowed hard and rubbed the back of my neck. "That's right.

I'm wondering if you might have some time to meet me for a follow-up interview."

There was a long pause on the other end of the line, and my stomach turned over with dread, for there was something noticeably standoffish in his tone.

"What exactly do you want to know?" he asked, warily.

"Um…" Again, I swallowed over a thick lump of unease, and strained to sound amiable and confident, but decided it was no use. I couldn't pretend to be conducting a follow-up interview about Seattle grad schools. I wanted to tell him the truth and let the cards fall where they may.

"Actually, it's not about the interview, per se," I confessed. "It's about something else, but I feel a bit strange talking to you about it on the phone. Would you be able to meet me for coffee or something?" He offered no response. "If you really want to know," I added, clearly beginning to ramble, but words spilled out of my mouth faster than I could stop them. "I'm right outside your office, sitting in my car. I just flew in from Seattle last night. I know that sounds crazy, but I sort of had a…I don't know how to describe this. I was in a cycling accident a year ago and I lost consciousness for a bit. Um…I had a vision or a premonition or a dream…I'm not sure what to call it. But you were in it, and I just want to talk to you and try to figure out what I saw."

There was another long pause. This one seemed to go on forever.

"Hello?" My heart was pounding thunderously in my ears. "Are you still there?"

"Are you okay?" he finally asked. "I mean, from the accident. Were you hurt?"

The question caught me off guard. "Only a bit. I had a few scrapes and bruises and a concussion, but I'm okay now."

He was quiet for a moment. "Did you go over the guard rail? Did you fall into a ravine?"

I sucked in a breath and darted a look at Bailey, who was watching me intensely.

"No, I didn't fall into a ravine," I replied, holding her steady in my gaze. "So you know something about that."

"I do," Chris replied. Then he fell silent again.

By now my heart was racing faster than wildfire. "Can we meet?" I asked. "I'd really like to talk to you. I'm right outside."

Again, he was hesitant. All I could do was wait and try to keep my breathing steady.

Finally, he spoke up. "Yes, I'll meet you. But I think the person you really want to talk to is my wife, Sylvie."

My eyebrows pulled together with bafflement, for there had been something strangely familiar about his wife in the wedding picture. Nevertheless, apprehension flooded my senses.

"Would she be willing to meet me?" I asked.

"Yes," he replied. "She's right here beside me, nodding her head. She works here as well. Can you meet us for lunch?"

"Absolutely. What time, and where?"

He was quick to lay out a plan. "There's a pub a few blocks south of here. It's called The Old Stone Keep. We'll be there at noon."

"Great, I'll see you then. And is it okay if I bring a friend?"

"Sure," he replied, and ended the call without another word.

I set my phone down on my lap and blinked a few times, struggling to clear my vision and calm my breathing.

"Did you get all of that?" I asked Bailey.

She stared at me in disbelief. "Yes, and I have to admit, I'm stunned. I thought you were imagining all of this, but how did he know about the guardrail and the ravine?"

"I have no idea," I replied. "I'm just as stunned as you are."

Bailey and I arrived at The Old Stone Keep fifteen minutes early. It was a classic English-style pub with dark wood paneling, heavy tables and chairs, and booths at the back. Bailey ordered sparkling water, but I ordered a glass of wine to help calm my nerves. I took a few large, unladylike gulps as soon as the waitress set it down in front of me.

"Slow down there, Sparky," Bailey said. "You don't want to stagger out of your chair when you stand up to shake their hands."

"No, definitely not. That wouldn't do at all." I removed my sweater and draped it over the back of my chair, and picked up my phone to check the time. It wasn't quite noon.

The bells jingled over the door and I jumped. Three men walked in.

"It's not them," I said to Bailey, who sat with her back to the entrance.

Taking a deep breath, I clasped my hands together on my lap and fiddled with the garnet ring on my middle finger, turning it around and around. Then I spotted a couple walk by the windows. They stopped out front, talked for a moment, and pulled the door open. The bells jingled again and I sat up straighter. "It's them."

They paused just inside and looked around. In those few brief seconds, I was able to take in Chris's appearance. Though it had been ten years since we last spoke in person, I felt as if I'd known him intimately, forever. Slim and fit, with light brown hair, he looked exactly as he had in my memories of our so-called marriage, and I felt as if I were being reunited with an old friend—a man of integrity, someone who had been good to me.

Someone I had foolishly betrayed. I felt a dreadful stabbing of guilt in my belly.

As for Sylvie, she was tall, blond and beautiful, and although she appeared to be about my age, I felt intimidated by the fact that she knew so much more about this than I did. At least, that's what Chris had implied on the phone.

They spotted us and approached the table. I rose from my chair and held out my hand. "Hi Chris. Thanks for meeting us." We shook hands, then I turned to his wife. "And you must be Sylvie. It's nice to meet you."

Our eyes locked and I felt a sudden rush of butterflies as we clasped hands, for there was something guarded in her eyes, an overall wariness in her manner.

"It's nice to meet you, too," she replied, nevertheless, mustering up a courteous smile.

"This is my friend, Bailey." I gestured toward her as we all sat down. "She's from Seattle as well. We've known each other since kindergarten."

Bailey shook hands with them over the table, and then the waitress arrived to take their drink orders. A moment later, we all stared at each other in awkward silence.

"Well," I said pointedly, leaning forward to break the ice. "I'm really curious to talk to you both. I mentioned on the phone that

I'd had a vision, of sorts, when I had my cycling accident, and for some reason, Chris, you were in it. When we talked on the phone this morning, you seemed to know something about my accident—that there was a guard rail and a ravine. Can I ask how you knew about that?"

Chris glanced at Sylvie and raised his eyebrows. "I *didn't* know, actually. It was Sylvie who told me about it."

She sat directly across the table from me. I met her gaze. "When?"

"It was almost a year ago," she replied, "not long after Chris and I started seeing each other."

"But how did *you* know about it?" I asked her.

She glanced uneasily at the other people seated in the pub. "It's kind of a strange story, and I'm not all that comfortable telling you about it, since we hardly know each other, not to mention the fact that you're a reporter. I've never told anyone except for Chris, and one other person."

I spoke gently, hoping she would warm up to me and trust me with whatever secret she was keeping. "Told anyone *what*?"

"How and why I know certain things. Why I knew who you were. And you have to give me your word that you won't use this for a news story. This is off the record. Otherwise I won't talk to you."

"I promise," I said without hesitation. "That's not why I'm here. I'm on vacation. This is completely personal."

Chris and Sylvie exchanged a look, as if they were deciding whether or not to reveal whatever she knew, then Chris leaned forward and rested his forearms on the table. At last, he began to explain.

"When Sylvie and I first started dating, she asked me if I knew anyone named Katelyn. I said no, and she then proceeded to remind me about the interview I did with you at UW. It was only then that I remembered you, but I didn't know why *she* had known about it, or why she was asking."

"I still don't understand," I said.

Sylvie sat forward as well. "Maybe we should start with you telling me what you saw in your vision, Katelyn. Or I could guess, if you like."

I leaned back and gestured with a hand. "Please, go ahead. I'm very curious."

Without wavering, she said, "Did you imagine that you were married to Chris, and that you had a son together?"

I felt the color drain from my face, and nodded.

"Was his name Logan?" Sylvie asked.

I frowned at the sudden ache of longing in my heart and spoke heatedly. "Yes."

Chris and Sylvie exchanged another look.

"Was he sick? With leukemia?"

I couldn't take much more of this. It was bringing it all back, making Logan real again. And if these people—who were complete strangers to me—knew about him, surely he had to be real. "My God, yes. How do you know that?"

Sylvie pushed a lock of her hair behind her ear. "I know it because it sort of...*did* happen."

I quickly shook my head, not knowing what to make of her latest revelation. *If it really were true, where was my son?*

"Wait a minute..." Bailey leaned forward as well. "*How* could it have happened? I've known Katelyn all my life, and she was married to a man named Mark. They never had any children. What are you talking about?"

The waitress arrived just then, set down Chris's and Sylvie's drinks and asked if we were ready to order.

My shoulders slumped at her terrible timing.

Chris picked up his menu. "We both have patients at 1:00 and have to get back to the office by then," he explained. Then he looked up at the waitress and handed the menu back. "I'll have the pan-fried haddock and vegetables with rice."

Sylvie ordered the same thing, and Bailey and I ordered chicken salads.

As soon as the waitress was gone, Sylvie continued. "I know this must seem crazy to you…"

"Trust me. It doesn't."

She nodded with understanding. "Either way, I think you deserve to know what happened—to me, at least." She sipped her water and set down the glass. "I had a strange experience last year when I experimented with lucid dreams. There's also a similar phenomenon called astral projection. I'm not sure what happened to me exactly, and it certainly wasn't a controlled experiment. I was completely on my own and didn't tell anyone what I was doing."

"What happened?" I wanted desperately to hear everything she had to say as quickly as possible, before they had to leave.

"I don't know," she replied, "but it seemed as if I traveled backwards through time and relived certain events from my past where I did something differently, and when I woke up the morning after, my life *was* different. I did it more than once, too."

Bailey inclined her head. "You mean like in *Back to the Future* when Marty McFly goes back in time, changes how his parents met, and it affects the future?"

Sylvie chuckled softly. "Yes, kind of like that. It's complicated to explain, because it seemed as if each time I woke up with a new life—always on the same day in the present—it was like an alternate reality. Each a parallel life, in a way." She inhaled deeply. "In one of those alternate realities, I met Chris, and he was married to you. Or at least, he had been. You were divorced, but you had a son named Logan."

"We were divorced because I cheated on you," I said to Chris, "which I would never do in real life. I'm very sorry about that. Seriously."

Chris shrugged. "As far as I'm concerned, it never happened. All I know is this life, right here." He reached for Sylvie's hand and squeezed it.

"*I* still remember it," she said under her breath, regarding me with hooded, mistrustful eyes.

I shifted uneasily in my chair and tried to speak lightly. "I'm happy for you guys, honestly, and I'm glad I'm not a cheater—in *this* life, at least. But still…." I paused. "I can't seem to let go of the memory of the son we had."

We all reached for our drinks and sipped at the same time.

"I'm curious," Sylvie said, "about your vision, Katelyn. Was it a dream? Were you asleep or unconscious when you had it? Chris said it happened during your cycling accident."

I nodded. "That's right. But I wasn't asleep. You know how they say your life flashes before your eyes at the moment of your death? I thought I was going over the guardrail and I panicked— obviously. But the life that flashed before my eyes wasn't my own. It was like this alternate reality you're describing. And then I saw myself falling into the ravine and waking up in a wheelchair. It was as if everything happened in slow motion."

"That must have been very frightening," Chris said.

"It was. But somehow, at the last second, I managed to contort my body so that I hit the rail instead and didn't go over the edge. I think I had an inkling of it and prevented it."

Sylvie swallowed uneasily. "I'm glad to hear that, because in that other life, you *did* fall into the ravine and you became paralyzed from the waist down. You're very lucky, Katelyn. I'm so glad that didn't happen to you."

I reached for my wine glass and finished it off. "Me, too."

The waitress arrived with our meals and set them down in front of us. As soon as she was gone, I picked up my fork and asked Sylvie another question. "If that truly was an alternate reality that I saw, why did I have that same accident in *this* reality?"

She shook her head. "I have no idea. It's still a huge mystery to me and I'm trying to move on, to live life in the present. But I also experienced the same thing, because there were events that happened in those other lives that repeated themselves in this one."

"Like what?"

She waved her fork around and chewed delicately while she spoke. "Like the hurricane that ravaged Maine last year. Three times, I went back, spent a few weeks in another reality. In one of them, we were hit by a hurricane. When I finally woke up, here in my current life, that same storm hit a few weeks later, on the exact same date. I was able to predict it and I knew exactly how bad it would be. Other things were the same as well."

"Like your grandmother needing surgery," Chris added helpfully.

Obviously Sylvie had shared everything with him.

"Yes," she agreed. "In that other life, my grandmother had to have some polyps removed, and when I woke up in this one, I asked her to get checked out, and sure enough, she was diagnosed with the same thing. She had to have them removed." Sylvie moved her food around on her plate and frowned slightly. "Still, other things were different. Like the sailboat. I don't know why."

"What sailboat?" I asked when she offered no further information.

Her eyes lifted and she seemed hesitant. "When the hurricane hit in that other reality, a sailboat was washed up onto the lawn of the house where I was living. We didn't know who it belonged to and had to track down the owners by the boat's name. But in this reality, when the storm hit, that didn't happen. No boats were washed ashore in that area."

I let out a heavy sigh. "This is really confusing." I shut my eyes for a moment, labored to comprehend everything, then I opened them again. "So when I had a near-death experience, I remembered one of these alternate lives that *you* sort of created for me when you had your visions?"

Sylvie glanced at Chris. "I guess that's a sensible conclusion. And I'm just as baffled as you are."

"So Logan doesn't exist at all?" I asked.

Sylvie set down her fork and regarded me with gentle compassion. "Not in this life. I'm sorry."

Feeling brokenhearted and resistant to simply let those memories go, I exhaled sharply. "But how did you *get* there? How did you reach those other lives? It's just that...after all this, I feel like he truly is my son and he's out there somewhere. I know it sounds crazy, but I've been wanting to find him, but now there's nowhere real to look. I don't know where to start."

"You're not crazy," Sylvie said. "But I know what you're thinking. I can see it in your eyes. You want to find a way to reach that other reality and be his mother again."

We all stopped eating, and I felt everyone watching me with concern and pity, which troubled me, because I never liked being *pitied*. That implied I was weak. Doleful. Unfortunate.

I tried to explain myself. "It's just that...I never had children, so I had no idea how strong the pull could be. It's shocking to me. Ever since my accident, it's like I've been living a life where my child went missing, or died. Bailey knows. I haven't been myself. I've been grieving, but trying to ignore or deny it."

Sylvie sighed heavily. "I'm sorry, Katelyn. I'm sorry that you were caught up in this, and I'm still amazed, to be honest, that you connected with those memories. But I'm pretty sure that you could never cross over to that other life."

"But how do you know?" I pressed, setting down my fork. "Are you worried that if I do go back there and change something, you won't be married to Chris?"

She and Chris regarded each other uneasily, then Sylvie bowed her head and wiped her mouth with her napkin.

"I have no idea what it would mean for this reality." She picked up her fork again and poked at her haddock on the plate. Then she looked across at me. "But the way I see it, there could be a billion possibilities and it's likely that one small change can have a ripple effect on how things turn out. Even if you ended up married to Chris again—if you dated him and didn't cheat on him—the odds of having the same baby are a billion to one."

I shook my head, denying that possibility. "My gut is telling me that our son exists, and he's waiting for me to find him."

Now, I *did* sound crazy.

Sylvie regarded me with sudden displeasure.

"I apologize," I said. "I didn't mean to imply that we have a son together." I glanced at Chris. "We don't even know each other."

"You don't have to apologize," Sylvie said with a kinder tone. "This is complicated. I admit, I'm feeling a bit threatened here, because in that other life, you *did* try to get Chris back."

"After he started seeing you?" I asked with a frown of disbelief.

She nodded and studied my expression, no doubt searching for my intentions. "And I lost him to you."

"I see," I replied. "I'm sorry, I didn't know. That memory never played out in my mind. But I promise you, I'm not going to try to steal your husband away. Not this time."

I shared a look with Bailey, feeling grateful that I had *someone* in my corner, here at the table. Someone who knew me well and understood I wasn't a husband stealer.

I made an effort to change the subject. "You still haven't told me, precisely, how you went back in time. I don't know anything about lucid dreaming. Is it really possible to—?"

"It wasn't the lucid dreams," she told me. "It was something else, or a combination of the lucid dream and a portal of some kind."

"Sylvie…" Chris spoke with a note of warning. "You said you weren't going to—"

"I think she needs to know," Sylvie explained to him, then she turned back to me again. "There's a sundial at a historic home in Cape Elizabeth—the same place where the sailboat washed onto the lawn. I believe the dial might have had something to do with it. The man who owned the house was a sea captain and he lost his wife at a young age when she was swept off the rocks during a storm. I did some research and learned that he spent his life trying to build a time machine, so that he could go back and prevent her death. I think that's what the sundial was supposed to be."

"Cape Elizabeth?" I leaned forward. "Which historic home? Is it the Fraser House Inn? Because that's where we're staying."

Sylvie dropped her fork and flopped back in her chair. "Are you kidding me? You're staying at the Fraser House Inn. What made you choose it?"

I shrugged and glanced uncertainly at Bailey. "I don't know. I saw pictures online and I liked the look of it."

Sylvie rested her elbow on the table and cupped her forehead in a hand. I found myself staring at the top of her head, worrying that she was about to bring this conversation to an end. "I've said too much."

"No, you haven't," I assured her. "Please, I need to know everything, because I'm already involved. There's no going back."

She lowered her hand from her face. "But isn't that the point? Trust me, I've done this. What matters is the future, not the past. Besides, I don't want to be responsible for what might happen if you tried to do what I did."

"Why not?"

"It's too unpredictable. What if you could never get back *here*, to this life? Do you want to risk losing everything you know and love?"

"Every single second of every day is unpredictable," I argued.

She turned to her husband, Chris, and regarded him imploringly, as if she hoped he would help her argue the point. He merely shrugged, leaving the decision up to her. And me, I suppose.

Sylvie turned in her chair to signal the waitress. "I'm sorry, we have to go. It's almost 1:00."

The waitress immediately crossed the pub with our bills and a wireless credit card machine.

"We're in a bit of a rush," Sylvie explained to her while Chris pulled his wallet out of his back pocket.

Bailey and I sat in silence, watching Sylvie and Chris pay their bill and rise from their chairs. "I'm sorry," Sylvie said. "It was nice to meet you, but…" She paused. "You should go home, Katelyn. Just be happy with your life. Be grateful for what you have." She gestured toward Bailey. "You have a wonderful friend here, and you're a beautiful, intelligent woman. You survived a terrible biking accident, and if you go back, you might not be so lucky next time. It's a second chance that you've been given. You should make the most of it by moving forward."

That's exactly what I'm trying to do. It's why I came here.

Chris laid a hand on the small of Sylvie's back and they walked out together. I continued to watch them while the bells jingled over the door and they moved onto the sidewalk. As they passed by the windows, walking quickly, he slung an arm around her shoulders and pulled her close, and she rested her cheek on his shoulder.

Despite everything she had just said to me, as I witnessed the connection they shared, all I could feel was…*envy.*

I turned to Bailey. "She made a lot of sense just now, about focusing on the future, not the past, but…Are you thinking what I'm thinking?"

"We need to check out that sundial," she said.

We both, simultaneously, waved the waitress over to take our credit cards.

A few minutes later, as we were walking back to the SUV, Bailey said, "Katelyn, I have to ask…You don't really believe it do you? That the sundial could be an actual portal through time? Surely there's another explanation for all of this."

I handed the keys to her. "I have no idea, but that's why I want to see it for myself."

A heavy and humid summer breeze had picked up by the time we returned to the Fraser House Inn and parked the SUV on the gravel lot.

Feeling as if there wasn't a moment to lose, I grabbed my purse off the floor and hopped out, pausing only briefly to scan the length of green sloping lawn that led down to the sundial, just before the shoreline. Two freshly painted Adirondack chairs— one red and one blue—stood empty beside it.

Everything seemed small in the distance, except for the ocean, of course. If a boat had been tossed up during a storm, I wondered if another rogue wave, sweeping in upon these rocks, might have swept the sea captain's wife to her death. Despite the summer heat, I shivered at the thought.

"Ready?" I said to Bailey as she got out of the vehicle and shut the car door.

"Yes."

Together, with the sun warm upon our shoulders, we strolled onto the stone path that meandered down to the water, and passed beneath a charming, white painted rose arbor with a but-terfly flitting about.

We noticed Angela on the far side of the property wearing a wide-brimmed straw hat and denim overalls. She was pruning a hedgerow with a giant pair of clippers. She waved at us and we waved back.

As we drew nearer to the sundial, I lifted my sunglasses to rest on top of my head. "It looks ancient," I said, stopping in front of it.

Slowly, I circled the stone dial plate and ran my fingers over the Roman numerals carved into its surface.

"The stand is pretty elaborate," Bailey commented.

I squatted down to inspect the column that stood upon a stone slab, and ran my open hand up and down the intricate designs. "I've never seen anything like it. This part looks Asian or Middle Eastern."

Rising to my feet, I turned to look out at the sparkling blue sea, and spotted a sailboat in the distance. Shading my eyes, I watched the boat for a moment, then walked forward to the edge of the lawn and looked over the rugged shoreline below. The tide was out and the rocks were covered in seaweed and barnacles. I breathed in the salty scent of the pebbly beach, then turned back to consider the sundial again.

"Well," I said, "we're still here."

Bailey pulled out her phone and swiped the screen. "And it's still August, 2016."

She pointed at a wooden deck on the far corner of the property with a few empty lounge chairs upon it. "Listen, do you hear that? I think those chairs are calling to us. Want to get into our bathing suits, grab a couple of drinks, and do some reading?"

I glanced at the deck. "That sounds good, but you go ahead and get changed without me. I'd like to talk to Angela first, to see if she knows anything about the sundial. I'll meet you on the deck. Save me a chair."

Bailey and I parted ways. She returned to the stone path while I started off in the opposite direction across the wide green lawn.

"A lot of guests ask me about that sundial because it's so unique," Angela said, as we began the short walk back to the house together. "My husband and I both wish we knew more. What we do know is that Captain Fraser was also an inventor late in life, and we found all sorts of fascinating Victorian contraptions in the attic when we bought the place. We donated everything to the local museum."

"That's interesting. Is there a display there? I'd love to take a look."

"Yes, they have a cabinet dedicated solely to his inventions, and they also have a number of items stored in their archives." Angela stopped, bent over and tugged a weed out of the grass, then we continued on.

"I heard that the captain lost his wife when they were still quite young," I mentioned, "and that he wanted to build a time machine so that he could go back and prevent her death. Do you know anything about that?"

"Yes, of course. I was the one who discovered it in the letters his children wrote to each other, which we found in the attic. That's her portrait hanging over the fireplace in your room. Sadly, the family destroyed most of his paperwork referencing his inventions and his travels during the last years of his life. They thought he was delusional in his old age."

"I suppose I can understand that," I replied, "but it's a shame those were lost."

"Indeed. When I think about how much we discard in our society today, not holding on to anything anymore, I wonder how much history we're throwing away."

We reached the stairs that led up to the enormous veranda, but Angela paused at the bottom. "I have to put these clippers in the carriage house, so you go on without me. If you need anything, my husband is just inside. Ring the bell at the front desk."

"I will. Thank you." I attempted to follow. "But wait…"

I wasn't ready to let her go just yet. There was still so much I wanted to know, because Sylvie had been more than upfront about the sundial being a doorway to another time and dimension. Surely, if that were true, the homeowner would know something about it.

"Do you think it's possible that the sundial has something to do with the time machine the captain was trying to build?" I asked, feeling ridiculous as soon as the words spilled across my lips. "It looks very ancient, as if it's meant to be magical."

She smiled at me and laid a hand on the top of her straw hat to keep it from flying off in a sudden gust off the water. "I've always thought so myself, but I've never heard any tales about it. We can always imagine."

With that she walked around the side of the house toward the carriage house, swinging her hedge clippers at her side and humming a cheerful tune.

I watched her for a moment, then climbed the steps alone, pausing on the veranda to shade my eyes and look out at the sea. It sparkled like diamonds under the sun.

The sailboat was no longer visible. I wondered where it had gone. Perhaps the owner had sailed farther out to bask in the freedom of the open water and the sound of the ocean rushing

past the hull. Or possibly back to one of the yacht clubs to finish
out the day with a glass of wine and a bowl of seafood chowder.

How wonderful that sounded. Turning to go inside, I promised myself that one of these days, I would learn how to sail.

Eighteen

⌒⌒

After spending the afternoon stretched out on the lounge chairs on the seafront deck—each of us immersed in a bestselling novel while listening to the waves on the rocky beach below—Bailey and I returned to our rooms to shower and dress for dinner. I was ready before she was, so I lay down on the bed to watch the *Portland Evening News*. When Bailey finally knocked on my door, she told me that Angela had recommended a few places to eat.

A short time later, we found ourselves seated at a cozy local restaurant called The Good Table.

Bailey ordered the lobster fettuccine and I devoured the rib-eye steak—delicious with horseradish crème fraiche, frizzled onions and a baked potato.

Afterward, we returned to the inn to take part in a card game in the library with Angela, her husband, and a few of the other guests, where we all drank Rusty Nails—equal parts cheap whiskey and Drambuie—and gambled with quarters.

There had been much animated talk about the weather forecast for the following day, which promised record-hot temperatures and high humidity. Bailey and I decided to head to Crescent Beach to lie on the sand all day, read our books, and frolic in the waves.

When we said goodnight to the other guests and retired to our rooms, I felt relaxed and slightly tipsy from the strong drinks, and laughed at myself as I tumbled, in my pajamas, onto the massive antique bed.

"You're drunk," I said to myself while gazing, blurry-eyed, at the portrait of Captain Fraser's young bride above the fireplace. I imagined how passionately and deeply in love they must have been for him to spend his life trying to invent a time machine to bring her back. It only served to remind me, yet again, that I had never known that kind of love. All I'd ever experienced was heartbreak and betrayal—a sense of not being everything my husband truly wanted me to be, because Mark had desired another.

Even Chris, in that parallel life I remembered, hadn't loved me the way I needed to be loved, and that's why I had been unfaithful to him. I was always searching, longing for something more. It was as if I had known we weren't meant for each other. That we were each meant for someone else.

Not that *that* was any excuse for my actions. Infidelity was a four letter word as far as I was concerned, and I despised myself for having given up on our marriage—even though my actions were completely fictitious. At least in this life.

In the next few moments, the bed began to spin. *Typical.*

"Good luck getting up tomorrow," I said to myself as I rolled onto my side. "You'll be hungover and you'll probably get sunstroke."

I closed my eyes and tried to fall asleep, but couldn't stop thinking about the sundial. I suspected Sylvie had kept something from me, because she didn't want me to go flying in and out of other dimensions and start messing around with her current reality.

Why would she want to chance it, when she was already married to the man of her dreams?

The last thing I wanted to do was destroy her life, or take anything away from her. But I couldn't help but believe that I had been drawn to this place for a specific reason, and I had my own destiny to seek and fulfill.

I decided to rise early and drag Bailey to the local museum before we headed to the beach, because there was still so much I wanted to know about this house and its mysterious sundial.

⋅ᴄᴄ⟋⟍⟍ɔ⟍ᵒ

I t took tremendous discipline, but I rose extra early to get my CNN application sent off to New York before heading down to breakfast. I then dragged Bailey to the Cape Elizabeth Museum, where we spent the entire morning in the back room, seated at a large round table, wearing white cloth gloves as we handled precious documents. I was surprised when the museum curator trusted us with the entire Fraser Collection—which consisted of one box of letters and a number of interesting contraptions from the inn's attic—but she remained seated nearby, working at her desk the entire time. She was also kind enough to answer any questions we had about the social history of Cape Elizabeth during the late-Victorian period.

We discovered that Captain Sebastian Fraser had inherited the house from his father, a sea captain himself, who had built it in 1840. Sebastian married his beloved, Evangeline, in 1878 when he was thirty-five years old and she was twenty-one. They had two children in the first two years of their marriage—a boy and a girl, who were unfortunately too young to remember anything about their mother after she died.

One interesting item I discovered was that she had been swept off the rocks at the Portland Head Light. This came as a surprise to me, for I had assumed she'd died on the property itself, in the place where the captain had erected the sundial.

Later in life, the children's letters to each other revealed how they lamented their father's perpetual grief over the loss of his young wife, and how they wished he would marry again.

The daughter, Amelie, wrote this to her brother about her efforts to find him a new bride:

> "Father is so stubborn and rude sometimes. He slams his book closed and walks out on me whenever I mention a pretty lady's name. He knows what I am up to. Then he sails off again for months on end. I worry about him, Nathan. He is obsessed with his regret, and I often catch him standing at the edge of the lawn, staring out at the waves on a stormy morning, no doubt thinking about how he couldn't save her…"

I read the letter aloud to Bailey, who sat back in her chair and laid both her white gloved hands over her heart. "Oh, to be loved like that."

"Tell me about it," I replied, carefully tucking the letter back into the envelope. "But it's so sad, how he couldn't ever be happy again. And the children, never having a chance to know their mother or see their father happy."

The curator glanced up from her work. "It is rather tragic," she agreed.

We discussed the rarity of such everlasting love, then Bailey and I continued poring over the rest of the collection. At last I came to a reference about the captain's desire to build a time machine.

In a letter dated September 1915, his son Nathan wrote this:

> "He's not well, Amelie. Last night I found that
> H.G. Wells book on his bedside table again. I thought
> he was all through with that, but he nearly electrocuted
> himself last week, fooling around with another one
> of his mad gadgets. I also snuck a look at his journal
> when he was out. There were notes and equations
> about time doorways and the alignment of the stars
> and the universe. I think you should come home…"

"I wonder what happened to the journal," Bailey said when I folded the letter and returned it to its envelope.

The curator glanced up again. "It was never found. We believe the children must have destroyed it, because at the end of his life, they were quite concerned about their father's mental state, and his reputation."

As I read through the remaining letters, I thought their assessment was a reasonable conclusion, based on Amelie's and Nathan's correspondence.

Sadly Captain Fraser died a few months later, from a severe fever, at the age of seventy. His descendants lived in the home until the 1950s when they couldn't afford to maintain it any longer and sold it to a family from Portland. It changed hands a number of times before Angela and her husband purchased it in 2009.

When Bailey and I walked out of the museum, it was almost noon, and scorching hot. "Are you hungry?" she asked. "I could go for a sub before we hit the beach."

"That sounds good," I replied, not wanting to reveal the fact that I would have preferred to skip the beach altogether, return to the inn and spend the afternoon napping in my room, because I felt deeply, inexplicably morose.

I decided to blame it on the aftereffects of the Rusty Nails.

"Of course, it's all very fascinating," I said to Bailey as we shook out our towels, laid them on the sand, and sat down. "But I didn't come all this way for a history lesson. I'm still just as frustrated."

"You mean you're still thinking about the son you had with Chris."

I sighed heavily and gazed out at the blue water for a moment before I squirted sunscreen on my palm and rubbed it on my shoulder. "It's not that I'm in love with Chris or anything. It's just..." I paused. "It's more that my memories of Logan are painful because he was sick most of the time and I was so afraid of losing him, and there was so little I could do to make him better. Now here I am, but he's not with me. It's like...my worst fear realized."

"But he's not real in your life," she reminded me, growing a little impatient. "Who knows what happened to Sylvie? Maybe the whole thing was just a dream for her, too, and you picked up on it somehow—maybe through some sort of psychic ability. I saw a documentary about that once, where scientists were studying how people's brainwaves could actually intermingle, where they would suddenly think of the same thing at the same time, like a steak dinner or something, or have the same dream. Maybe that's what happened to you."

I sat forward, hugged my knees to my chest, and stared at the horizon where the water met the sky. "You're right. It probably *was* just a dream. It's crazy to think otherwise, right? And she did mention that it happened because she was experimenting with lucid dreaming." I turned to Bailey, who was stretched out on her back with her mirrored sunglasses on. "What is that, anyway? Lucid dreaming…"

Bailey raised a knee. "I think it's where you're half-awake, and consciously, you know that you're dreaming, so you can control what happens in the dream."

This idea went off like an exploding lightbulb in my brain, raising all kinds of possibilities. I turned slightly on my towel and raised my sunglasses. "Have you ever done it?"

"It's not something that you *do*. It just happens. And yeah, I've had them. Haven't you?"

I faced the water again. "I'm not sure." For a long while I watched families on the beach, wading into the water with their small children, and listened to the distant sound of a portable speaker playing rock music. I breathed in the scent of coconut sunscreen on the air, then noticed a colorful seashell in the sand. I picked it up and studied it closely. Completely fascinated, I stuffed it into my bag.

Then I turned onto my stomach and rested my cheek on my arm. "Sylvie said she was experimenting with lucid dreaming, which suggests she had been *trying* to make it happen. I wonder if that's how she did it. I wish I could remember everything she said, but it's all running together in my mind."

"You could always call her and ask."

I considered that for a moment, knowing that Sylvie wouldn't be thrilled to hear from me again. "You remember what she was like yesterday. She won't want to discuss it with me."

Bailey leaned up on her elbows and flicked her blond hair off her shoulder. "Not that I'm *encouraging* you or anything—but you're a news reporter. It's your job to ask people questions they don't want to answer."

I smiled at her and dug my phone out of my purse.

"Thank you for taking my call," I said a few minutes later as I walked down the beach, along the water's edge, holding my cell phone to my ear. "I hope I didn't take you away from a patient."

"I'm just waiting for the next one to arrive," Sylvie said. "He's a bit late."

There was an awkward pause, and I cleared my throat. "I see. Well, I just wanted to ask you a few more questions if you don't mind. Yesterday, you said you experimented with lucid dreaming, and that's how you ended up in those alternate realities. How, *exactly*, did the sundial play into it?"

"I can't really answer that," Sylvie replied, "except to say that it always happened when I went to sleep *trying* to dream about the thing I wanted to remember or revisit. Then I would float out of my body and…I know it sounds far-fetched, but in my dream, I would fly to the sundial and take hold of it, and the next thing I knew, I was living another life, and not always remembering the old one. But like I said, I couldn't control it.

I never intended to go to the sundial. It just happened after I drifted off."

"What were you trying to remember, or revisit?" I asked.

"That's another story altogether." She paused. "Things from my past—my *actual* past. Choices from my youth that I regretted and wished I had handled differently."

A volleyball came flying at me and landed in the water. I fetched it and threw it back to a group of teenagers on the beach, then returned my attention to Sylvie on the phone.

"So you were trying to return to your actual past," I said to her. "I wonder what would happen if I tried to dream about a past I never actually lived."

Sylvie was quiet for a moment. "Please, Katelyn, just let it go. You could end up screwing up your whole life. And you should know that I haven't set foot at the Fraser House Inn since I found Chris, because I'm afraid I'll get swept away again, and that scares the daylights out of me—because I like where I am right now. Just thinking about it and talking to you about it has me worried that it's going to happen again. I really have to go. Please don't call me again. I don't want to talk about it, and you should go home."

Click.

She'd ended the call. I lowered my phone to my side and gazed out at the water again, realizing that any sane person would accept that she was right, and understand that it was madness to fixate on a life that wasn't real.

But maybe I wasn't sane, because all I could think about was one of the last things she said to me: *I like where I am right now.*

She was happy because of her experience with the sundial.

I wanted happiness, too.

Which required me to reunite with my son, as crazy as that sounded.

So I did what any intelligent woman would do in my situation. I sat down on a large piece of driftwood and googled "how to lucid dream."

Evangeline

CHAPTER

Twenty-one

⚜

1878

It's rather peculiar, don't you think? How one particular memory can take hold in your mind and never grow dim, even years later when you've lived a full life and thousands of other memories have piled on top of it. What is it that makes certain experiences more relevant, more vivid than others? To the point that they are burned, as if by a branding iron, onto our brains forever?

This knowledge and understanding had not yet occurred to me as I walked along the sandy beach a few miles south of my parents' new home in Cape Elizabeth, Maine, where I had been dragged—quite by force—a week earlier. At twenty-one years of age, I was still somewhat immature at the time, because the most relevant, enlightening moments of my life were yet to occur. And I was still terribly angry with my parents for not involving me in the decision to pack up and leave our brick townhouse in Boston where I had been born and raised, in order to migrate to a tiny fishing town on the absolute edge of nowhere.

I couldn't understand it. I was no longer a child. Why hadn't they given me some notice, or at least time to prepare myself for what would surely be my sad and wretched fate on this desolate, rocky coast? Now I was completely dependent upon them for company and conversation, because I knew no one else here. Nor was there any sign of good society in this hapless backwater.

We had been here a full week and I had yet to meet a single neighbor of a certain standing. "One would probably have to travel to Portland for that," Father had mentioned at dinner the night before, "or even back to Boston."

Mother had kicked him under the table.

That was the moment I knew—my life, as I'd known it, was utterly over.

My name is Evangeline Hughes, and I was the youngest of six children who all went on to independent, illustrious lives and successful marriages. It's obvious to me now that I was an unexpected accident, born ten years after the previous youngest offspring—who was currently a banker in San Francisco, married with three children.

I, on the other hand, was still at home with parents who should have been free to enjoy their elder years without the encumbrance of a daughter who needed to be married off—and sooner rather than later. At twenty-one, I was no longer a fresh-faced young debutante. I was, in fact, due to our unexpected removal to this place, in serious danger of being put "on the shelf."

For that reason, *why* they decided to leave Boston at that crucial stage in my social progress remains a mystery to me. I half suspect that Papa realized I was the last child who would live under his roof, and he was refusing to let me go, because we made each other laugh.

Or perhaps he simply couldn't pay the rent on our townhouse in Boston. That was more likely the case, for he'd been ill much of the past year, and might very well have been dismissed from his position at the bank.

I doubt I will ever know the particulars. He refers to this adventure with the fish and lighthouses as his "glorious retirement," and I would not dare to press him for the truth. So, a *glorious retirement* it shall be.

⁓

As I made my way along the sandy beach, stepping over giant piles of brittle seaweed and skipping to avoid the flat, foamy waves that pushed aggressively up the beach, I could not pretend to be happy about my current situation, one without friends or any romantic prospects. Perhaps it was time I simply accepted my fate to become a companion to my parents in their old age.

Suddenly, a seagull swooped low over my head and I ducked. Then I looked down and spotted a colorful seashell in the wet sand at my feet. Wondering what sort of creature would dwell in such a home, I crouched to pick it up, rinsed it off in a tiny pool of seawater, and slipped it into my pocket to take home with me.

As I walked, a fierce gust of wind blew my skirts around my ankles, causing them to flap like a ship's sail. I looked up to discover the sky had turned gray with thick, low-lying clouds rolling in from the sea. The gull was now floating in one spot on the wind just over my head, his wings spread wide, as if he had no desire to travel anywhere. He was simply basking in the indulgence of flight, taking pleasure in holding steady over my head.

In the distance, a flash of light over the horizon caused my heart to beat a little faster, then a deep rumble of thunder had me dashing up the beach to return to the coach road. A few cold, hard raindrops struck my cheeks, and I wished I had not walked such a distance from home, for I was at least two miles from the shelter of our front door.

I barely made it up the path, beyond the dunes and sea grasses, before the clouds emptied their coffers, dumping buckets of cold hard rain on me. There was nothing I could do but surrender to the hostile conditions and accept that I would soon be drenched to the bone. I might as well have waded into the water and swam home.

After walking a mile in the heavy downpour, I began to shiver. My teeth chattered and my upswept hair hung heavy and limp. My shoes made squishing sounds with every step, and I tried to distract myself from the chill by rubbing my thumb over the ridges in the seashell in my pocket.

Soon, the distant sound of horses' hooves and the rumble of an approaching vehicle caused me to turn. Sure enough, from around the bend, a shiny black brougham appeared with a team of two black horses and a well-dressed driver out front. He wore a black cloak and top hat, and held a long whip in one hand, the leather reins in the other.

I moved to the side of the road to allow the impressive vehicle to pass, and noted the shiny gold mountings, the green striped moldings and morocco trimmings at the back as it drove past.

Suddenly it pulled to a halt just ahead, causing a rush of unease in my belly, for I was alone in a remote location and could not be sure of my safety. I glanced into the woods to my right, half-tempted to dash into the trees and escape, but the foliage appeared thick and prickly, so I decided to take my chances with the inhabitants of the coach.

The door flung open and a striking gentleman with wavy, black hair stepped out, top hat in hand. He appeared to be in his mid-thirties and wore a fine, charcoal-gray jacket with a high, stiff white shirt collar and crimson cravat. He wore no gloves, but settled the hat upon his head before he spoke.

"Are you all right, miss?" he asked. "May I be of some assistance?"

"I'm quite all right, thank you," I replied with chattering teeth.

He stared at me a moment, his blue-eyed gaze traveling down the length of my body to the mud-stained hem of my peach-colored skirt, and back up to my soaked bodice, and the condition of my sopping hair, which had to be falling down in clumps around my face.

"You're shivering," he said, closing the door. "Please allow me to offer you shelter. I will take you where you need to go."

I shook my head, rather frantically, for I was not in the habit of getting into coaches with strange men, however handsome and gentlemanly they appeared.

Who *was* he? He certainly didn't look like any of the rough and weathered fishermen I'd seen about the village. I felt rather overcome.

"Please," he said. "I give you my word that no harm will come to you. I only wish to help, and I cannot, in good conscience, leave you here on the road when the temperature is dropping." He glanced up at the clouds. "I fear it's not going to let up for a while." He took a careful step forward. "Where do you live?"

When I stretched out my arm and pointed further down the road, I realized my hand was shaking uncontrollably. "That way."

The man's expression revealed that he would not take no for an answer. He strode toward me, removed his hat, and bowed slightly at the waist. "My name is Sebastian Fraser and I live here on the Cape, near the head light. Please, you must permit me to drive you somewhere."

Feeling numb and shivery from head to foot, and dreading the thought of walking another mile in such blustery weather, I reluctantly agreed and allowed him to escort me to his coach.

My rescuer—it makes sense, now, to call him that—opened the door for me, and I peered in at the luxurious green, deeply buttoned upholstery and matching tasseled blinds on the windows.

Mr. Fraser handed me up into the cozy interior, where I sat down gratefully, arranged my skirts and brushed the dampness from my sleeves. He then swung himself inside, shut the door, took a seat beside me and reached into his pocket for a clean white handkerchief, which he kindly offered to me.

I used it to dab at my face and hair. "Thank you, Mr. Fraser. I am in your debt."

"Do not be silly," he replied, tapping the handle of his walking stick on the ceiling while regarding me steadily. The vehicle lurched forward and we were suddenly on our way. "But I would like to know your name and where I should instruct my driver to take you."

"Of course. I do apologize. My name is Evangeline Hughes and I am new to the area. My father is George Hughes. We recently took up residence in the Vaughn Blackstone Cottage."

"Ah yes," he said. "I know the place. It's not out of the way at all. I must inform my driver." Mr. Fraser lowered the window glass and removed his hat before leaning out into the wind and rain. He shouted instructions while the wind blew a part in his thick black hair.

"What a spectacular day," he said as he closed the window and sat back. "Tell me more, Miss Hughes. What brings you and your family to Cape Elizabeth?"

Clearing my throat, I endeavored to speak in a steady voice, which was no easy task when I was still shivering from the cold. "My father has retired from his position at a Boston bank, and he wished to live close to the sea. He's a bit of a romantic that way. I think he's always dreamed of being captain of a sailing ship and traveling around the world. As it happens, Mr. Blackstone is an old family friend, and he offered us his cottage while he is abroad, indefinitely."

I refrained from mentioning that I'd overheard my parents discussing our financial situation late one night—that it was a charitable offering from Mr. Blackstone, for we were in dire straits and could not afford to pay our rent.

"Then please allow me to welcome you to Cape Elizabeth," Mr. Fraser said. "I am sure you will be very happy here. It's glorious in the summer months, but I must warn you—it can be bitter cold in the winter, when the ground freezes and the trees are coated in ice. You'd best have plenty of firewood on hand."

My eyebrows lifted.

"I do beg your pardon." He chuckled, and I couldn't help but admire the dimples in his cheeks. "That was rather tactless of me. I've frightened you, haven't I?"

"Not at all. We had 'spectacular' winters in Boston as well."

He smiled. "Indeed."

At this point, I would be remiss if I did not point out that my belly had exploded into a mad flock of nervous butterflies—which began the instant Mr. Fraser passed me the handkerchief and our fingertips touched briefly—for he was the most handsome man I had ever encountered in my young life.

To begin with, his eyes were a pale shade of blue, the likes of which I'd never imagined possible on any living human being. They brought to mind an aqua-marine gemstone with flecks of golden sunlight, beaming from within. His lips were full and moist, his mouth friendly, and his nose was perfectly proportioned. He had a strong jaw, bold cheekbones and a proud brow.

I, with my freckled complexion and burgundy hair, was positively mesmerized by his dark features and the deep timbre of his voice. He was like a hero out of a romantic legend, or a dream.

But of course, I thought he must be married or promised to someone. He was far too handsome to have escaped the clutches of some brilliant, ambitious young lady.

Like me?

"Miss Hughes, may I ask…?" He inclined his head slightly. "Were you named after Longfellow's poem, *Evangeline*?"

"I was," I replied matter-of-factly. "My mother is also a romantic, I profess. My parents are a perfect match. But I've always wondered why she chose to name me after such a tragic character. I hope I will not suffer a similar fate. I would prefer to live a happier life and not spend the whole of it searching for a lost love."

Mr. Fraser tapped his finger on his knee and gazed out the window. "Yes, we should all be spared that." Then he met my gaze again. "Did you know Longfellow spent time, during his younger years, at the Portland Head Light? I believe his poem *The Lighthouse* was inspired by his affection for the place. Do you know that poem?"

"Year after year," I said, "through all the silent night, burns on forevermore that quenchless flame, shines on that inextinguishable light."

He leaned forward slightly. "Forgive me. Of course, you would know it, considering you are named after Longfellow's greatest epic work."

I sighed. "It is both a blessing and a curse, for my mother was always reading his poems to me when I would have preferred to run down to the pond with the boys and catch frogs."

Mr. Fraser laughed and sat back. "A noble pursuit for a young lady," he replied with a charismatic smile that caused my heart to flutter anew.

I swallowed hard in an effort to calm my spirits. "And what about you, Mr. Fraser? Have you lived in Cape Elizabeth all your life?"

"I have," he replied. "My father was a sea captain—as am I."

I raised my fingers to my lips. "Good gracious. Have I already blundered? Should I be addressing you as *Captain* Fraser?"

"Probably," he replied. "Although I rather enjoyed the sound of *Mr.* Fraser across your lips. I don't know why."

His words struck me like a lightning bolt. Feeling suddenly shy, I lowered my gaze.

"Now it is my turn to apologize," he said. "That was rather uncouth of me. It must be the weather, knocking me off balance. Or perhaps it's your charming company. It's a delight to encounter a fresh face on the Cape. We don't see many like yours. You're quite lovely, Miss Hughes."

I cupped my hands together on my lap, and felt rather daring all of a sudden. "And I suspect there are not many faces like yours either. But now I am flattering you, quite shamelessly. Enough of that. You were saying…about living in Cape Elizabeth all your life?"

His shoulders rose and fell with a deep intake of breath. "Yes. My parents built our home six years before I was born, and when they passed, they left it to me, as I was the eldest."

"My condolences. When was that?"

"Almost ten years ago."

I gazed out the window for a moment and realized I had stopped shivering. A warm glow had settled around my heart. "You have siblings?" I asked, turning my attention back to the captain. "How many?"

"Three sisters and a younger brother," he replied. "My sisters reside in Portland, and my brother lives in London. He manages our British shipping interests."

"You own ships?"

"Yes. Eight of them. All steamers."

"How exciting. Do you see your sisters often?"

"I do. And that is, as you put it, both a blessing and a curse."

I laughed out loud and relaxed back on the soft upholstery.

Just then, a fierce gust of wind shook the carriage, and rain-drops, like tiny pebbles, pelted the glass.

"My poor driver," Captain Fraser said. "Thank heavens he's a tough old chap."

"In that regard, thank you for insisting that I accept your kind offer of assistance," I said. "I don't know how I would have managed to make it back on my own. I shouldn't have walked so far, but the weather was pleasant, at the time."

"That's the thing about Cape Elizabeth," he said. "If you don't like the weather, simply wait a few minutes."

I laughed again. "Perhaps I shall meet your sisters...I am looking forward to getting to know this place. It has suddenly become more interesting than I first imagined it would be."

Our gazes locked and held, and for a few seconds I felt transported, as if I were floating like that seagull on the wind—coasting on the air with natural ease and rapture.

In the very next instant, I felt giddy, wishing I could leap to my feet and dance a jig, right there in the coach.

Heaven help me. Was I already doomed to a mad infatuation, after only a few short minutes in this man's company?

Get a hold of yourself, Evangeline. You know nothing about him. He could be a disreputable rake, or married.

The carriage leaned to the side, and Captain Fraser peered out the foggy window. "I believe we have arrived," he said. "Blackstone Cottage."

The carriage wheels bumped over the uneven drive, then we pulled to a slow halt.

"I will escort you inside and introduce myself," he said, "for I must welcome your parents to the area."

He swung the carriage door wide open, got out and offered his hand. I stepped down and we fought our way through the wind and rain. Seconds later, introductions were made in the entrance hall, Captain Fraser was apologizing for dripping on the carpet, and my mother responded with: "Please! No apologies are necessary, sir! Won't you come in for tea? And please, allow my housekeeper to hang your coat to dry by the fire in the kitchen."

My gallant rescuer accepted her invitation and joined my parents in the parlor while I hurried upstairs to change into something dry and tidy my hair.

A short while later—after the captain's driver was sent around back to warm himself and take some tea in the kitchen—I returned to the parlor where Captain Fraser was engaging my parents in conversation about the area and places worth visiting. He stood up when I entered, and my heart fluttered as our eyes met.

When we were all seated again, conversation resumed, and he described his career as captain and the proprietor of a number of merchant ships he'd inherited from his father. He was cool, collected, and charming, and I found myself growing quiet and still inside as I listened to the silky tone of his voice and marveled at every fascinating word he spoke about his travels, around the world.

"So many magnificent experiences for a man your age," my father commented. "Unless you truly are an ancient mariner and have discovered the Fountain of Youth!"

Everyone laughed.

"Tell me, Captain," Mother interjected as she raised her delicate china teacup to her lips. "Is there a *Mrs.* Fraser at home?"

And there it was—the bold and fundamental question I had wondered about at least a dozen times during the past hour.

"Not yet," he replied with friendly optimism, and finished his tea.

My heart rejoiced!

"It must be difficult to feel settled," Mother said with understanding and compassion, "when you are away from home so much of the time."

"Indeed."

My still-rejoicing heart drummed with excitement, and suddenly I was grateful to have left dirty old Boston behind for this idyllic seaside paradise.

Thank you, Papa.

When it came time for the captain to take his leave, he thanked my mother for the tea, and we all moved together into the entrance hall.

"I shall take the liberty of sending over an invitation later today," he said as the housekeeper handed over his coat, "for dinner and a musical evening at my home this Saturday. It will be a small gathering of close friends and acquaintances—about twenty people I am sure you would enjoy meeting, since you are new to the area."

Mother laid a hand over her heart. "Oh, how can we ever thank you, Captain Fraser? You are most kind."

"I hope you can all attend." He turned to me in that moment, gave me a private look that was not meant as a good-bye, but rather an unspoken message: *I look forward to seeing you again soon.* He then bowed to both my parents before he placed his hat on his head. "And now I must brave the storm. Good day to you all."

With that, he was gone into the twilight.

"My word, what an impressive man," my mother said as soon as the captain drove off. "With an equally impressive coach, if I may say so. How fortunate you were, my darling girl, to have been rescued by him when you were in such peril."

"I wouldn't call it *peril,*" my father interjected as he returned to his chair by the fire to continue reading his book. "It's only rain. And he merely pulled over and offered our girl a ride home, as any decent person would do."

Mother rolled her eyes heavenward. "He could have simply driven by, but he didn't." She linked her arm through mine, led me up the creaky stairs to help me put away the wet clothes I'd left on my bed, and spoke softly, so that Father wouldn't hear. "And he invited us to a musical evening at his home next Saturday. He must have been very impressed with you, dearest, which is hardly surprising at all. You are a beautiful, intelligent young woman. How wonderful, Evangeline! Finally, we will meet some new people, and I dare say, he will know the right sort."

She entered my room and crossed to the window to look out. "I knew, if we were patient, we would find our place in society here. I am sure the captain knows *everyone* of good standing in

Cape Elizabeth and Portland as well. Well done, darling." She moved to the bed, shook out my wet gown, and hung it over the back of a chair. "Of course, I am very sorry that you were caught in the downpour, but sometimes these things happen for a reason. Perhaps you were meant to meet the captain, and this will be an important turning point in your life."

Mother was a firm believer in fate and destiny—to the point of forgetting, sometimes, to take hold of the wheel herself.

"Only time will tell," I casually replied as I began to unpin my hair, and consciously turned my back on my mother in an effort to conceal my own excitement and romanticism.

In that instance, I believe my mother was right—that certain things happen for a reason, and that my experiences in the months and years following my arrival in Cape Elizabeth would play a significant role in shaping the future. Not just my own, but others' as well. I wouldn't know that at the time, for I was still young and had yet to learn the joys and cruelties of life. I had also yet to truly understand its magic.

And so it was, on the night I dressed for the dinner party at Captain Fraser's mansion overlooking the sea, I was certain of one thing at least—that my fate had already been sealed. That it was my destiny to meet this man and fall madly, hopelessly in love with him.

"These are just the sorts of tales I'd dreamed I would hear when we moved into our splendid little seaside cottage," my father said at the dinner table, after the main course had been served. He raised his glass to Mr. Harvey, the lighthouse keeper, who had been a fisherman all his life until he retired from that career to accept the post at Portland Head Light.

Mr. Harvey had just regaled us with a thrilling tale of a ship that had run aground during a storm, directly in front of the lighthouse tower. Mr. Harvey and his stalwart assistant keeper, young Mr. Williams, had used ropes and ladders to rescue all those aboard. Mercifully there had not been a single casualty.

"Mind you, that sort of thing doesn't happen every day," Mr. Harvey added. "Some days are unbearably dull, and if a man is in the wrong frame of mind, the tedious, relentless roar of the ocean can drive him stark raving mad." A hush fell over the table. "Not me, though," he added. "When you grow up with it, the rhythm of ocean waves becomes like the sound of your own breathing."

Captain Fraser, seated at the head of the table, raised his glass. "Hear, hear. To the eternal breath of the sea."

"To the sea!" we all agreed as we sipped our wine.

In that moment, my gaze fixed upon Captain Fraser's, and we shared an intimate acknowledgement of each other. It was not the first time I had caught him watching me during dinner, and the glimmer of attraction I recognized in his eyes filled me with euphoria.

Feeling restless, and with my blood sizzling through my veins, I turned my attention back to the white-haired gentleman seated next to me. His name was Jeffrey Danforth, and he was a wealthy businessman from New York who spent his summers in Cape Elizabeth with his stunningly beautiful wife, Cecilia.

Mr. Danforth, a congenial man who seemed genuinely interested in others, kept me engaged in conversation throughout the meal, asking me questions about my life in Boston, and talking to me about activities I might enjoy in Portland. "Do you like the theater?" he asked.

"Very much so."

"Well, I am sorry to say there isn't much of a theater district in Cape Elizabeth—not like in Boston and New York—but my wife Cecilia has a wonderful singing voice and I hope you will stay to hear her entertain us later." He leaned close and spoke conspiratorially. "When I met her, she was lighting up the stage in New York, until she finally surrendered to my persistent proposals and agreed to become my wife."

"How wonderful." I regarded her with interest across the table. She was a slender, golden-haired beauty in her mid-thirties, while Mr. Danforth must have been in his late sixties, at least.

"I look forward to hearing her sing," I added.

Later, when we all filed into the drawing room where chairs had been set up in a semi-circle facing the grand piano, and a footman was making his way around the room with a tray of drinks, my mother leaned close and whispered in my ear. "I heard she's Mr. Danforth's third wife, and by far the youngest. He has ten children by his previous two wives, who are no longer with us, but he has no children with the current Mrs. Danforth, even though they've been married for seven years. As you can imagine, there is much speculation as to why that might be."

"Mother!" I whispered harshly. "That is none of our business."

Turning with a friendly smile toward the footman, Mother accepted a glass of brandy. As soon as the man turned away, she whispered, "And to think I imagined there would be no good gossip in Cape Elizabeth. At least not the delicious sort. Thankfully, I was mistaken."

"Mother, please stop at once. I do not wish to hear it."

Again I glanced discreetly at Captain Fraser who stood in front of the window, conversing with other guests. He sensed my eyes upon him and gave me a smoldering look that heated my blood. Feeling suddenly exposed, I lowered my gaze, demurely.

When I looked up again, he was still watching me with pleasure and amusement.

At last, Mrs. Danforth began to sing a piece from Mozart's opera, *Figaro.* I was intensely moved by her voice and understood why her husband had fought so hard to win her. She was breathtaking in every way, and for a moment, I wished selfishly that she were not the center of attention, for I was falling more passionately in love with my handsome host every passing moment, and I wanted every other woman in the room to disappear.

Again, I couldn't resist the compulsion to glance over at him. This time, he was alone against the back wall, appearing relaxed, still watching me with those compelling, magnetic eyes.

I felt a tremor of arousal deep in my belly, for he was so much more of a man than any of the young gentlemen who had flirted with me at balls and assemblies in Boston. Sebastian Fraser was an experienced sea captain. He had led crews of men around the world, earned their respect and shouted commands as he gripped the wheel in his strong, capable hands and steered the ship through the waves. I imagined him as a romantic hero with the wind in his hair and the salty spray in his face, his deep, masterful voice cutting through the roar of the wind in the sails. I was positively enraptured.

By that time, Mrs. Danforth had finished her song and my blood was on fire, my cheeks no doubt flushed with color. Everyone began to clap and murmur with appreciation.

Captain Fraser held me in his gaze the entire time, clapping slowly while he mouthed the words, "Meet me outside."

I felt breathless and exultant—and in that moment, I knew.

He *would* be mine, and I would be his.

Katelyn

That night, after our day at the beach where I spent far too much time on my phone googling "how to lucid dream," Bailey and I enjoyed another evening of cards and sipping Rusty Nails in the library of the inn. When it came time to say goodnight, we returned to our individual rooms, but I secretly ventured back out again on my own to have another look at the sundial—this time at night.

The sky was clear with a half moon and plenty of starlight, and the ocean was calmer than it had been on the night of our arrival. The violent storm and the cab driver's disturbing tale of manslaughter in the house had been rather unsettling. Tonight, there was only a constant, gentle murmur of waves lapping the shore, which eased my mood as I walked down the stone path, under the rose arbor, to the edge of the property.

I came to a halt, about ten feet away from the sundial—for Sylvie's warnings came suddenly to mind. What if she were right, and this was a mistake? Maybe I shouldn't even touch it. What if I was taken somewhere I didn't want to go?

But did I truly believe that this ancient timekeeper was a portal to another dimension? It still seemed like the stuff of fantasy, even to me, who had come all this way across the country in search of answers to questions I didn't even understand.

As I slowly, cautiously moved closer, my rational mind insisted that the portal idea was exactly what my mother had called it: a lot of mumbo jumbo. So I stood over the sundial with confidence and defiance regarding its power, and reached out to run my open hand over the top of the dial plate, as if I were dusting it clean with a damp cloth. Then I traced the clock numbers with the tip of my index finger, feeling the depths of the grooves.

I moved, full circle, around it, never lifting my hand or breaking contact with the stone, while I listened to the waves on the beach and the chirping of the crickets in the cool grass.

Finally I backed away from the stone and looked up at the big house, all lit up in the night, as if there were a party going on inside. I imagined what it must have been like to live there in a time without electricity, when women wore corsets and men wore top hats and traveled in horse-drawn carriages. I gazed up at the veranda and pictured Captain Fraser and his beloved young wife standing at the balustrade, drinking champagne, gazing up at the moon. I wondered about their courtship and how long it had lasted. Was it love at first sight? Or was it an arranged marriage where their love took time to grow?

History was a fascinating thing, I thought, as I returned my attention to the sundial and rubbed my hand over the top of it again. The past seemed like such a different world, and yet it wasn't. It was this very same world, with the same smells and sounds and textures. The same ocean breezes. The same emotions.

Love. Hate. Jealousy. Joy.

Grief.

Suddenly I felt the loss of the son I'd never had—at least not in this lifetime—which sounded completely insane, even to my own ears.

Maybe I should consider therapy when I went home. It would probably be a good idea.

But first, I thought stubbornly, as I returned to the stone path and walked back to the house, I would see if I could find a way to have a lucid dream. Maybe, just maybe, new experiences and answers existed out there, somewhere in the ether.

Evangeline

Twenty-six

1878

I remained in my chair for a moment, waiting for the captain to exit the drawing room. Then, while Mrs. Danforth and her husband flipped through pages of music, I leaned toward my mother and whispered in her ear, "Will you excuse me for a moment?"

She watched me rise from my chair. Thankfully Mrs. Danforth began to sing as I reached the door, so my mother could not possibly follow without offending the performer.

I wandered to the grand entrance hall and noticed that the front door was open. Taking a deep breath and striving to prepare myself for a private rendezvous with a man I desired passionately—to the point that it felt almost reckless—I strode forward and stepped onto the wide veranda that overlooked the sea.

Captain Fraser stood at the white painted balustrade, gazing up at the stars and the half moon in the sky. He raised a glass of champagne to his lips, and I noticed another glass perched on the rail, waiting for me.

He turned as I approached, and without a word, he handed it to me. As I accepted it and gently clinked glasses with him, I was keenly aware of the soft murmur of the surf, surging onto the rocks at the edge of the lawn, even though it was a calm, almost windless night. Crickets chirped in the grass below.

"It's a perfect half moon," he said.

I looked up at the stars, twinkling in the sky. "What a beautiful night. Thank you for inviting us to your home, Captain. I love everything about it."

He met my gaze with a tenderness I did not expect. "Tell me."

I grinned at him, for I understood he was seeking my approval, that he wanted assurance that I could, potentially, be happy there. Perhaps it was over-confident and presumptuous of me, but I felt there was a connection between us that defied reason and experience. I felt as if we knew each other intimately, even though we'd only spent a few hours together. And I was convinced he felt the same way—that I had swept him off his feet just as powerfully as he had swept me off mine—and he was already considering the future.

"I love the vastness of it," I said, looking up at the massive portico above us and the white Roman columns that supported it. "There is a perfect balance in the architecture. One side of the house is a mirror image of the other." I looked out, beyond the railing. "And the wide green lawn and view of the sea…I love that with only the light of the moon, I can see all the way to where water meets sky. It's like seeing to the very edges of the earth. And your staff seems so loyal and devoted to you. Footmen in Boston are not nearly so cheerful." Captain Fraser chuckled softly at that.

"Your mother's crystal is exquisite," I added. "Where did she get it? I've never seen anything like it before."

"My father brought it back from Singapore when they first married. He purchased it during an estate auction. It had belonged to an aristocratic Englishmen living with his concubine in the Far East."

"Good heavens," I said. "How positively scandalous. My mother would go mad for that story."

He chuckled with amusement.

Inside the house, Mrs. Danforth continued to sing, and we listened for a moment.

"I wonder if she ever regretted leaving her glamorous career on the stage for married life here in Cape Elizabeth," I said.

Captain Fraser shook his head. "She has everything a woman could ever desire," he replied. "Her husband's as rich as Croesus, and they only come here during the summer months. Otherwise, they're in New York, and he doesn't forbid her from performing. He encourages it, actually."

"That sounds very modern and liberal. They do seem happy, despite the age difference."

"I believe so," he replied, "which is how it should be. As they say—the soul is ageless."

"Is *that* what they say?"

He casually shrugged a shoulder. "I've heard it a time or two."

While he regarded me intently in the glow of the moon, I took another sip of champagne and felt a pleasant warmth pour through my body. I was far too relaxed. My body felt like liquid.

I looked away. "Forgive me. I was nervous tonight. I drank too much wine and now I am a bit lightheaded."

"Why were you nervous?" he asked, though I suspected he already knew the answer.

"Because I was looking forward to seeing you again. I didn't know what to expect."

He leaned casually upon the balustrade. "I was looking forward to seeing you again, too, Miss Hughes. You came into my life rather unexpectedly, standing at the side of the road as you were."

"Like a drowned cat," I replied, making fun of myself. "Shivering."

"Thank heavens for that, or you wouldn't have accepted assistance from me, a complete stranger."

"You mustn't remind me. It was rather frightening for a moment or two. I had no idea what your intentions were."

"I assure you, they were completely honorable."

"Well, of course I know that *now*."

He smiled again, and Mrs. Danforth stopped singing. The guests inside applauded and cheered.

"We should go back," I said, finishing my champagne. "I feel guilty, keeping you from your party."

"But this is where I want to be. Right here."

"As do I. But we should go inside before my mother takes to worrying and causes a scene."

"Very well."

We turned away from the sparkling moonlit sea and crossed the wide veranda, moving slowly to the door.

The captain touched my arm. "I would like to call upon you, Miss Hughes—with your permission of course. Perhaps on Monday. It would give me great pleasure to escort you and your parents to the lighthouse for a tour. I am sure we could arrange it with Mr. Harvey this evening."

"That sounds lovely," I replied as we entered the house and returned to the drawing room just as Mrs. Danforth was curtsying before her captivated, adoring audience.

CHAPTER

Twenty-seven

Portland Head Light, Monday

"As you can see," Mr. Harvey said, leading us up the cast iron spiral staircase, "the tower is lined with brick, which was an improvement in '55. And what you are about to see is a second-order Fresnel lens which was installed in '64, after the wreck of the *Bohemian,* where forty immigrants perished. I wasn't the keeper back then, but I've heard the tales."

Our lighthouse tour proved to be a fascinating escapade, but equally fascinating was Captain Fraser's continued ability to make a brilliant impression on my parents—my mother especially—who seemed to think she was the instigator and constant navigator of my budding romance.

"Mark my words," she whispered in my ear when we first arrived at the lighthouse and stepped out of Captain Fraser's luxurious carriage. "I'll do whatever it takes to see you at the altar before the snow falls, because he is the catch of the century."

"But it's not up to *you* to make it happen," I replied, knowing it was my pride talking, for I couldn't abide the idea of my mother taking credit for Captain Fraser's affection for me. *She* wasn't the one who had inspired him to bring his carriage to a halt, throw open the door, and step out into the rain. If it weren't for me, she would never even have made his acquaintance.

Later, after our journey up and down the tower stairs, followed by a leisurely walk along the cliff, Mr. Harvey invited us
back to his single-story keeper's cottage—a modest stone dwelling at the base of the tower. He offered us tea and biscuits, and
while the water boiled on the iron stove, he entertained us with
more thrilling tales of his life as a fisherman.

Then, suddenly, in the middle of one of his exciting an-
ecdotes, the door swung open, and a young man, who appeared to be about my age, stepped into the light. He carried a
load of kindling and wore a gray woolen cap. His windblown,
honey-blond hair was in desperate need of a trim, for it nearly
reached his shoulders.

Abruptly, he halted his stocky frame in the open doorway.
"Good morning," he said, appearing surprised by our presence in
the front room.

Mr. Harvey beckoned for him to step inside. "Come in, come
in. Close the door behind you and say hello to Mr. and Mrs.
Hughes, who are new to the area, and their charming daughter,
Evangeline. You already know Captain Fraser. Everyone, this is
my nephew, Laurence Williams."

Mr. Williams moved across the room to the woodstove,
where he set the firewood down with a clatter in a wooden box.
Straightening, he wiped his hands on the front of his tattered wool
jacket, stepped toward my father with his hand outstretched, and
said, "It's a pleasure to meet you, sir."

Father stood to shake the young man's hand, while Mr. Harvey
continued to explain: "Mr. Williams is assistant lighthouse keeper.
He's been with me for the better part of a year, and if it weren't for
him, I wouldn't have the luxury of accepting generous invitations
to fancy dinner parties and musical performances."

Captain Fraser, seated at the table with one long leg crossed over the other, said, "Williams, one of these days I will invite you instead, and Mr. Harvey can be the one to hold down the fort."

Mr. Williams smiled. "That would be very good, sir. And I wouldn't feel guilty about it. Not one bit."

The men laughed and Mr. Harvey slapped his nephew on the back. "Poor lad hasn't had a day off in six months. Join us for a cup of tea, son. You've earned it."

Mr. Williams pulled a chair away from the wall, spun it around and sat astride it. "So you're new to the area?" he asked me directly.

"Yes, we're from Boston," I replied. "My father just retired."

"Ah. Well, you picked a good place for the next chapter of your life, sir," Mr. Williams said to my father. "There are plenty of decent people in this town who would give you the shirt off their backs. And it's just about the prettiest place on earth in the summer months when the flowers are blooming, the breeze is blowing, and the water is warm enough for a swim."

"It's never quite *that* warm," Mr. Harvey disagreed as he removed the kettle from the stove and filled the teapot. "Once you've bathed in the turquoise waters of the Caribbean, it spoils you for the North Atlantic, even in August. Sometimes I wish I'd never taken that plunge."

My mother perked up excitedly. "Oh, do tell us about that, Mr. Harvey. What was it like, swimming so close to the equator? I cannot even imagine."

He described the climate in St. Thomas and Mexico, and the extreme heat that could make a robust man faint dead away on his feet. The conversation was lively and relaxed as we sipped our tea and enjoyed biscuits with strawberry jam.

Soon it was time for us to go, and we rose from our wooden chairs to thank Mr. Harvey and his nephew. They walked us outside toward Captain Fraser's coach, but halfway there, I realized I had forgotten my gloves on the table.

"I'll fetch them for you." Mr. Williams jogged back to the little stone house. I waited a moment or two in the yard while Mother and Father climbed into the vehicle, causing it to bounce slightly under their weight. At last, Mr. Williams reappeared in the doorway.

"I can't find them, Miss Hughes!" he called out to me. "Are you certain you don't have them?"

I quickly checked my reticule, and sure enough, I had stuffed them into the bottom. "I do beg your pardon, Mr. Williams! Here they are!" I quickly pulled them out, waved them at him, and tugged them on.

He ran back to meet me. "It's just as well, because I found this on the floor. Is it yours?"

He opened his rough, callused hand to reveal a pearl earring in a drop setting.

"Yes, it's mine. Gracious, that's never happened before." I reached up to check my other earlobe, to make sure that earring was still in place. "These were a gift from my late grandmother. I would have been heartbroken to lose them." I plucked the earring from his palm and dropped it into my reticule. "I will have this checked before I wear it again."

All the while, Captain Fraser was conversing with Mr. Harvey outside the coach, waiting for me to join them.

"Have you made many new friends since you arrived, Miss Hughes?" Mr. Williams asked me. "Sometimes it's difficult in a new place, to meet people your own age. If you like, you could come to a corn boil on Saturday at the Smiths', around 7:00. They live at Smuggler's Cove."

"Smuggler's Cove...That sounds a bit dodgy."

He laughed. "Nothing to worry about. The Smiths are decent folk. Their son's a fiddle player and it's always a rip-roaring good time. I hope you'll come. You can bring your parents, of course. Mr. Smith would be happy to meet them. He's friendly and hospitable."

Mr. Williams stopped and faced me, not far from the open door of the coach, and waited for an answer. My eyes roamed over his sun-bronzed face, golden hair and bright blue eyes. There was something youthful, energetic and lighthearted about him, yet something that suggested experience and wisdom as well.

"I will think about it," I replied. "Thank you for the invitation. I enjoyed meeting you."

I turned and laid my gloved hand upon Captain Fraser's. With a handsome, charming smile, he assisted me into the vehicle, then entered and sat beside me. The nearness of his strong, muscular body caused a shock of awareness in me, and I swallowed hard, hoping my cheeks were not suddenly flushed with color.

A moment later, as we rolled away on carriage wheels that bumped over the rutted lighthouse road, I realized I felt very at home in this place and excited about the future. That clarity helped me to realize how foolish we can be at times—to fear the unknown, when occasionally the unknown can be far better than anything we ever imagined. I decided from that moment on never to resist change or steer away from new horizons.

I glanced at my mother just then, seated across from me. She frowned with disapproval.

"What were you thinking, accepting an invitation from that crude young man when you were in the presence of the captain? What must he be thinking?"

"I didn't accept Mr. Williams's invitation," I said, as I fumbled around the top of my straw hat for my hatpin, found it and yanked it out. "I told him I would think about it. And he wasn't crude. He was very polite. He found my earring for me. I am grateful for that. You should be, too. It was Grandmother's earring." I tossed the hat onto my bed.

"His clothing was dirty and threadbare," she argued, "and did you see the way he plunked himself down on that chair, *astride,* without even removing his cap?"

I turned to the dressing table and removed my bracelet and necklace. "We're not in Boston anymore, Mother, and I don't see why we cannot overlook a few breaches in rules of etiquette. It's not as if we were in the presence of royalty. And Mr. Harvey was perfectly hospitable. You mustn't complain. It was a wonderful day. I enjoyed myself tremendously, and I believe the captain did as well."

Mother paced about the room. "So is that your plan? To play them against each other? To try them both on for size and see which one you prefer? It would be a pointless exercise, Evangeline, because there is no comparison."

"That is not my plan at all," I calmly replied, aiming to pacify her. "Mr. Williams was merely acting as a good neighbor should. He was very welcoming. And you needn't worry. Just now, when Captain Fraser said good-bye to me on the front porch, he asked if he could call again on Saturday. He wishes to take us all out for a sunset sail. I told him yes. I hope that was all right."

Mother's face lit up like the impressive Fresnel lens we had just seen at the lighthouse. "Saturday! Why didn't you say something sooner?"

"I'm saying it now."

She gave me a sneaky, satisfied grin—as if this were an elaborate game of chess and we'd just captured the king. Striding toward me, taking my shoulders in her hands, she said, "So you have made your choice. You won't be free to attend Mr. Williams's corn boil, for you will be sailing the high seas with a handsome gentleman who might as well be royalty in this part of the world."

"Yes, I have made my choice. Although…he is older than me, Mother. Do you think that is an issue?"

"Certainly not," Mother replied. "I doubt he's a day over thirty-five, and that is young by my standards. You did the right thing to accept his invitation."

How could I *not* have accepted? I was feverish with constant dreams of him, and I could barely contain my desire to see him again.

Back at the lighthouse, when he had taken hold of my hand and assisted me into the coach, all my senses had leapt to life, and I felt like a breathless girl of fifteen.

What would it be like to be held in his arms? I wondered languorously as my mother picked up her skirts and hurried downstairs to tell Father the good news—that on Saturday, we would not be attending the corn boil at Mr. Smith's at Smuggler's Cove. We would be sailing around Casco Bay on Captain Fraser's luxurious yacht.

I flopped onto my bed and smiled.

Two months later, when the leaves turned red, yellow and gold, and the air grew crisp in the mornings, the summer residents left town and everything felt quieter and more serene in Cape Elizabeth. Except for my heart, which caused a continuous commotion in me.

Captain Fraser had been courting me formally since the night he took us sailing, and since then, my feelings for him had grown stronger and more passionate with each passing day. He paid regular calls to our seaside cottage, and invited us to his mansion for dinner with prominent members of local society. Occasionally, he and I arranged to meet secretly when I took afternoon strolls to collect seashells on the beach. We would walk together and talk, until it was time for me to return home.

Mother never questioned the propriety of my solitary afternoons. Perhaps she believed Cape Elizabeth was a safe place for a young woman alone, or perhaps she knew I was meeting the captain and did not wish to interrupt the speed and progress of our courtship. Some might have considered her lack of interference to be negligent and irresponsible, but I was not one of those critics, for nothing mattered more to me than being in the presence of the handsome, beloved captain of my soul.

Looking back on it, I probably shouldn't have felt so romantic about the whole affair, as if I were living in a fairy tale. Perhaps it would have been wiser to maintain a more judicious attitude and be prepared for future hard times and disappointments, which would undoubtedly come.

Eventually.

⸺

"I was about to give up on you," I said to Captain Fraser late one October afternoon, when I met him on top of the sand dune on my way off the beach. The sky had turned overcast and the wind gusted, whipping my skirts around my ankles. I gathered my shawl more tightly about my shoulders. "I've been walking up and down the beach for almost an hour, but you never came, and now I have to go."

"I'm sorry to be late," he replied, striding forward onto the dune with purpose and determination.

Though I was angry with him for keeping me waiting—for he had promised to arrive well over an hour ago—I couldn't help but marvel at how handsome he looked in his dark, tailored jacket and blue silk neckcloth. Just the sight of him in the gray light of the afternoon filled me with rapture and melted away all my fears and frustrations—for he had not stood me up after all.

How little it took for me to forgive him.

"I was on my way out the door," he explained, "when my solicitor arrived unexpectedly, needing me to sign something. I couldn't turn him away." Captain Fraser glanced up at the sky. "Will you come into my coach, Miss Hughes? I wish to spend time with you. I was hoping we could walk together, but it looks like rain."

"I really should start for home," I said, "or I will be late, and Mother will worry."

"Allow me to drive you."

I hesitated and pulled my shawl even tighter about me. "She doesn't know we are together. I don't want her to feel the need to start setting rules, forbidding me to walk alone, unchaperoned."

My walks had never been a problem before—not as far as my mother was concerned—and I don't know why I was making a fuss about it today. I suppose I was still recovering from my hurt feelings over the past hour, when I had slowly come to the conclusion that the great love of my life had brushed me off.

Captain Fraser strode closer and reached me on top of the dune. My pulse quickened, for there was a constant physical longing inside me that could not be satisfied, especially when he stood a mere arm's length away.

"Do you forgive me?" he asked, and the troubled, regretful look in his eyes broke me completely. I realized I was soft putty in his hands, but I didn't care. Not as long as I mattered to him.

"Yes, I forgive you," I replied on a sigh, "because it wasn't your fault. I'm sorry if I was angry. I was disappointed, that's all. I didn't know why you weren't here. I thought perhaps you'd forgotten me. I fear I may be too young for you. There is a fourteen-year age difference between us, sir. Perhaps I am not worldly enough."

His head drew back as if I had swung a punch at him. "Too young? Not worldly enough? My darling Miss Hughes—that is what I love most about you. Your youth and innocence. You have charmed me completely. You make me feel more alive than ever before, and you have helped me to remember how to laugh, and to recognize and not take for granted how remarkable our world is. I am constantly moved by your fascination with a colorful seashell, for instance." He waved a hand through the air. "Or the movement of a wispy cloud, fast across the sky. *Forgotten* you? Never, Miss Hughes. I live for our walks on the beach."

Emotion rose up within me, and I could have wept at the sound of those words on his lips. I took a desperate step forward and suddenly found myself spilling out my whole heart to him.

"I live for them, too, Captain Fraser. If you must know, I miss you all the time. I think of you day and night. And when you didn't come today, I was so afraid this was over—as if I had been wrenched awake, out of a perfect dream. I don't know what I would have done if you wanted to end it."

He laid a hand on my cheek, and I inhaled sharply at the contact, for this was the first time he had touched me, aside from offering his arm or a gloved hand to assist me in some way. The captain had behaved with perfect propriety over the past eight weeks.

Until this moment…

"I feel it too, Miss Hughes," he said, his voice husky and low. "And I am afraid I cannot go on like this much longer."

"What do you mean?" I asked, terrified that he was about to put a stop to this. That he was going to tell me I was too young for him, or too emotional. Too demanding.

"I mean that you have become everything to me," he said, "and I am completely besotted—and utterly, woefully, heart-breakingly in love with you."

I bit my lip to stifle a cry of delight, and before I knew what was happening, he had gathered me into his arms and pressed his lips to mine.

Pleasure radiated through me and I felt transported, as if I were rising up on a floating cloud. I'd never been kissed like that before—with passion and ferocity. I'd only been kissed by one boy in a childish experiment outside the fish market in Boston. I had been fourteen at the time.

That was nothing like this. Today, I was being kissed by a real man who knew how to hold me, how to make me open up to him, how to seduce me completely.

His lips parted, and even though a part of me knew this was wicked and dangerous—and if anyone saw us, my reputation would be reduced to rubble—I couldn't say no to him. There was nothing in the world that could keep me from the pleasure of his touch and the ecstasy of knowing that he loved me. I would have done anything for him in that moment. I would have given him everything—my heart, my body, and my soul.

Perhaps he already owned it.

When he stepped back, he left me trembling and dizzy. My lips parted. My eyes opened wide as saucers. I blinked up at him, half thinking this was a dream.

"Miss Hughes." He took both my gloved hands in his and rubbed the pads of his thumbs across my knuckles. "From the moment I stepped out of my coach and saw you on the road, shivering and drenched to the bone, I knew I was done for. I believe I fell in love with you in that instant, before you spoke a single word. It was like a lightning bolt, and I am still in its grip." His eyes lifted and his hypnotic, blue-eyed gaze met mine. "I've been alone in that big house of mine for many years, because I have never found a woman who has inspired me to pursue her, unreservedly. I feel as if I've been waiting for you all my life, and it boggles my mind that we have only just met." He paused and took a deep breath. "I want very much to have you with me, at my side, so that I can be content at last, with the woman I am destined to love. I believe you are that woman, Miss Hughes, and that we are meant to be together, forever. Until the end of time."

My chest was heaving. I could barely breathe.

"I wish to ask you a very important question," he continued, "but first I must ask your father for his permission and his blessing. Is he at home today?"

I nodded frantically. "Yes, he is."

"Then would you permit me to drive you home and speak with him? Please tell me now if this is not what you want. If that is so, I will understand and say no more about it. But if you have feelings for me, Miss Hughes…If what you say is true—that you miss me when we are apart…" He regarded me lovingly while the savage ocean breezes swirled around us, and my heart exploded with happiness.

"Would you make me the luckiest man alive, and be my wife?"

I threw my arms around his neck and buried my face in the firm wall of his chest. "Yes, Captain Fraser! *Yes!*"

He clasped my body tightly to his. "Then it is time, my darling Evangeline, for you to start calling me Sebastian."

I drew back to lay my gloved hand upon his cheek. "Nothing would make me happier. Now, please, let us go. You must speak with my father before you change your mind."

"Never," Sebastian said. And like the perfect gentleman he was, he offered his arm and escorted me down the slope of the sandy dune to the path that would take us to his coach.

CHAPTER

Thirty

❧

O n New Year's Eve, 1878, with giant snowflakes falling from the sky like confetti, I married my one true love.

The ceremony was a simple affair in the Cape Elizabeth Chapel, with only our closest friends and family in attendance. This included my parents, a few special aunts and uncles, Sebastian's sisters and their families from Portland, and Mr. Harvey, the lighthouse keeper.

I wore a white velvet wedding gown with a fur muff instead of flowers, and a matching mantle of soft white rabbit fur. After the ceremony, our guests and the minister followed us to Sebastian's home for an intimate reception and dinner, where toasts and speeches were delivered. Then we all danced until midnight to ring in the New Year.

Much champagne was consumed, but it did not dull my senses, for I was jubilant the whole night long, and not the least bit tired when it came time to say goodnight to our guests and retire to my husband's bedchamber. As man and wife—at last.

―᷒

The first day of 1879 dawned majestically before my eyes, for I was transformed. I was now a married woman, and pleasure took on a whole new meaning for me. When I rose from bed that morning, donned my robe and gazed out the frosty window at the cold, winter sea, I was warmed by the sensation of Sebastian's arms around me as he joined me there to watch the sunrise. Soon, we climbed beneath the covers again, fell back to sleep, and woke up to breakfast in bed.

By noon, a frigid wind rattled the glass panes and snow mixed with ice-pellets began to fall. As cozy as we were in bed, it was difficult to believe that a severe winter storm was beginning its violent assault across the state.

Temperatures dropped to record levels, and three feet of snow fell in a twenty-four-hour period.

What was there to do as newlyweds, but remain in our warm bed until it was time to dig ourselves out?

Over the next two years, I bore my husband two healthy, beautiful children—a boy, Nathan, and a girl, Amelie—and we were as happy as any family could be. Sebastian's shipping company continued to prosper, and most days, I felt as if I were living in a picture-perfect dream, for I never imagined I could be so deeply and passionately loved. Everything felt right and as it should be. I must have been thoroughly blessed indeed, for he was not only my best friend and my lover, but the one true mate of my soul.

Katelyn

For three nights in a row, I used the information I had gleaned online about lucid dreams and astral projection, and went to bed straining to recall another life: the one I had seen as I flew over the handlebars of my bicycle, in which I had a son named Logan. But each morning I woke from a dreamless sleep—or at least it seemed that way. If I dreamed, I could not remember, and unlike what happened to Sylvie, I did not wake with new knowledge or wisdom about my existence, or my true destiny in this lifetime. Everything was the same. I was still Katelyn Roberts, recently divorced television reporter who was probably insane because she yearned to have her imaginary son back.

Bailey was supportive as always, but there wasn't much she could do to help me. The best we could do was try to enjoy our summer vacation together in Maine.

And so, we went down to breakfast each morning in the dining room at the inn, socialized with the other guests, then spent the day at the beach or touring the area. We visited the Henry Wadsworth-Longfellow House in Portland, and afterward, went shopping for clothes and souvenirs.

On another day, we visited the Portland Head Light Museum, where Captain Fraser's wife had been swept off the rocks over a century before. It was a stunning, ruggedly beautiful location on a point of land that jutted out into the ocean, and as we went through the displays inside the museum—a large Victorian dwelling built in 1891—I found myself intensely moved by the history of the place. I read about the shipwrecks and storms and stories of adventure, and about all the lighthouse keepers who had dedicated their days and nights to keeping the tower lit—and to warning others of danger on the rocks.

Afterward, Bailey and I went outside. We stood at the fence and looked out over the jagged coastline to the blissfully calm sea beneath a bright blue sky. Still curious about so many things, I approached one of the attendants.

"Can you tell me where Captain Fraser's wife was standing when she was swept off the rocks in 1881?" I asked. "There was only a brief mention of it inside."

"We're not sure exactly," the woman replied, "but we think she might have been standing over there." She pointed down at a small cove, north of the tower. "We have no idea why she would have been down there on such a cold winter morning. Her husband and the assistant lighthouse keeper were nearby, which must have been an awful thing for them to witness."

"For certain," Bailey said as she lifted her sunglasses to look down at the rocks.

I moved slowly along the fence. "It's hard to imagine something like that happening today, when the water is so calm. It looks harmless down there."

"It's a very different sight during rough weather," the attendant told me, "especially when the tide is in. It's terrifying to see how violent the ocean can become. Poor Mrs. Fraser wouldn't have stood a chance, especially in the winter. She was from Boston, I believe, so she didn't grow up in Cape Elizabeth. She might not have understood how unpredictable the ocean can be."

Later, Bailey and I took the "cliff walk" and enjoyed the rest of the park, and as usual, ended up on a blanket at Crescent Beach with our books and sunscreen.

That night, after we said goodnight to the other guests at the inn, retired to our rooms and got into our pajamas, I turned on the local Portland news. But then Bailey showed up at my door with two tiny bottles of Baileys Irish Cream and a couple of bubble base tumblers.

"Interested?" she asked, holding them up with a smile. "It's my namesake drink."

I chuckled. "I certainly don't need the calories, and you are a terrible influence...but definitely yes." I stepped back, invited her in and shut off the television.

She poured each miniature bottle into a glass, and we climbed onto the bed to talk about our week.

"Only a couple more days," she said. "Then we'll be flying home again. Are you going to be okay?"

I inched back against the comfortable array of thick feather pillows and crossed my legs at the ankles. "I don't know. I guess so. I came here thinking I was going to uncover something mind blowing about my past or my future, but not much has happened, even after talking to Sylvie and learning what she went through—*allegedly*. Now I'm starting to wonder if she was delusional, thinking the sundial was some sort of portal through time. And apparently, I somehow tapped into her crazy brain waves through telepathy or something—like what you saw in that documentary." I sipped my drink.

Bailey, sitting at the foot of the bed, tucked her legs under her and leaned on one arm. "I'm sorry you haven't found what you were looking for. But maybe all of this will make sense to you one day. Maybe there's a reason you're here. It might be a stepping stone to something. Who knows? Maybe you'll write a book about it, or do a story on lighthouses, or sundials, and win a big award for it."

"Maybe so." Holding my drink in my hand, I gazed up at the portrait of Captain Fraser's young wife over the fireplace. "Do you think she looks like me?" I asked, tilting my head to the side.

Bailey slid along the bed to sit beside me against the headboard. She crossed her legs at the ankles as well and stared up at the portrait. "Yes, actually. I wouldn't have noticed it until you said it, but wow. Yes. There's something in her eyes. And her hair is the same color."

I took another sip of my Irish cream. "Do you remember, after I had the cycling accident and I was trying to figure out what I saw, that I did some research online about reincarnation and past lives?"

"Yes," she replied.

"It totally creeped me out at the time, because there were actual documented cases of children who insisted they had different names and different families. When the parents did some investigating, they found those other families and discovered that they had actually lost a child shortly before the new child was born. The other parents were convinced the young child was their own teenage son or daughter, reincarnated. And then, to top it all off, the kids grew up to look very much like the son or daughter who died. It was so freaky."

Bailey blinked a few times. "Why are you telling me this? Do you think you're this woman, reincarnated?" She raised a finger. "Ah hah. Maybe *that's* why we're here—because you wanted to sleep in your own bed again." Bailey nudged me playfully.

I chuckled. "I'll probably need therapy after this."

The air conditioning came on just then, and we both jumped with fright, then burst out laughing.

"This has been a wild trip," Bailey said, glancing around. "I wonder, if on top of everything else, this place is haunted. Remember the story the cab driver told us? I wonder how many other people have died in this house."

I nudged her hard in return, nearly knocking her off the bed. "Stop it, or I won't sleep a wink tonight, and you'll have to deal with my early morning cranky edition."

"I'm sorry," she said, still laughing. "Blame it on the Baileys."

"Sure. Let's blame it on the Baileys."

As it happened, my conversation with Bailey turned out to be the perfect nightcap.

For the first time since my arrival in Cape Elizabeth, I did not struggle to make sense of what I had envisioned on the mountaintop during my cycling accident, nor did I attempt to dream lucidly about a life I never actually lived. I let it all go and relaxed into the soft feathery pillows, gazing up at the portrait of Evangeline Fraser.

My thoughts then turned to the CNN job in New York.

As I rolled to my side and hugged the pillow next to my cheek, I began to feel that it was time I set sail toward unknown horizons. I shouldn't fear it, because a fresh start could turn out to be far better and more fulfilling than anything I'd experienced in my past. Perhaps my destiny was not here in Cape Elizabeth, but in New York City, and I had simply needed this trip to help me learn to look forward, not back, otherwise I might have remained stuck in the same place forever. And in a terrible rut.

Sylvie had certainly tried to convince me to move on. Perhaps *she* was the person I had needed to meet. A part of my destiny, in a sense.

As I fell asleep, the young woman in the portrait over the fireplace reminded me that life was short and every day was precious—because you never knew when a rogue wave might come out of nowhere and sweep you away. I didn't want to get swallowed up by the past. I wanted to live each day to the fullest.

Feeling liberated by these thoughts, I drifted off to a place where my spirit felt light, without burdens of any kind. I dreamed I was walking down to the sundial, just before dawn. I put my hands on it, but then I felt cold and began to shiver. My teeth chattered. I wished I had worn gloves.

Evangeline

Spring, 1881

"I wish you didn't have to go," I said to Sebastian as we stood on the dock in South Portland, while his trunks and bags were loaded onto the ship. "The children are going to miss you terribly."

"You'll miss me too, I hope." He raised my gloved hand to his lips and kissed it.

"Of course, more than anything. Perhaps, if Mother feels better in the next few weeks, we'll be able to join you."

"I'll pray for it."

It had not been an easy year thus far, for my mother had fallen ill with a severe fever that lasted for days, and she had not yet fully recovered. Due to her continued lethargy for more than a month, the doctor feared it might be some form of cancer. We were still awaiting a diagnosis.

At the same time, Sebastian's brother Marcus, who operated the London office for their shipping company, had suffered a health crisis. His eyes were failing him, and blindness was a distinct possibility, which was why Sebastian was leaving me to cross the Atlantic and take up the reins in his brother's stead.

A horn blew on the steamship, and I squeezed my husband's hands. "It's time for you to go, isn't it?"

I could hardly bear it. My heart was breaking at the thought of being separated from him.

"I'm sorry, my love. I will write to you as often as I can, and please keep me apprised of your mother's health, and the children's."

"I will. And give my love to Marcus. I hope he'll be all right."

Sebastian kissed my hands again, then pulled me into his arms and held me tight against him. "Take care of yourself." With that, he bent to pick up his leather portfolio, backed away from me and stepped onto the gangplank.

I remained on the crowded dock to watch the steamship pull away, and waved to Sebastian, who stood at the rail.

"Safe travels," I softly said, knowing he couldn't hear me above the noise of the steam engines and the voices of the passengers and people on the dock, waving good-bye to their loved ones.

I remained on the dock until the ship left the harbor and I could see it no more. Then, wiping tears from my eyes, I returned home to our children.

Over the next three months, my mother's health slowly deteriorated, and there was nothing to be done but visit her often, read to her, and help her through the pain. When it became too much for my father to bear alone—and since I, too, was alone with my children—I sent for my parents to come and live with me for as long they wished.

I wrote to Sebastian about the situation, and he replied with more news of Marcus's worsening vision and the fact that the company's accounts had suffered from his inability to focus over the past year. The books and employee records were in a terrible state, and there was some concern over embezzlement by a previous bookkeeper who had taken advantage of Marcus's ailment. Sebastian warned me that he would be unable to return home until at least the fall.

And so, I spent the summer months caring for my dying mother and relying on the household staff to help me through those difficult times. Our nanny was especially helpful in keeping the children occupied.

"Perhaps a visitor might lift her spirits," my father said one evening after dinner, when he and I sat alone together in the drawing room, sipping brandy. "She always enjoyed Mr. Harvey's tales of the sea. He has a sweet spot for you, Evangeline. Perhaps you could encourage him to pay a call."

"That is an excellent idea," I replied, sitting forward in my chair. "Tomorrow, if the weather is fine, I will pack up a basket of goodies—some of our fresh strawberries and Mrs. Cooper's delicious rum cake—and pay him a visit."

It felt good to have a plan, for I had been feeling rather lost in recent weeks.

I decided to walk to Portland Head Light, rather than take the coach, for it seemed a lifetime since I'd walked any substantial distance alone. Life had become too busy in the wake of marriage and motherhood. There was so little time to simply be quiet and reflect.

Hooking the basket handle over my arm, I ventured down the veranda steps in my peach morning dress, comfortable walking shoes and wide-brimmed straw hat, with the full intention of forgetting my woes for the next half hour while I journeyed along Shore Road, past Chimney Rock and our neighbors' homes facing the sea. Before long, the steady sound of the surf on the rugged shoreline relaxed the inner workings of my body and I breathed deeply the scent from chamomile along the edges of the lane.

By the time I spotted the sturdy lighthouse on the point—like a beacon of hope to bring my husband home—I felt calmer and stronger, and believed I would somehow find the strength to weather these hard times of loneliness and grief.

With purpose, I strode to the little stone house at the base of the tower and knocked firmly on the front door. No answer came, and I wondered if Mr. Harvey might be inspecting the light in the tower, or perhaps he was fishing off the edge of the cliff.

Just then the door opened, and I found myself staring at his nephew, Mr. Williams.

He appeared disoriented and disheveled, as if I'd just woken him from a deep slumber. Running his hand through his tousled hair and reaching quickly for his jacket on the hook by the door, he shrugged into it and said, "Good morning, Mrs. Fraser. How nice to see you."

"I'm very sorry, Mr. Williams," I replied. "Perhaps I've come too early." I tried to remember what time it had been when I left the house. It must be at least 9:30.

"Not at all," he replied, stepping back and opening the door wider. "Please come in."

I entered to discover the front room was tidy and clean. The stove did not appear to have been lit that morning.

"I don't usually sleep this late," he said, "but I was up most of the night trying to fix the tower door. It came right off its hinges in a sudden gust of wind."

"My word. It certainly *was* windy last night."

He yawned and rubbed the back of his neck.

Clearing my throat, I set my basket down on the table. "Well. Today is a new day. I thought you and Mr. Harvey might like some fresh bread, strawberries and rum cake. Is he here?" I glanced around. "I would like to speak to him, if I may."

Mr. Williams glanced eagerly at the basket on the table. "I'm sorry, but my uncle's not here. He had to travel to Boston. An old friend of his passed away, and he wished to pay his respects."

"Oh, I'm very sorry to hear that. Were they close?"

Mr. Williams regarded me for a long moment before his broad shoulders rose and fell with a heavy sigh. "I'm afraid so, Mrs. Fraser. It was a *lady* friend—a woman he'd loved all his life but could never be with because she had married someone else. They were sweethearts in their youth and remained friends. I think she loved him too, even though she remained faithful to her husband. They wrote to each other for over fifty years."

"How sad," I replied. "Why in the world did she marry that other man if she loved Mr. Harvey?" I asked innocently.

"Well…the man who asked for her hand was very wealthy. My uncle was just a fisherman. In the end, I don't think he begrudged the choice she made, until he found out she'd died. I swear on my life, there was no consoling him. I think only after her death did he realize he'd always held out hope that she would be a widow one day and they could finally be together. But now, that will never come to pass."

"Oh, dear me." I covered my mouth with the tips of my gloved fingers. "What an excruciatingly sad story."

I don't know what came over me in the next moment, but my eyes filled with tears and a jagged, painful lump formed in my throat. Perhaps it was all the hardships I had endured in recent weeks, with my mother's suffering and my constant longing for my husband who was on the opposite side of the Atlantic. I was normally in control of my emotions and had always maintained a stiff upper lip in situations such as this, but that day, I had reached the end of my tether.

I covered my eyes with my white-gloved hand, bowed my head and shuddered with despair.

Almost instantly, a handkerchief appeared before me. I opened my eyes to find Mr. Williams holding it out, his brow furrowed with concern. "I didn't mean to upset you."

I took it and dabbed at the corners of my eyes. "It's not *your* fault, Mr. Williams. Good gracious, I didn't realize I had become so fragile."

He watched me carefully. "I understand your mother is ill. I hope she'll feel better soon. She's a kind and lovely lady, and I am sure she is very grateful to have you at her side."

Again, I fell apart, without warning, like a piece of crockery hurled upon rocks. "I don't know what's come over me," I said, apologizing profusely while I wiped my eyes with the handkerchief.

Before I could comprehend what was happening, Mr. Williams stepped forward and wrapped his arms around me. He held me close, with tenderness, and I set my cheek upon his broad shoulder and wept for many minutes in the privacy of the little stone house.

Finally, I gathered my composure and withdrew from his embrace.

"Please…" He pulled a chair out from the table and waited for me to take a seat. As soon as I did, he sat across from me with his hands clasped together on the table, saying nothing, simply waiting for me to collect myself.

For a long while, I fiddled with the balled up handkerchief on my lap, then at last, I lifted my gaze to meet his. "Thank you."

"No need," he replied.

We continued to sit in silence while the ocean roared like a beast outside the windows.

"It's been a difficult time," I explained, dabbing at my eyes again. "I'm sure you know that Captain Fraser has been in London throughout all of this, ever since the spring. He was already gone when I learned how serious my mother's illness was. I don't think she's going to last much longer, Mr. Williams, and I feel very alone." I paused and took a breath. "Of course, I cannot blame Captain Fraser for not being here. His brother needs him as well, and so does the company. It's necessary for him to be there. It's just a bad time, that's all."

Mr. Williams nodded. "Sometimes life saves up its worst and doles it all out at once."

I nodded. "Everything seemed so perfect and wonderful for the longest time. I supposed I knew it couldn't last forever. Life can't always be roses and sunshine."

"Sometimes it's dark clouds and hurricanes."

I managed a small smile. "Indeed."

"Would you like some tea?" Mr. Williams asked. "My mother always said a hot cup of tea can make anything better than it was five minutes ago."

I inhaled deeply and nodded. "Thank you. And perhaps a little rum cake will improve the day even more?"

Mr. Williams grinned at me as he lit the stove. I made myself useful by emptying the contents of the basket onto the table. Then I moved about the room, searching for plates and a knife with which to slice the cake. Mr. Williams pointed to where I could find the items I needed.

A short while later, he was pouring my tea and I was feeling much better.

"What did you want to speak to Mr. Harvey about?" he asked as he dug into his cake with a fork. "Is it anything I can help you with?"

I set my teacup down in the saucer with a soft clink. "I was hoping he would pay a visit to my mother. As you can imagine, her spirits are very low, as she is confined to her bedchamber. But she always enjoyed his stories of the sea. I thought it might cheer her up, at least for a little while."

"I am sure he will be sorry to have missed your call."

"Do you know when he'll return?"

"I have no idea. He was going to visit his brother as well, in New Hampshire. I told him to take his time. That I have everything under control here."

"I am sure that you do." I took another sip of tea.

The waves continued to explode on the cliff below the tower, while the rum cake in my mouth tasted sweet and moist.

Mr. Williams finished his tea. "Please tell me, Mrs. Fraser, if there is anything I can do for you. It cannot be easy for you to manage everything, with your husband out of the country."

"Thank you, Mr. Williams. You've always been such a good friend to me."

We had encountered each other many times over the past few years, at local events, passing each other on the road, here and there, with me in my luxurious coach and Mr. Williams on foot, walking along with a sack of supplies slung over his shoulder. I took advantage of opportunities to stop and chat with him, as he was always so cheerful and friendly. I valued our conversations.

"I hate to see you unhappy," he said.

"You are very kind."

Neither of us spoke for a long moment, and a tight knot formed in my belly. When I lifted my gaze, he was watching me intently, with great caring and concern for my welfare. I sensed— or rather I *feared*—that he was about to reach across the table and squeeze my hand.

Suddenly, I became aware of how alone we were, and something about this felt wrong. Nothing had ever seemed improper with Mr. Williams before, but today was different. Nothing was quite the same as it had been.

"I must go," I said, finishing my tea and setting the cup down in the saucer. "It's a long walk back, and I am sure my mother must need me."

"Of course." His chair scraped across the plank floor as he quickly rose to his feet.

I collected my empty basket, hooked it over my wrist, and allowed him to escort me to the door. "Will you tell Mr. Harvey that I came by? If he returns soon, I would welcome a call from him."

"I am sure he will be knocking on your door the moment he returns." Mr. Williams followed me into the yard. "And please, Mrs. Fraser, do not hesitate to come and see me again if you require anything at all. I want to be of service, if I can be."

"I appreciate that, Mr. Williams. Good day to you." I turned away and started off down the lane.

As I walked, my heart felt lighter, for I had allowed it to open up and release some of the pain inside. And while a part of me still felt foolish for weeping so despairingly upon Mr. Williams' shoulder, I did not wish to think that there had been anything untoward about our encounter. I was confident in Mr. William's integrity, discretion and genuine concern for my welfare. He was a kind-hearted and decent man. Always a true friend.

October—normally my favorite month of the year—came and went without my usual awareness of the colorful changing leaves, the crisp, juicy flavor of a fresh apple, or the rich, royal blue of the autumn sky. Instead, it was a bleak and lonely time, for my mother passed away in her bed during the second week, and a few days after her funeral, my father announced his intention to return to Boston and work for a former colleague as an office clerk in a tannery.

"I cannot stay here without her," he told me as we stood at the balustrade on the veranda one foggy evening after the children were asleep. "Your husband will soon return home," Father continued, "and I do not wish to be a hanger on. I don't wish to return to Blackstone Cottage either, for there are too many memories there. The house will seem so empty and lonesome without her."

"But the children and I will miss you terribly," I said, reaching for my father's hand. "I hope you know that you can stay here as long as you like. Forever, if it pleases you."

He raised my hand to his lips and kissed it. "I will miss you, too, my sweet pea, but it's only a train ride away. We can visit each other." He paused. "But I simply must return to some form of work and prove myself worthy of something. Otherwise, without your mother's constant chatter to fill my days, I fear I will just wither away in silence. She always kept me so amused with her silly ideas and laughter."

We were quiet a moment, thinking of her.

"I understand," I said, "and please know that what I want most of all is your happiness."

I had spoken the truth, but what left me uneasy about our conversation was the fact that I still didn't know when Sebastian would return to me, for whenever I received a letter from him, he always promised it would be just a few more weeks. He had been saying that for months.

Perhaps it was my mother's passing that inspired my husband to make the necessary arrangements at the London office, so that he could return home to me at last. He hired a new manager to take over most of Marcus's duties, and boarded a ship which arrived in Portland Harbor on the first Monday of November.

When I finally heard the hired coach rumbling up the long tree-lined drive to our home, I ran down the stairs and out the front door without even pausing to check my appearance in a looking glass. All I cared about was seeing my beloved husband again—stepping into his arms and breathing in his familiar, masculine scent that always enchanted me.

The coach pulled to a halt in the driveway and the door was immediately flung open. I froze on the spot, at the top of the veranda stairs, looking down as Sebastian stepped out.

Dressed in a fine, black traveling jacket with a new blue paisley neckcloth, he looked up at me and laid his hand over his heart.

My own heart leapt with joy, and tears spilled from my eyes as I descended the stairs and walked into his waiting arms.

"I'm so sorry about your mother," he whispered into my ear, nuzzling me close for a few seconds before he kissed me deeply and ardently on the mouth. I was still grief-stricken and so grateful for the comfort he offered, that I barely noticed the coachman climbing down from the driver's seat, and the flurry of activity as the servants emerged from the house to collect the trunks and bags and welcome their master home.

When we finally stopped kissing and stepped apart, I could not yet smile, for though I was overjoyed to have him home, I was damaged from recent events and still heartbroken over our separation.

"I wish you had been here," I softly said. "I needed you."

He nodded. "I am home now, my darling, and home to stay."

With those comforting words—spoken with a hint of guilt and regret I did not yet understand—he wrapped his arm around my waist and walked up the veranda steps with me. We went straight to the nursery to see the children.

My husband and I had been apart for six months, and upon his return, I came to believe that the old adage was true: absence *does* make the heart grow fonder. Our first night together was as passionate and exciting as our wedding night had been, and for the next seven days, Sebastian did not leave our home to attend to any business matters or travel anywhere beyond the perimeter of our ocean property. Nor did we invite anyone for dinner or cards or any such activities that required us to pay attention to others. All we wanted was to be together, just the two of us with our children, and to quietly grieve for our recent hardships. We wanted to spend every waking moment together as a family with Nathan and Amelie. We took them for long strolls—Amelie in the pram and Nathan toddling about. We played games with them in the afternoons, went sailing at sunset, and made intimate, tender love after dark.

There was a time I had believed I could not be any happier than I had been in those early days of our marriage, but I soon learned that even in the wake of sorrow, love and joy could prevail. And though I was never cured of my grief completely that first week, the pleasure and comfort that my husband brought home with him dimmed my feelings of loss. Soon, I began to believe that in time, my pain would diminish, and the sun would come out again.

Sadly, however, not long after Sebastian's return, something in me sensed another round of dark clouds and thunder rumbling on the horizon, threatening to roll in from somewhere across the sea. I don't know why I felt such foreboding, but I was reminded of Mr. Williams' words that day at his kitchen table when I suggested that life couldn't always be roses and sunshine.

"Sometimes it's dark clouds and hurricanes," he had replied.

I was about to discover that not even the most wonderful life could be absolutely free of stormy weather.

"You've been home for a month," I said as I slid onto Sebastian's lap at the dinner table, where it was just the two of us, sipping wine by candlelight after the dishes had been cleared. "We've been living like a couple of hermits, which has been wonderful in many ways, but perhaps it's time we hosted a dinner party. Or a musical evening. It's been ages since we had the Danforths over, and last night, I noticed that their summer house was all lit up. It's odd that they are here this time of year. If they are, we must invite them over."

Sebastian kissed me on the lips and shifted me to sit more comfortably upon his lap. "Why must we invite anyone over, when all we need is each other?"

I laughed and kissed his eyelids, his cheeks, his ears. "I agree that we are more than enough for each other, but the poor neighbors, going without our splendid social evenings for so long. We must get back in the saddle and provide them with entertainment."

He chuckled again. "I vote we go to bed, get thoroughly undressed, and discuss it in the morning."

My body tingled with anticipation. "You are a terrible influence when I am trying to be an upstanding leader of local society. We must not allow ourselves to sink into an oblivion of private activities, where we soon lose sight of what exists outside these walls. Please, Sebastian. I need this. I've been living too long in the shadow of loss. It's time we did something fun. I want to laugh again."

He pushed a lock of hair away from my face and stared deeply into my eyes. "I would love to host a dinner party," he said. "But I doubt the Danforths are here. They never come in the winter. I suspect their servants were just testing the lights. Or perhaps hosting a party of their own. You know what they say: While the cat's away, the mice will play."

"Fine," I said. "I will come up with some other form of entertainment. And though I adore Mr. Harvey, I suggest you make good on your promise and invite Mr. Williams, so that he may enjoy an evening out, without guilt, as long as Mr. Harvey is back to man the light. Do you remember how he jested about that when we visited the lighthouse a few years back? We have never had him over. Not once."

Sebastian bowed his head in defeat. "I forgot about that. But the poor lad won't know a dinner fork from a dessert fork. He won't feel comfortable."

"We will make him feel at ease, because we are excellent hosts. Please say yes, Sebastian. I feel a terrible need to start living again. I want our old life back."

My husband kissed the side of my neck. "All I want is to see you happy and satisfied. Will you be happy if I say yes and give you permission to order the most expensive champagne we can get our hands on? And perhaps caviar?"

"I will most decidedly be happy," I replied, "but I will only be *satisfied* when you take me upstairs and remind me why I married you."

Sebastian threw his head back and laughed. Soon I was being carried up the wide, ornamental staircase, praying that one of the servants wouldn't catch a glimpse of my skirts flying up over my kicking legs.

As it turned out, the Danforths had indeed returned to Cape Elizabeth during the deep chill of late November, when ice began to form on the roads and winter weather was a constant threat. I wouldn't have known they were in town, except that the mystery was niggling at me. Why would their house be so brightly lit if they were in New York? Was their butler secretly running a gentleman's club or some other operation on the sly? Concerned about the situation, I marched up to the front door one afternoon, and knocked.

The butler answered and informed me that Mrs. Danforth was indeed at home. I was surprised to find her there, and she was equally surprised to see me. She offered her condolences over the death of my mother, and invited me in for tea. I took the liberty of asking her to join us the following Saturday for dinner at 8:00, and I requested that she and her husband honor us with a musical performance after the meal.

Knowing of my mother's recent passing, Mrs. Danforth respectfully asked what sort of tone might be right for the evening. Should it be celebratory or reflective and mournful?

After an intimate conversation about my travails during the past six months—where I expressed far more than I intended about my loneliness and frustration due to my lengthy separation from Sebastian—I left it open to her and Mr. Danforth to determine an appropriate program. Perhaps a mixture of lively tunes and sentimental favorites?

She agreed that that would be an appropriate choice, then rose to her feet and kissed me on both cheeks before walking me to the door.

⁓

Our musical evening was a resounding success, and for the first time in months, I felt almost like my old self, eager to socialize and laugh and engage in interesting conversations with people I hadn't seen in a long while.

Mr. Williams attended as well, and though he could not, like his uncle, regale us with stories from the sea, he certainly had many interesting tales about daily life as a lighthouse keeper.

After dinner, Mr. Danforth—who had been conspicuously quiet all evening—sat down at the piano to accompany his wife, who brought tears to my eyes when she sang *Lorena*—one of my mother's favorite ballads. *Had she known?*

Seated in a chair at the back of the room, I bowed my head and discreetly wiped a tear from my cheek. When I lifted my gaze, I locked eyes with Mr. Williams, who had been watching me during the performance. He nodded his head, to let me know he understood and sympathized.

Afterward, when the audience began to applaud, I noticed his chair was empty. Fearful that he felt uncomfortable—as Sebastian had predicted he would—I rose and ventured out to the main hall.

Not finding him there, I checked the dining room and library, but Mr. Williams was nowhere to be found. The last place I thought to look for him was the veranda—for it was late November and most of the guests preferred to crowd around the warmth of the fire—but there he was, bent forward with his fore-arms resting on the balustrade, his hands clasped together while he gazed out at the cold, dark sea.

"Mr. Williams." I opened the door to join him and hugged my arms about myself as the chill touched my flesh. "What are you doing out here?"

"I needed a moment," he replied, turning to face me. "But you shouldn't be out here. It's freezing."

"Yes, but that makes you the pot calling the kettle black, doesn't it?"

He smiled. "Indeed. Please, take my jacket." He shrugged out of it and swung it around my shoulders. I relished the warmth from his body, deep in the weave of the fabric.

"Thank you," I replied, "but now *you* will be cold."

"I am the son of a fisherman," he proudly replied with a grin that reached his eyes. "This is nothing."

"You may be the son of a fisherman," I argued, "but you are also a gentleman, straight to the bone. Thank you for the jacket."

He watched me uncertainly for a moment, then turned to look out at the moonlight reflecting off the ripples on the water.

"Are you enjoying yourself?" I asked him.

"I am. Dinner was wonderful. I don't think I've ever tasted so many interesting flavors in one sitting. I ate things I didn't know the names of. No idea what they were."

I chuckled. "Our cook is very talented."

"And what about you?" he asked, turning to look at me. "Are *you* enjoying yourself?"

I thought about how I'd become sentimental during Mrs. Danforth's rendition of *Lorena*, and took a breath. "I am, even though I did feel some melancholy earlier. But you, of all people, must understand…"

"Yes." He gazed out at the dark water again.

"I am just glad Sebastian is back and life can finally return to normal," I added. "I will be glad to put this year behind me. Although, certain things still don't feel quite as they used to."

"How so?" Mr. Williams asked.

I gathered his jacket more snugly about my shoulders. "Oh, I don't know. Something felt off tonight. I don't know how to explain it."

"Try."

I turned around to lean against the balustrade and face the house. "You are going to think I'm foolish, but at dinner, Mr. Danforth mentioned that he took Mrs. Danforth overseas on a business trip last summer, and they visited Paris, London and Rome. I was a bit…oh, I don't know."

"Tell me," Mr. Williams insisted.

I exhaled sharply. "What hurts me is that her husband took her with him on a luxurious business trip to Europe, while I was forced to stay behind. I realize it wasn't Sebastian's fault that I had to remain here to care for my ailing mother, but I am jealous for some reason. It's petty of me. I don't know why I am confessing this to you, Mr. Williams. You must think me a spoiled child."

"No, Mrs. Fraser. I could never think that. You are the most incredible woman I've ever known."

I felt my cheeks flush with heat and worried suddenly that I had been mistaken about his feelings for me. That he was not simply a friend I could rely upon to listen to my most personal, emotional confessions. I began to worry that he felt more than friendship toward me, and that I was encouraging him.

I hadn't wanted to think such a thing before, because I enjoyed our conversations very much. I did not wish to feel compelled to avoid him in the future. That would be absolutely…

Absolutely what?

Tragic.

I hoped I was mistaken. He was only trying to be kind.

But still…

I looked away. "You shouldn't say such things."

"Why not?"

"Because they aren't proper. They sound like a flirtation. I might even go so far as to say a seduction, and that could cause trouble, Mr. Williams."

He shook his head at me, as if I should know better.

I felt suddenly embarrassed and ashamed of what I had said and what I was implying. *Seduction?* We were friends, and he had paid me a compliment. That was all.

Please, let it be all.

I let out a long, heavy sigh and endeavored to change the subject completely. "Oh, my dear Mr. Williams. I don't know what I am saying tonight. My thoughts are all in a jumble. Perhaps I've had too much wine. And I don't know why I am worrying about things that happened in the past. Things that cannot be changed. But I did find it odd that Sebastian was so against hosting this party tonight." I turned to face the water again, and bent forward to rest my forearms on the rail, mirroring Mr. Williams' stance.

"He didn't even want to invite Mrs. Danforth to sing," I continued. "He tried to convince me that she and her husband weren't here in Cape Elizabeth, when they *were*. She hasn't graced us with her lovely singing voice in almost two years. Now I am wondering if there was some disagreement between my husband and Mr. Danforth. A business conflict perhaps. Because Mr. Danforth was not his usual friendly self at the dinner table this evening. He was silent and reserved. Almost standoffish. Did you notice? I felt it created some tension in the room. Or was it just me? Perhaps I am being foolish again."

Mr. Williams stared at me for a moment, then he gave me an apologetic look. "I should probably go." He turned away from me and started off, then seemed to realize his social blunder and halted. He faced me again and bowed slightly at the waist. "Thank you for having me, Mrs. Fraser. It was a delightful evening. Please say goodnight to your husband and thank him for his hospitality." He turned and descended the veranda steps.

"*Wait!*" I was bewildered and flabbergasted. "Where are you going in such a hurry?"

I followed him down the steps, my shoes tapping quickly as I went.

Mr. Williams let out a heavy sigh and turned around—almost as if it were a terrible inconvenience to do so. "I'm sorry, Mrs. Fraser. You know how I feel about you, but I don't belong here. I'm a simple man. This isn't my world."

"You live simply, but you are not simple," I argued, realizing he had walked off without asking for his jacket back. I pulled it off my shoulders and handed it to him. "You're as brilliant and worldly as any person in that drawing room. Just because you don't wear a silk neckcloth or sip single malt scotch in the evenings, that does not make you any less worthy of my friendship, or anyone else's. Please do not go."

"I really should," he replied, slipping his arms into his jacket. "Again, thank Captain Fraser for me. And tell him I was…not feeling so well." Mr. Williams then surprised me by reaching for my hand. He raised it up and kissed it. The touch of his lips lingered for a moment, and I felt slightly breathless. "Good night, Mrs. Fraser."

"Good night," I said as he turned away and strode off down the driveway, melting slowly into the darkness.

A chill came over me suddenly and I saw my breath, like puffs of rising smoke that disappeared instantly on the air. I folded my

arms at my chest to keep warm as I whirled around, climbed the
veranda steps and hurried back inside.

Later that night, when Sebastian slipped into bed beside me,
I was still cold. I curled into him and rested my cheek on his
shoulder. "It was fun tonight, don't you think? I thought everyone
had a good time."

"It was a great success." I waited for him to say something
more, but he was quiet.

Swallowing uneasily, I lifted my cheek and rested my chin on
my hands to look up at him. "I didn't know that the Danforths
were in Europe over the summer. Mr. Danforth said they went to
London. Did you see them while they were there?"

Sebastian ran his thumb back and forth across my shoulder.
"Yes, once or twice at a few social gatherings."

"I'm surprised you never mentioned it in any of your letters.
How long were they there?"

His eyebrows lifted, as if he had to think about it. "Oh, I don't
know. A couple of weeks, maybe? As I said, I only saw them a few
times. I was very busy, trying to get the company back on track."

He yawned and rolled to his side to turn the key in the lamp.
Even after the flame sputtered and went out, the room remained
bathed in the flickering, golden light of the fire in the hearth.

It was nearly three in the morning, and I thought perhaps
Sebastian might wish to go to sleep right away, but he slid close to
me, took me into his arms and whispered in my ear how much he
loved and treasured me….

Thirty-five

A few days later, Sebastian traveled to South Portland to meet with one of his captains about his oldest and most prized steamship, which was in need of a full refurbishment. He rose early and left before dawn.

A light snow began to fall by mid-morning—the first snowfall of the year—so Nanny and I took the children outside to play in it. Though there was only an inch or two on the ground, we had a marvelous time building tiny snowmen until Nathan got snow on his wrists and wailed in agony. I took his hand to lead him inside and change his mittens, but stopped at the bottom of the veranda steps when I spotted something shiny in the garden.

"Wait, sweetheart," I said as I let go of his hand and moved to pick it up. Wearing my black leather gloves, I brushed the snow off it and held it in my palm. "Look what I found. Someone lost an earring."

I recognized it immediately. It was the emerald and diamond set Mrs. Danforth had worn to our dinner party. It must have fallen off as she descended the stairs at the end of the night, perhaps when she was gathering her fur mantle tightly about her shoulders.

I was reminded of how grateful I was to Mr. Williams that day in the keeper's cottage when I was unaware I had lost an earring and he had found it for me.

"This belongs to one of our guests from the party the other night," I said to Nathan. "I must see that it is returned. But for now, let's go inside and get you a dry pair of mittens so we can build some more snowmen." I took hold of his hand and led him up the steps.

Later that afternoon, when the children went for their naps, I asked John, one of the footmen, to take me to the Danforth's house in the small Stanhope buggy. By then the sky was blue and the sun had come out, but it was still wickedly cold. The snow had not melted and the water was peppered with whitecaps, so I dressed warmly with a fur scarf and hat, and covered my legs with a thick woolen blanket.

When I arrived at the Danforth's mansion, I hurried up the walk and rapped on the brass knocker. Their butler opened the heavy oak door and informed me that Mrs. Danforth was not at home. I then asked to see Mr. Danforth, so that I might return something of value, which belonged to his wife.

"I'm very sorry, Mrs. Fraser," the butler said, leaving me to shiver outside in the bitter wind blowing off the ocean, "but Mr. Danforth has returned to New York."

My eyebrows lifted. "I see. And what about Mrs. Danforth? Is she gone as well?" It surprised me that they hadn't at least sent a note to thank us for the dinner party and say good-bye until next summer.

The butler spoke matter-of-factly. "Only to Portland for the day, to do a little shopping I believe. I would be pleased to pass the item on to her the moment she returns."

Portland.

I felt suddenly overheated and swallowed hard over my rising apprehension.

No. I did not wish for my thoughts to run off in an unpleasant direction. Perhaps it was a coincidence that Mrs. Danforth had traveled to Portland on the same day as my husband. But why had Mr. Danforth returned to New York without his wife? Why would he leave her here alone?

Feeling both flustered and disconcerted, I fumbled through my reticule for the earring, which I had placed in a small box, tied with a ribbon. Still standing on the stone terrace, my cheeks going numb from the icy wind, I held out the box.

"It's an earring," I explained. "Mrs. Danforth wore it to our dinner party last week. She must have lost it on her way to the coach at the end of the night."

The butler accepted it and bowed gratefully. "I will see that she receives it."

"Thank you." Turning away, I strode to the buggy and asked John to take me home, straight away.

As we drove along Shore Road, I went over everything in my mind and felt shaken by what I had just learned. I loved my husband desperately—and I trusted him. I also believed he loved me equally, in return. Therefore I did not wish to believe what my instincts were suggesting. Surely I was imagining things.

Please God, let it be so.

Sebastian arrived home shortly after 7:00, in time for dinner. When I appeared in the front hall to greet him, he removed his overcoat, handed it to the butler, strode forward, and kissed me on the cheek. "It's good to be home. How was your day?"

I was tempted to confess how my mind had run rampant all afternoon with images of his infidelity and betrayal, but I did not wish to sound ridiculous, or heaven forbid, hysterical. What I wanted was to observe him for a brief time and try to ascertain if it were possible that he was keeping secrets from me.

"It was lovely," I replied, walking with him to the drawing room for a drink. The footman, John, was there, waiting to serve us. I accepted a glass of sherry from the silver tray he held out.

"The children and I played in the snow all morning," I said, "and then I took a drive over to see Mrs. Danforth."

I glanced at my husband as I sat down on the sofa. He stopped in the center of the room and gazed at me for a moment. "What on earth for?"

"I found one of her earrings in the garden below the veranda," I explained. "I recognized it from the other night when she was here. She must have lost it as she was getting into her coach afterward. I wished to return it."

Sebastian picked up the whisky glass from John's tray and held it in his hand. "And did you?"

"Yes. John was good enough to drive me over in the buggy, but I am afraid Mrs. Danforth was not at home. Her butler said she had gone to Portland for the day. Just like you. And Mr. Danforth, for some strange reason, has returned to New York without her."

I stared at Sebastian directly, while my blood began to prickle through my veins, for it was more than obvious to me that I had caught him off guard. I had never seen him so lost for words. He lowered his gaze and sipped his drink.

I sat for a moment, my mind burning with questions and suspicions.

"John, would you excuse us please?" I said.

"Of course, madam."

I waited for John to exit the room, then I set down my sherry glass, stood up, crossed to the double doors and pulled them closed. Turning to face my husband, I said, "Please tell me that I am being foolish and imagining things. Because it has been a difficult year. I do not think I can bear any more heartbreak."

Sebastian inclined his head questioningly. "What do you believe you are imagining?"

"Surely you must be able to guess." I returned to pick up my glass of sherry. "Because you are as white as a sheet."

On the surface, I probably appeared in complete control of my displeasure, but deep down, it was far more than displeasure I felt, for I was coming apart at the seams and wanted nothing more than to fall at my beloved husband's feet and cry my eyes out—to beg him to tell me that it was all a silly mistake and he loved me more than anything, and that he would never betray me or stray to another woman's bed. Not in a thousand years.

But he said nothing like that, and I did not collapse at his feet. We stood facing each other in a heavy, stressful silence.

"Did you see her today?" I asked, point blank.

"Who? Mrs. Danforth?"

"Of course, Mrs. Danforth. Who else have we been talking about?"

Sebastian downed the entire contents of his glass and strode to the sideboard to pick up the crystal decanter. He poured himself another glass and replaced the stopper with a noisy clink.

"You should probably sit down," he said as he faced me.

Oh Lord.

Overcome by a sudden, sickening wave of dread, I moved to the sofa and took a seat.

Drink in hand, Sebastian paced around the room. Then he stopped and faced me. "I probably should have told you this before," he said, "but before you and I met each other, Mrs. Danforth and I…" He paused. "We were involved."

"What do you mean…*involved*?" I asked. "Are you telling me that you were lovers?"

"Yes."

I inhaled sharply. "But she is a married woman. She has been married to Mr. Danforth for a number of years."

"Yes, and I am not proud of what occurred between us, but there it is. It happened. It cannot be changed."

I took a moment to process this. "How long were you involved in this…illicit affair?"

"A few years."

My head drew back and anger came rushing in. I set my glass down on the end table beside me. "*My God*, Sebastian." I gazed up at him with pleading eyes. "Did you *love* her?"

For a moment, he did not answer the question. He simply stood motionless, except for a muscle flicking repeatedly at his jaw. At last, he spoke. "Yes, I believed I did."

My breath came short, for it was not easy to imagine that my husband could ever have loved anyone but me. I was the great love of his life. *Wasn't I?*

"What about the first musical evening I attended with my family," I asked, "when she sang for us? Were you sharing a bed with her then?"

He hesitated, and then nodded.

Oh, God. I began to feel nauseous and laid a hand on my belly. "Were you still seeing her when you proposed to me?"

"No," he assured me. "As soon I realized I was in love with you and that I wanted to marry you, I ended it. That is why she and Mr. Danforth have not returned to Cape Elizabeth since our wedding, until now. She was angry and hurt."

My feminine wiles rose up in umbrage—for how *dare* Mrs. Danforth be angry and hurt, when she had no claim whatsoever on my husband? She had no right to feel *anything*, for he did not belong to her. She had her own husband.

"Did Mr. Danforth know?" I asked.

"Not until very recently," Sebastian replied.

I bowed my head and shut my eyes, struggling to keep my anger in check, when what I really wanted to do was pitch my crystal sherry glass across the room and hit my husband in the face with it.

I fought to control myself, even though my stomach was churning with nausea. "How did he find out? What happened recently to bring it to light? And why was she in Portland today? You never answered my question. Did you see her?"

Sebastian took a deep breath and sat down on the sofa. "Yes, I saw her today. She came to my office to speak to me, but I did not invite her to come, and nothing happened."

"What did she want to speak to you about?"

"She wanted to…" He paused. "To resume our affair. But I told her no."

"Well, thank you ever so much," I replied haughtily.

He reached for my hand, but I pulled it away. "Please, Evangeline, you must believe me. I love you. I would never do anything to jeopardize our marriage."

Struggling to control my anger, I made an effort to listen to what he had to say, because the rational part of my brain was telling me that it was not his fault if Mrs. Danforth still carried a torch for him. How could I blame her for that? He was the most handsome, charming man on the face of the earth. And if their affair had occurred before he met me, I could hardly call that a betrayal. And he told me that he put an end to it when he realized he wanted to marry me.

"You say nothing happened," I mentioned. "Am I a fool to believe you? To accept your word that it is all in the past?"

He bowed his head, and again, my stomach churned, far worse than before. I covered my lips with the tips of my fingers. "My God. What are you *not* telling me?"

His eyes lifted, and he regarded me with shame and regret. "I made a mistake, Evangeline. In London."

I shook my head at him, wanting this to stop. I did not want him to continue, because once those words were spoken—once he admitted it—there would be no going back to what we were.

"She followed me there," he said, "knowing I had left you behind. I thought nothing of it at first because she was traveling with her husband. I thought we had become friends at last, but there was a night, when I was lonely and we…" He stopped. "God, I don't know how to say this to you."

I raised my hand. "Please don't. I don't want to hear it."

Rising to my feet, I strode to the fireplace and stood with my back to him, fighting against the wild thumping of my heart and the sickness in my belly.

My husband loves me. He would never do such a thing.

"I am so sorry, Evangeline," he said. "It was never my intention to hurt you."

I whirled around to face him. "What does that have to do with anything? Of course it wasn't your intention to hurt me. What you did had *nothing* to do with me. I wasn't even the tiniest, niggling thought in your brain when you were having your fun." I stopped to catch my breath. "What happened, exactly?" I asked, suddenly wanting to know everything, for there was no point living in denial, refusing to hear the truth. "I assume you went to bed with her. How many times?"

He shook his head at me, as if he didn't want to say, and even through the fog of my escalating rage, I could see that he was sorry, that he didn't want me to suffer, that he wished this was not happening.

But it *was* happening. My husband had been unfaithful to me—with a woman he had once loved. He had broken our marriage vows and bedded another man's wife.

"I trusted you," I said with disgust.

"It was only one night," he quickly replied. "And it was a terrible mistake. I knew that as soon as it was over and I regretted it immediately. I'd had too much to drink because of everything that was going on. Marcus's illness, the theft in the company, and I was missing you. But then I couldn't take it back. It was done. It happened quickly. I'm so sorry."

"Where?" I asked. "*Where* did it happen?"

I don't know why I wanted to know all the ugly, sordid details, but I couldn't survive without the whole truth. My imagination would become a torture chamber otherwise.

"It's not important," he said.

"Yes, it is. You would know that if the shoe were on the other foot. You would need to know everything."

Sebastian shifted uneasily but kept his eyes locked on mine as he spoke those putrid words that ate away at my soul.

"It happened in my coach," he said, "after a ball in Mayfair at the home of one of our partners. She'd had too much to drink as well. Her husband had left early, so I escorted her back to her hotel."

"Did you spend the night in her room?"

"No. Her husband was there. Everything happened in the coach. But I believe that is when he learned the truth, after that night."

I feared I might be sick. Laying a hand on my belly, I turned my face away. "I can't even look at you right now. Please go, Sebastian. Just leave."

He stood and approached me, touched my arm. "Please, Evangeline. I must have your forgiveness. I never meant to hurt you."

"Oh, stop saying such a stupid thing!" I replied, shaking him away. "I don't care what you meant or didn't mean to do. You slept with another woman—a woman you once loved. Maybe you still do. Obviously you still desire her. How *could* you, Sebastian?"

My heart was breaking into a thousand pieces, and there was nothing he could say or do to mend it. I loved him too much, too deeply, and I'd thought he loved me, that I was the only woman in the world for him. But he had slept with another. *Oh, God*, I couldn't breathe. I wanted to vomit.

Turning away, I ran from the room.

"Please, Evangeline." He followed me up the stairs.

I stopped halfway and slammed my open palms into his chest, pushing him back. He had to grab onto the railing to keep from tumbling down the staircase. It was lucky he didn't break his neck.

"Stay away from me," I said. "I will never forgive you for this. You have broken my heart, Sebastian. *You*—the man I trusted more than anyone in the world. The man I loved. The father to our children. How could you have done this to me when my mother was dying and I was here all alone, caring for our children, in agony the entire time? I am repulsed by you!"

I had never felt so full of hate.

Dashing up the stairs, I entered our bedchamber, shut the door and locked it.

I heard him in the corridor a second later. He knocked and spoke softly. "Please, Evangeline. Let me in. Talk to me. I must tell you again how sorry I am, and how badly I wish I could take it back. If only I could turn back the clock and travel back to that moment…"

"Go away," I said. "I don't want to see you. Not tonight. I need to be alone."

He continued to plead with me through the door until I told him firmly, in no uncertain terms, that I would not forgive him that night. I needed time to calm myself. I told him that if he came in, I would only shout and throw things, and we would wake the children.

Finally, he retreated, and I curled up in a ball on our bed, weeping my eyes out until the wee hours of the morning.

Then, just before dawn, I rose from a brief and fretful sleep, still wearing my clothes from the night before. I ventured downstairs, donned my cloak and fur hat, and walked out the front door into the winter chill.

CHAPTER

Thirty-seven

I still don't know why I went there—why I was propelled like a spirit, sleepwalking, as if in a dream, down the veranda steps to our wooded drive and beyond, into the predawn gloom. My flesh tingled under my clothes, like pins and needles, all the way to my fingertips. I was strangely unaware of the crunch of fresh snow under my boots, and recalled nothing about my life. Then, as I grew more lucid and aware of my surroundings, I remembered what had occurred the night before and shivered with despair.

I thought of what I was leaving behind in that white, symmetrical mansion, and felt as if I were choking in the throes of a nightmare. All I wanted was for my legs to take me away, to the very edges of the earth, where I could look forward into the future, beyond the horizon, where there would be no memory of this night.

I reached the road and walked briskly along the frozen, rutted ground, making my way toward the Portland Head Light. What was I doing? Searching for a shoulder to cry on? A true friend?

Or was it something else that drew me there like an invisible hand, beckoning me toward the powerful ray of light that would shine for miles and miles into the distance?

All I could do was follow. Obey my instincts.

Most of the walk passed in a blur, for when I found myself standing on the front door of the lighthouse keeper's cottage, I realized I was trembling uncontrollably. The frigid wind off the water had chilled me to the bone, and only then did I realize that I had not worn mittens. I could barely close my hand to knock. I had to pound with the edge of my fist, for my tiny knuckles could not possibly compete with the roar of the ocean upon the cliff, just beyond the tower.

The door opened quickly, and I found myself staring, in a daze, at Mr. Williams, whose eyes grew wide with shock. Still tucking his nightshirt into the waistband of his trousers, he said, "Mrs. Fraser. What the devil are you doing here at this hour? Is everything all right?"

He reached out, took hold of my arm and pulled me across the threshold, then quickly glanced back outside, left and right, to see if I had come alone. Discovering no one else in the yard, he shut the door.

"You're as cold as ice." He raised my bare hands to his lips and blew on them. He rubbed them between his palms to generate warmth and blew again. "Where are your gloves?"

"I don't know," I said. "I must have left home without them."

He regarded me with dire concern, then led me to the table where he sat me down. Then he moved quickly to light a fire in the stove.

I glanced toward the back room, embarrassed suddenly in case Mr. Harvey should emerge and discover me sitting there at such an ungodly hour, in a tremulous, emotional state.

"He's not here," Mr. Williams said, as if he read my mind. "He won't be back until Friday. But tell me what happened. The sun's not even up yet. What were you doing, walking all the way here, alone, in the cold?"

"I couldn't stay there," I explained, as I removed my fur hat and set it on the table. "I was too angry. I hate him."

"Hate who?" Mr. Williams asked, squatting down to strike the match inside the fire chamber. He got a flame going, blew on it, closed the door, then rose to his feet and adjusted the damper in the flue.

"Sebastian. He broke my heart."

Mr. Williams stared at me, speechless, before he dragged a chair around the table to sit down facing me. He leaned forward and warmed my hands again, rubbing at them furiously.

"I found out that he and Mrs. Danforth were lovers," I explained.

Mr. Williams's eyes lifted to meet mine, but he remained silent.

"Did you know about that?" I asked.

For some reason, I was not surprised when Mr. Williams nodded. "But that was before he married you," he mentioned.

"But how did *you* know about it," I asked, "if her husband didn't even know? Were Mr. Danforth and I the only two people in Cape Elizabeth who were blind to it?"

"Oh, he knew," Mr. Williams informed me. "Mr. Danforth used to come out here to fish off the rocks with my uncle. They'd get into the gin and Mr. Danforth would confess everything, ask for advice. I think he always believed that she was too young and beautiful for him, so he turned a blind eye to her indiscretions, just to hang on to her, so she wouldn't leave."

I lowered my gaze. "That is very sad for Mr. Danforth. And terribly dishonorable of my husband." Anger returned, and I frowned as I looked up.

"You must understand, I am in shock this morning, because I always believed he was a man of integrity. It's why I fell in love with him. And I thought he loved me just as deeply in return. I thought we were destined to be together—that he had never loved anyone...not truly—until he met me. That's why he never married, or so I thought. But he admitted that he'd loved her, and no doubt he would have proposed to her if she had not already been married. Perhaps that is the only reason he married me—because he couldn't have *her*. All along, I was second choice. I still am."

Mr. Williams rubbed my hands more gently, and I felt the heat returning to the tips of my fingers. "I believe he does love you, Mrs. Fraser. Otherwise he wouldn't have ended his affair with Mrs. Danforth. If I am correct, this is the first time they've returned to Cape Elizabeth since your wedding day."

I let out a sigh of defeat. "Yes, but I am afraid you are missing a few puzzle pieces, Mr. Williams. I don't think you would be defending him if you knew what he did."

Mr. Williams's eyebrows pulled together with agitation. "What was that?"

I leaned back in my chair, and for reasons I will never understand, I took perverse pleasure in revealing the filthy, scandalous details to Mr. Williams.

For once, I wanted honesty—honesty without concern for propriety.

"He was with Mrs. Danforth again in London this past summer. In fact, he made love to her in his coach after a ball. There, look. I've shocked you. I apologize, Mr. Williams."

He stood up and paced around the room. "He told you this?"

"Yes," I replied, "but I doubt he ever would have if I hadn't found her earring in my garden yesterday morning. I tried to return it to her in the afternoon, only to discover that she had driven to Portland—when *he* happened to be there as well. He confessed everything, of course, when he came home for dinner and I confronted him." I stood up as well. "But if I hadn't found that earring, I believe I would still be in the dark, living a lie. I might never have known the truth."

I turned away from Mr. Williams and tried to squelch the nausea that rose up in my belly. "I feel like such a fool."

"You are not the fool," Mr. Williams softly said, crossing the plank floor to reach me. He touched my arm. "*He* is."

My heart began to pound faster, for I was intensely aware of Mr. Williams's touch and his overall physical presence behind me as I turned my cheek to the side. I was afraid to turn my body around completely—afraid to look into his eyes.

By now the sun had come up, and a soft gray light appeared in the windows. The little stone house had grown warmer with the heat of the fire, and I realized I was still wearing my heavy cloak. I began to unbutton it.

Mr. Williams removed it from my shoulders and draped it over the kitchen chair behind him. At last, I found the mettle to turn around. A tear spilled across my cheek.

Mr. Williams wiped it away with the pad of his thumb. "Please don't cry, Evangeline," he whispered, and it was not lost upon me that he addressed me by my first name. "Everything will be all right."

"Will it?" I asked. "It doesn't feel that way. Not today."

A wave exploded on the rocks outside—then another, and another, like the angry beating heart of the unsettled ocean. Mr. Williams pulled me into his arms. Again, I found myself weeping on his shoulder, grateful for the comfort he offered, for the safe harbor I always knew I could come to when my world was falling apart.

He squeezed me tightly against him, and I clung to him with inexplicable desperation, fisting great clumps of his shirt in my hands. I wanted to thank him for being there. For holding me so steadily and solidly.

After a moment, I gathered my composure and stepped back, but my hands remained resting on his broad shoulders as I looked uncertainly into his eyes. I noticed the little flecks of gold within the blue that surrounded his pupils, and I couldn't resist the desire to reach up and lay my hand on his cheek, touch the rough stubble at his jaw.

"Come away with me," Mr. Williams said suddenly. "You must know how much I love you. I've loved you since the first moment I saw you, and I swear I would never hurt you like he has. I would cherish you always. I would never leave you or betray you."

I stepped back. "Mr. Williams. *Please*…you mustn't."

"Why not?"

"Because I am married."

His face flushed with color. "I know that, but he has broken his vows and he cannot possibly make you happy. Not after this." Mr. Williams paused and wet his lips, took a deep breath. "You and I could leave here and start over somewhere else where no one knows us. We could go to New York. I would take care of you, Evangeline. I promise. We could leave this morning. You would never have to go back there, never see him again."

I regarded Mr. Williams with horror. "But my children…"

He nodded quickly, as if he were struggling to iron out all the details. "We could take them with us. Sneak them away."

I shook my head. "No, I could never do that. I'm Sebastian's wife."

"But you hate him."

"No, I don't."

His lips parted. "You just said you did."

Oh, God... I looked away, toward the back room. "I'm so sorry. I hate what he did," I tried to explain, realizing I was making a terrible mess of things. "But I still love him."

Mr. Williams closed his eyes and pressed the heels of his hands to his forehead. For a long moment, he stood in the center of the room without speaking.

"Forgive me," he said at last, looking up. "I don't know what came over me. I just thought...perhaps..." He turned away and sank, forlorn, onto one of the kitchen chairs. He rested his elbow on the table and buried his forehead in his hand.

Overwhelmed by regret for my inability to recognize the depth of his feelings—and how my presence here under the circumstances might affect him—I hurried to kneel before him and took his hands in mine. "Please do not apologize. You have been such a good friend to me, always. You mean so much to me, Mr. Williams. Truly. It was lovely that you said those things to me. That you want to be my hero. I will never forget it."

"I *will* be your hero," he said, "if you ever need me to be."

I sat back on my heels and regarded him for a painful, tremulous moment. "I shouldn't have come here," I said. "I should go home now."

I saw the disappointment in his eyes, followed by acceptance as he nodded.

Offering a hand to help me rise, he walked me to the door, where we stood facing each other, hands clasped between us.

"Before I fetch your cloak and hat," he said, "I want you to know that I meant what I said. I do love you, Evangeline, and I always will. I will be right here waiting, if you ever need me."

As he squeezed my hands in his, I was overcome, yet again, by heartache and regret, for I could not bear the thought of causing this man further pain. He was good and kind. He did not deserve to be unhappy.

"Please, Mr. Williams. You mustn't wait for me. You must find your own happiness. I couldn't bear to think of you suffering in any way."

Like his uncle.

Mr. Williams raised both my hands to his lips and kissed them devotedly.

And if not for the roar of the surf, perhaps things might have turned out differently. Perhaps we might have heard the thunder of hooves as a rider entered the yard, dismounted, and strode to the front door to look in the window.

We might have had a chance to at least step apart.

CHAPTER
Thirty-eight

⌒⌒⌒

When Mr. Williams opened the door, shock reverberated through my body at the sight of a tall dark figure on the stoop—my husband, looking every inch the well-to-do-gentleman in his top hat, overcoat with fur lapels, shiny black boots and riding crop at his side.

"Sebastian," I said. "What are you—?"

His eyes blazed with fury as he threw his riding crop to the ground, stepped over the threshold and grabbed Mr. Williams by the shirt collar. "Take your hands off my wife."

Dragging Mr. Williams outside, he shoved him away. Mr. Williams fell backwards, onto the freshly fallen snow, and shook his head as if to wake himself.

"Sebastian, stop it!" I shouted as I followed them outside.

His big black horse was stomping around skittishly, tossing his head in the air, wanting to bolt. I hurried to take hold of Sebastian's arm, but this gave Mr. Williams an opportunity to scramble to his feet and retaliate. I had no choice but to move out of the way as he came barreling toward my husband. He threw himself forward and tackled Sebastian, who fell onto his back. His hat flew off and Mr. Williams proceeded to pound him in the face and shake him repeatedly by the lapels, saying, "You lousy cheat! You're all alike, men like you, flaunting your fancy carriages and silk hats, looking down on the rest of us. You don't deserve her!"

"Stop it!" I shouted.

Sebastian managed to rise up and toss Mr. Williams away, and get back on his feet. They circled around each other, glaring like a couple of wolves, ready to fight to the death.

Sebastian pointed his finger at Mr. Williams. "I've seen the way you look at her. Right from the beginning, since the day I brought her here, you've had your eye on her."

"I certainly have," Mr. Williams replied. "I won't deny it for a second. But I never laid a hand on her, because I'm a better man than you, Fraser. I don't steal other men's wives."

Thinking back to our conversation in his kitchen a short while ago, I realized it was a bald-faced lie, for Mr. Williams had asked me—quite plainly—to run away with him.

"Mr. Williams, *please…*" I said, though I didn't know what, exactly, I was pleading for. For him to refrain from punching my husband in the face again? Or perhaps there was a part of me that feared he would reveal how I'd welcomed his arms around me on more than one occasion.

"If you're referring to Mrs. Danforth," Sebastian said, "that was over a long time ago." He wiped a spot of blood from his lip.

"London wasn't so long ago," Mr. Williams reminded him, and Sebastian gave me a look of deep disappointment.

"You told him that?"

"I was angry with you," I explained. "I needed to talk to someone, and he's a friend. And how can you insinuate that my telling him was a betrayal, when you did far worse?"

He regarded me with exasperation in the hazy morning light and finally stopped pacing. He bent to pick up his hat, brushed the snow off it and placed it back on his head. "It's time to go home," he said, striding toward me.

I backed away. "I'm not going anywhere with you. Not after what you did in London."

His eyes flashed with remorse. "Evangeline, please come home with me and we will discuss it further. We will work everything out. Give me another chance and I promise I will spend my life making it up to you, proving how much I love you. I will never betray your trust again."

"Why should I believe you when I cannot possibly trust you?"

"You can, because I assure you, regret is a very powerful teacher."

I continued to back away, shaking my head at him.

He followed and took hold of my arm. "Please, Evangeline, I cannot lose you."

"Let her go!" Mr. Williams shouted from across the yard. "She doesn't want to go with you."

Sebastian turned and pointed a warning finger at him. "Stay out of this, Williams. It's none of your affair."

"It *is* my affair, because I love her, more than you do." He came striding quickly toward us.

Sebastian let go of my arm and prepared to defend himself again. "There is not a single chance in hell that is true."

"I wouldn't do what you did," Mr. Williams said. "Not to *her*. Now get off this property. She's staying right here."

"I'm not staying, or going, anywhere!" I shouted at both of them as I turned and marched angrily across the yard toward the snow-covered beach. I stepped onto the sloping rocks and realized with more than a little unease how slippery it was. There were patches of ice beneath the snow. The wind bit into my cheeks, but I did not wish to turn around. I wanted to escape the hurt and anger I had felt when I looked into my husband's eyes and realized there was nothing he could do or say to reverse what he had done. He couldn't change what happened. It would never go away. He would be apologizing to me for the rest of our lives. It would haunt us forever.

Gathering my skirts in my fists, I stepped over the fault lines in the ledges of bedrock, careful not to slip. I would climb back up off the rocks when I was further from the lighthouse, for I wanted them both to understand that I did not belong to either of them, that they did not control me. I would make up my own mind when I was fully prepared to do so.

A fierce gust of wind blew at my skirts, and the ocean roared like an angry beast. Stopping for a moment to catch my breath, I looked out at the raging water that churned, hissed, and foamed before my eyes. A gull screeched over my head, flapping his spread wings.

Then something happened. My head began to spin and I felt sick and dizzy. The pins and needles returned, and I held my bare hand up to my face to stare at the intersecting lines of my palm. Blinking repeatedly, I could barely focus my eyes.

I looked out at the sea again and recognized the slow swell of an approaching wave, far bigger than any other, like a demon making its way toward me. For reasons I could not comprehend, I felt paralyzed by a strange fascination with it. I was unable to turn away. Then my vision blurred and I knew it was coming for me—this monstrous rogue wave that wanted to carry me away and take me down into its cold, dark depths.

I saw my death before it happened.

I had once heard from Mr. Harvey that in the moment before death, your life flashes before your eyes in an instant.

I did indeed experience a flash of images—a white sailboat where I stood at the helm with my long red hair blowing in the wind. The house I shared with Sebastian where our children were born, though it looked different, with dazzlingly bright lights. There was a sundial in the yard which I did not recognize. I put my hands on it, and touched the smooth surface, then ran my fingertips along the grooves where the numbers had been etched into the stone.

Then suddenly I was riding in a strange vehicle—a shiny white horseless carriage with my sister. Or perhaps she was a friend…

As the wave drew closer, I laid a hand on my belly and knew somehow—by some miracle of communication with God perhaps?—that I was carrying another child. A son.

I whirled around and looked up at my husband. He shouted at me as he ran toward the snow-crusted cliff, waving his arms at me, warning me to get off the rocks. I could barely hear him above the roar of the surf. It didn't matter. I already knew the danger.

Then I frowned, for I could not understand why the life that had just flashed before my eyes was a life I did not recognize. It was a life that was not my own.

Katelyn

I woke with a start and sat up in bed, my pulse racing. The sun was up. My room was bright and my hands were tingling.

I had dreamed of the night Evangeline Fraser died. I had watched the wave approach and knew it was coming to end my life.

Panic and terror continued to burn in my chest, for it had felt impossibly real, as if I had been standing on the rocks just now, powerless to do anything to stop that monstrous wave from coming to sweep me under.

In the dream, I was upset, hurt and confused after walking through the frigid predawn darkness to visit the assistant lighthouse keeper, who had held me in his arms to comfort me about something. Then the captain arrived—my husband—and they fought in the yard.

Good God.

I tossed the covers aside and swung my legs to the floor.

What a dream that had been. So remarkably realistic. I felt such compassion and grief for that poor young woman who had experienced a tragic and frightening death. I could only imagine how cold the water must have been when it took her under, how desperate she must have felt when the surging, foaming ice water swept her off her feet. The gasping and flailing and kicking legs...

Squeezing my eyes shut to block out the horror, I rubbed my forehead with the heel of my hand, for the memory was causing me terrible, burning anxiety, even though I knew it was only a dream.

I looked up and tried to focus on the flat-screen TV on the desk, where I had watched the Portland Evening News each night. There was a bowl of foil-wrapped candies next to it, as well as a black leather binder with information about the services at the inn.

Feeling more grounded as the dream began to recede from my memory and my heart slowed to a more natural rhythm, I blew out a breath and stood up, but sank back down onto the mattress again when I felt dizzy. In a daze, I held my fingers up to my face and stared at them. I could barely focus.

This is what happens when you stand up too fast.

I took a moment to breathe deeply and waited for the light-headedness to pass.

"I was just about to go upstairs and knock on your door," Bailey said a short while later when I entered the dining room. She was the only person left seated at the breakfast table, and was just finishing a cup of coffee while reading the newspaper.

I glanced at the clock on the mantel. It was almost 10:00 a.m. I was probably the last guest to come down.

"Sorry. I had a weird dream," I explained as I moved to the sideboard to serve myself some scrambled eggs, cottage cheese and fruit salad. "Actually, it was more like a nightmare. I dreamed I was in the body of Captain Fraser's wife when she got swept off the rocks at the lighthouse. It was really scary."

"You dreamed she got swept off the rocks? Yeah, that would be awful. What a horrible way to go."

I reached for a blueberry muffin and moved to sit across from Bailey at the table. "In the dream, I went to visit the lighthouse keeper, who was this young, hot, rugged guy—a bit rough around the edges—and I was crying on his shoulder about something... Wait, I remember now. I had told him about how my husband cheated on me."

"You were telling him about Mark?" Bailey asked, interrupting my story.

"No. Captain Fraser," I clarified, "although there is a common theme here, don't you think?" I stabbed a grape with my fork and dipped it in the cottage cheese.

"So then what happened?" Bailey asked, setting down the paper to pay closer attention.

"Captain Fraser arrived and caught us, and he dragged the lighthouse keeper outside, and then the lighthouse keeper tackled him and punched him. I got really upset—"

"Naturally."

"And then I ran down onto the rocks just to get away from them."

"I don't blame you," she said.

"Exactly. Right?" I ate some eggs and waited until I swallowed before I continued. "That's when it got really scary—when the wave came toward me and I knew, with every inch of my soul, that I was going to die."

"Yikes." Bailey set down her cup. "Thank God it was just a dream."

"Tell me about it."

She picked up the newspaper again. "I wonder why you dreamed that."

"Probably because of our visit to the lighthouse yesterday, when we saw where it really happened. And we were all wondering what she was doing there in the first place, on such a cold winter morning. I guess subconsciously, I wanted to come up with a theory." I broke my blueberry muffin in half and spread some butter on it.

Bailey set down the newspaper and frowned at me. "What do you mean?"

I took a bite of the muffin. "I mean...I was probably freaked out by that."

"By *what*?"

"By seeing where she actually died. Where the wave took her off the rocks."

Bailey shook her head at me. "That's not how she died, Katelyn. She lived to be an old woman and died of old age, here in the house. You know that."

I set down my fork and knife. "What are you talking about? You and I spent the whole morning at the museum the other day, doing research on the captain and his wife. She died young, and that's why he was trying to figure out how to build a time machine. Because he loved her so much."

Bailey started to laugh. "What is wrong with you? I think you're dreaming right *now*."

I waved my fork through the air, trying to help her remember. "No, no. The sundial in the yard. We think that's why he put it there—remember? To find a way back in time to prevent his wife's death."

Bailey's expression darkened, and she leaned forward over the table and spoke quietly. "Are you okay? Because that's not what happened. You and I *did* do a bunch of research on the sundial, but it was *Mrs.* Fraser who was obsessed with time travel. *She* was the one who insisted they travel to Asia to find it. She didn't die at the lighthouse."

I sat back in my chair and frowned. "No, you're wrong."

"No," Bailey replied. "*You're* wrong. Don't you remember?"

"Of course I remember. It's *you* who doesn't remember."

She stared at me with concern. "Well, come on then." She rose from her chair and directed me to follow. "Let's go check out the picture in the hall."

I threw my napkin onto the table, slid my chair back, and followed her.

She stood in the entrance hall gesturing toward a black and white photograph in a pewter frame, perched on a side table. I hadn't seen it before. It showed Sebastian and Evangeline seated before a set of drapes—probably in a photographer's studio—surrounded by five children. Evangeline looked older than she was in the painted portrait in my room. Here, she looked to be in her mid-to-late-thirties.

We looked even more hauntingly alike.

I moved closer, squinting at the details of the photograph, and my eyes fixed on a young boy about nine or ten years of age. He stood beside Evangeline with his hand resting on her shoulder. "Who is that?"

"One of their children," Bailey said.

"What's his name?"

Bailey bent to look closer. "I'm not sure. I can't remember all their names."

My stomach began to roll with shock and nervous energy. "Do you remember why we came to Maine?"

"Yes." She followed me to the front desk, where I rang the bell frantically, over and over. "Because of that vision you had."

"Yes—and that's him," I said. "I recognize him."

"Who?" Bailey asked.

"The flashback I had on the mountaintop," I explained, "where I had a son named Logan. That's him in the picture. I'm sure of it."

Angela came hurrying out of the kitchen at the back of the house. "Is something wrong?"

"No. I'm sorry, Angela. I didn't mean to be so aggressive with the bell. I was just wondering…" I led her to the photograph in the front hall. "Do you know the names of all the children in this picture?

"Yes, of course." She moved closer to point at each one. "That's the oldest, Nathan, and this is Amelie, Henry, Sarah, and John."

"John." I bent forward and looked more closely at the boy I recognized from my flashback. "His name is John?"

Not Logan?

"That's right," Angela replied. "He was their third child, I believe, after Nathan and Amelie."

I backed away, trying to make sense of my perceptions and emotions, which were insisting that the boy in the portrait was the same boy from my flashback on the mountaintop.

I felt a hand on my shoulder. It was Bailey. "Are you all right?"

Nodding, I said, "I just thought I recognized him. He looks exactly the same."

I didn't know what else to say, how to explain what I was feeling, for I was confused and bewildered, yet overjoyed to have discovered that the boy I'd imagined was real. Or at least he *had* been real, at one time. Here was concrete evidence of his existence, although it made no sense to me that his name was John. Why not Logan? And was I insane to think that this boy was somehow my son? He was born as John Fraser, to a mother named Evangeline and a father named Sebastian.

In the late 1800s.

CHAPTER

Forty

⌒c⌒⌒

"**J**ust when I was beginning to think I was ready to move
on from all this, I have a dream that changes everything."
Bailey and I walked outside to the veranda and down the
stairs. It was a sunny, breezy morning.

"I have to admit," she said, running her hand down the white
painted railing, "I'm getting a bit worried about your state of
mind, Katelyn, because you're remembering the past week very
differently from how I remember it. You have this whole story in
your head about Captain Fraser's wife dying young, when that's
not what happened at all. They lived a long and happy life together and had five children. We've known that all along."

"I didn't know it," I said. "As far as I'm concerned, since yesterday, the history of this house has changed completely."

Which had me wondering…How much of it was a dream?
Or had the sundial played a part?

We stepped onto the stone path that would take us down to
the ancient timekeeper, and walked under the rose arbor. When
we reached it, I stood back for a moment, afraid to touch it or
even go near it.

"What's wrong?" Bailey asked. "You look very intense."

"I'm just thinking," I said. "When I first fell asleep, I dreamed I
came down here by myself. I ran my hands over the top of the stone,

then I got really cold, and the next thing I knew, I was dreaming I was Evangeline, walking down the driveway on a cold winter morning."

"Do you think it was one of those lucid dreams," Bailey asked, "or astral projection, like what happened to Sylvie? Do you think it's possible that you actually went back in time?"

I shrugged. "I don't know. I wasn't *trying* to make it happen. I went to sleep feeling very content for the first time in ages, and happy to move on from all this."

We strolled to the two Adirondack chairs and sat down to look out over the water. A fishing boat motored past, about a mile out.

"It was like I was actually inside Evangeline's skin, living her life," I said. "I was so upset and hurt by what my husband had done—cheating on me with that other woman—and I felt guilty about him catching me with the lighthouse keeper."

"What was the lighthouse keeper's name?" Bailey asked.

I wracked my brain, trying to remember. "Mr. Williams, I think."

She shook her head. "No, I'm pretty sure that wasn't the name of the keeper at that time. There were pictures at the museum, and I remember…It was another man. His name was…" She paused. "Harvey, I think."

The name struck a chord in me. "*Harvey*." I thought about that for a moment. "It sounds very familiar." I continued to watch the fishing boat and listen to the hollow clang of a buoy's bell somewhere in the distance. "I remember my parents from the dream. I was grieving for my mother who had died recently. She was sick for a long time, and then my father left to live somewhere else. And the woman my husband was in love with—I know it sounds crazy, but I still feel jealous, like it happened only yesterday. It's all coming back to me, in little bits." Again, I struggled to remember. "He was in love with her before he met me, but he ended their affair when he proposed to me, but then she tried to get him back after we were married. She followed him to London and they slept together over there. In his coach."

"Oh, that sucks," Bailey said. "But I can't believe it—that Captain Fraser would do that. Everything we've read makes it seem like they were true soulmates, devoted to each other forever."

I swallowed over a sick feeling of jealousy and heartbreak, then tried to remind myself that it wasn't real. He wasn't my husband. He had never cheated on *me*.

"What was he doing in London?" Bailey asked.

"Taking care of his shipping company, because his brother couldn't manage it anymore. He was losing his vision or something."

Bailey let out a deep breath and sat forward. "You keep saying 'my parents' and 'my husband,' as if you're Evangeline. But it was just a dream. And in another century."

I snapped out of my reverie. "I know. Of course, you're right. It just felt so real."

We both sat back in our chairs and listened to the waves roll gently onto the shore.

"Well," Bailey said, tapping a finger on the armrest, "we know one thing. There was no lighthouse keeper named Mr. Williams, and there's no record of Mrs. Fraser getting swept off the rocks that day."

"Danforth!" I shouted, slapping the armrest with the palm of my hand. "That was the name of the woman Sebastian had an affair with. She was a singer who performed at our house."

"*Whose* house?"

I pointed my thumb over my shoulder. "The inn."

She nodded her head, though she seemed a bit concerned about the things I was saying. "I see."

Sitting forward in the chair, I felt as if there were other important details I had yet to uncover. Things that were hovering at the fringes of my memory.

. "Would you mind going back to the museum with me?" I asked. "I want to look up some of this stuff."

"Which stuff?" she asked.

I stood up and started walking back to the house. "All of it."

The museum curator remembered us from our visit earlier in the week, and allowed us, with no questions asked, into the back room to delve into the Fraser House Collection a second time. We pulled on the white gloves like a couple of seasoned historians and waited at the work table for her to fetch the box.

I was shocked, however, when it wasn't just one box she delivered. She brought out one box after another, each one full of documents and pictures—a whole lifetime of memories—all donated by Angela Carrington when she purchased the house in 2009. It was far more extensive, and completely different from the collection I had examined before.

There were dozens of letters exchanged between all five children and their parents, where they discussed things like social engagements, milestones concerning the grandchildren, holiday plans. There was some talk of politics from the youngest son, Henry, who evidently had a passion for current events.

I devoured every word, as if they were my own long-lost children and I hadn't heard from them in years.

Everyone seemed perfectly content with every aspect of their lives. There were no letters of concern between Amelie and Nathan, worried for their father's sanity. According to this version of history, their father had lived a long and happy life without need for a time machine to bring his wife back from the dead. He hadn't spent his life inventing strange gadgets. To the contrary, Evangeline had been the one to insist upon a trip around the world, by steamship, shortly after the end of the First World War. The sundial had been their most treasured souvenir from that journey, though there was no mention of time machine anywhere. Perhaps they knew it would have made them sound crazy. Or maybe they didn't want strangers coming around to use it recklessly.

There was a black-and-white photograph of the two of them standing next to it, holding hands. It was dated 1924. I stared at it for a long time, mesmerized and wishing I could remember more of Evangeline's life beyond that final night at the lighthouse when I woke from the dream.

After more than an hour of focused, borderline-obsessive reading, I finally looked up. Bailey was asleep with her head on the table.

I glanced at the curator, who sat at her desk with her back to us, then poked Bailey lightly with my finger. "Hey," I whispered.

She sat up groggily and stretched her arms over her head. "Are we all done?"

I set down the photograph. "I feel terrible for dragging you back here. You must be so bored."

"No need to apologize," she replied. "It's just not as interesting for me the second time around."

"Because you've read all this before." I sighed, accepting that I was either completely bonkers with short-term memory loss, or I had in fact traveled back through time and changed the present-day world.

Which was it?

I turned to address the curator. "Can I ask you a question?"

She swiveled in her chair to face me. "Certainly."

"I'm wondering if there was ever a woman named Mrs. Danforth who might have visited Cape Elizabeth in the 1880s. Is there any way we could search for that name in your records?"

I just wanted to know if I'd dreamed the whole darn thing.

"Of course," she replied cheerfully. "Although we don't have to do much searching. What would you like to know? I could probably tell you anything, because I wrote an article about her a few years back. She was a singer on the New York stage and married a wealthy older gentleman who owned a summer house here."

I glanced at Bailey, whose lips parted with surprise.

"Well, that's interesting," I said. "Do you know if she might have been romantically involved with Captain Fraser at any point?"

And there were so many more questions I had. I felt suddenly as if time were rushing by too quickly. Soon, Bailey and I would be boarding a plane back to Seattle. Surely there weren't enough hours in the day to learn all the answers I was seeking.

The curator inclined her head curiously. "Not that I know of. Why do you ask? Did you read something that would suggest it?" She began to roll herself closer in her chair. "I've read everything there is to know about Captain Fraser and his wife. There was never any mention of anything like that. There is a 'thank you' card in the collection, however, for a musical evening at the captain's home. She provided the entertainment. But there is certainly no mention of any infidelities on her part, or Captain Fraser's. That's an interesting thought, though. They were about the same age, both very attractive and charismatic. And good heavens. Mr. Danforth sold his property quickly, well below market value. I always wondered why he was in such a hurry to leave Cape Elizabeth."

Feeling a strange unbidden urge to protect Captain Fraser's reputation—and that of his marriage—I waved a hand, dismissively. "Oh, don't listen to me. I don't even know why I'm asking that. There was nothing here to suggest it. I'm just dreaming. Obviously Captain Fraser was very much in love with his wife."

She smiled warmly. "Oh, yes. Theirs is one of Cape Elizabeth's most treasured marriages. They were together always. He absolutely worshipped the ground she walked on until the day he died. We wouldn't want to turn *that* one upside down."

"Good heavens, *no*," Bailey replied, and I kicked her under the table for making fun of the curator's old-fashioned romanticism.

I, on the other hand, was deeply moved and affected by her words—for it appeared that if, indeed, there had been an indiscretion between Mrs. Danforth and the captain, he had spent the rest of his life trying to win back Evangeline's trust and love, and she *had* forgiven him in the end. It was obvious from the photographs and letters. She *did* love him.

I felt that love beating strongly in my own heart.

Yet I couldn't help but wonder what had become of Mr. Williams.

"What about a lighthouse keeper named Mr. Williams?" Bailey asked—which had been the next question on the tip of my tongue. "We visited the Portland Head Light yesterday, but I don't recall seeing that name. There was a large photograph of a man named Harvey who manned the light around that time."

"That's right," the curator said. "Mr. Harvey was the keeper, but Mr. Williams was his nephew and the *assistant* lighthouse keeper. I believe there's a photograph of Mr. Williams in one of the books at the Head Light Museum," the curator added, "but there's no mention of him in the displays."

All at once, my blood began to race and my belly churned with nervous knots, because surely this proved that I knew things I shouldn't have known.

Suddenly, more precise details from those final moments came hurtling back at me. It was no longer a vague recollection. I remembered every word of my conversation with Mr. Williams in the keeper's cottage—how he had asked me to run away with him to New York and promised he would take care of me—and then the heated argument that occurred between him and my husband.

I had dashed onto the rocks to get away from them, and as the wave approached, my life had flashed before my eyes. I saw things and knew things I couldn't possibly have known.

Good Lord.

Suddenly, the room was spinning.

I pulled off the gloves, bent forward in my chair and stuck my head between my knees.

"Are you okay?" Bailey asked, leaping from her chair to circle around the table. She knelt beside me and placed her hand on my back.

"Yes," I said. "I just felt a bit dizzy, that's all. I think I need some protein."

"You didn't eat much breakfast," she commented.

Forming my lips into an O to breathe steadily in and out, I sat up again. The curator had gone to fetch me a glass of water. She moved the documents aside and set it down on the table in front of me.

"Thank you." I picked it up and took a sip, then we thanked the curator for all her help. I asked if it would be all right for me to return another time, before I flew home, because I was certain I would have more questions. She said yes and walked us to the door.

A short while later, Bailey and I got into our rental car. She took the keys from me and started the engine, while I closed my eyes and tipped my head back.

"What's going on?" she asked, as we pulled away from the curb. "You look gray, like you're going to be sick."

"I was pregnant," I said, lifting my head, "on the rocks that day at the lighthouse."

"*What?*"

I stopped, paused a moment to gather my thoughts into something a little more sensible and coherent, and began again. "What I mean to say is that *Evangeline* was pregnant on the day she was swept off the rocks, but she didn't know it. No one did."

"But she wasn't swept off the rocks," Bailey reminded me.

"I know that," I replied, "because I went back in time, knew what was about to happen, and I saved myself. Or rather, *she* saved herself and got off the rocks before the wave hit. But just before that, she saw a life flash before her eyes, but it wasn't her life. It was mine."

Bailey's eyebrows pulled together in a bewildered frown. "How do you know all this? From the dream? Or was there something you read just now?"

I shook my head. "It was the dream, if that's what it was. I don't know. But she sensed it, I guess, because I was in her head. And just before the wave hit the rocks, she realized she was carrying a son."

"But how would she know that?"

I shrugged. "I don't know. That part is still a mystery to me."

"Only *that* part?" Bailey asked as she turned toward Portland Head Light so we could seek out the photograph of Mr. Williams.

—⸺⸙⸺—

"What do you think all this means?" Bailey asked as we pulled out of the parking lot after our visit to the Head Light Museum.

The attendant had been kind enough to direct us to a book in the gift shop which contained the photograph of Mr. Williams, who exactly matched my memory and the description I'd given Bailey. In the photograph, he was a young man, muscular and rugged-looking, posing with his uncle outside the front door of the little stone dwelling, which had later been replaced by the larger Victorian home that now stood in the same location. His arms were folded at his chest. He was not smiling.

I asked if they knew what had become of him. Evidently, a few months after Evangeline's third child was born, he resigned from his position as assistant lighthouse keeper and left Cape Elizabeth. Unfortunately, there was no record of him after that. At least not at the lighthouse museum.

I wondered if he had ever crossed paths with Evangeline again.

"I don't know what it means," I replied to Bailey's question as a deep melancholy settled into my heart. "But I wonder if I'm reincarnated from her, and that's why I was able to reach her through the sundial. Maybe she had traveled the world to find it because I was in her head that morning on the rocks, and she saw the future through my eyes and knew everything I knew. Most importantly, she knew to hurry and get off the rocks." I gazed out the window at the passing landscape. "It was just like what happened to me during my cycling accident—there was a burst of adrenaline—except that I saw an alternate reality, and she saw a future one. If she was anything like me, she wouldn't have been able to let it go, and probably spent her life trying to find answers and figure out what it all meant.

"Maybe she had other visions, too—later on—and eventually realized that I had reached her through the sundial." I looked at Bailey in the driver's seat. "Because, think about it—if she didn't die that day, her husband wouldn't have been obsessed with time travel, and he would never have put the sundial on their lawn. But without the sundial, she *would* have died that morning, because I wouldn't have gone back to be inside her head and warn her." I raised my finger. "That's why *she* made sure they went together and found the sundial. She did that for *me*. So that I could find a way back to save her from dying that day, so that she could live a full life, have a chance to forgive her husband, and give birth to John, the son she was carrying."

Bailey drove us back to the inn, turned off the car engine, and we both unbuckled our seat belts. "It's very complicated," she said, "and there are a lot of maybes in your theory."

"I know. It's not exactly something I can prove."

We got out of the car, shut the doors and started walking toward the veranda steps.

I stopped and touched Bailey's arm. "Wait a second. You know how some people say we keep surrounding ourselves with the same souls from one life to the next, and we learn things from each other. Maybe my son John came back as Logan to somehow connect me with Chris and Sylvie, which is what lured me back here—to save his mother, and allow him to be born."

Bailey considered that for a moment, and nodded. "What did Evangeline see, exactly? In her vision, when the wave was coming toward her?"

We slowly climbed the wide staircase. "She saw most of my life, but the last few images were of the rental car we've been driving this week, and the sundial, and me at the helm of a white sailboat."

"But you don't sail." Bailey said.

"Not yet," I replied. "But maybe I will someday. I've always wanted to learn."

ailey and I went to our rooms to change into our bathing suits, with the intention of meeting on the cushioned lounge chairs on the sea deck to decide what—if anything—I should or could be doing about all this.

I arrived before she did, sat down and kicked off my flip flops. I raised my sunglasses to the top of my head to dig through my beach bag for sunscreen. My fingers closed around the colorful seashell I had found on the beach a few days ago, and again I marveled at its beauty before resuming my search for the sunscreen.

When I finally found it, I made an attempt to squirt some onto my palm, but it was empty.

"Typical." Stretching out on the chair, I lowered my sunglasses, and for a while, I sat in silence, gazing out at the ocean, watching the swells.

A part of me still believed I might be losing my mind and none of this was real. But I had Bailey as a witness and she didn't seem to think I was crazy. She hadn't tried to drag me to the hospital or have me committed. *Did she believe it too?* Or was she just humoring me until she could get me home, get in touch with my mother and call in professionals to deal with the issue?

Just then, I thought I heard the call of a seagull, but then I recognized Bailey's voice and swung my legs to the deck floor to turn around.

She was clumsily running down the sloping lawn with her hand on the top of her giant, wide-brimmed pink sunhat, her beach bag flopping around while she struggled to keep the strap on her shoulder. I couldn't help but chuckle, until she started to wave her arm wildly. I realized she was desperate to tell me something.

She was out of breath when she arrived. "I need to go to the gym more," she said as she dropped her beach bag onto the deck floor and flopped into the chair next to me.

"You look like you have something important to say. Did you bring sunscreen?"

"I did," she replied. "It's the spray-on stuff. And yes, I thought of something important as I was coming down the stairs." She huffed and puffed for a few seconds. "At least I think it's important. Maybe it has nothing to do with anything."

"What is it?" I asked.

She sat up cross-legged on the cushion. "Do you remember when we had lunch with Sylvie and Chris, and she talked about the things that were the same when she came back to this reality, versus other things that were different?"

"Yes."

"She mentioned the hurricane that hit on the same day here in Maine as it had in her so-called alternate reality. Remember that?"

I nodded.

"She also mentioned a sailboat that washed ashore on her lawn in that reality, but not this one, and that they had to track down the owners. I don't know why I'm making this connection or why I feel like it's relevant, but Evangeline did envision you on a sailboat."

I sat for a moment, staring at Bailey. "You're right. I wonder if Sylvie can remember anything else about it. Do you think she'd freak out if I called her again?"

"I think she'd be interested to know what you've been up to since the last time you spoke. Assuming she's still married to Chris after you went back and changed the past." Bailey raised an eyebrow as she reached into her bag for the sunscreen. "Fingers crossed you didn't mess *that* up."

"I'm so sorry to bother you again, Sylvie," I said when she answered the phone, "and thank you for taking my call. But first, can I ask—are you still married to Chris Jenson?"

"Of course," she said with an uneasy laugh. "Why would you ask that? Oh, wait. Did you—?"

"Yes," I replied matter-of-factly. "Assuming you're referring to the sundial?"

She was silent on the other end of the line. "Where are you now?" she asked.

"I'm still at the Fraser House Inn," I replied, "but we fly out the day after tomorrow. I'm just trying to figure out what happened. I still can't believe it and part of me thinks I dreamed the whole thing."

She paused again. "I think we should meet in person. I have a couple more patients, then I'm done for the day. Can we meet for a drink at 5:00?"

"Absolutely," I replied, giving Bailey a quick nod. "Where?"

"How about the same pub where we met last time? I'm sure you can understand why I can't come there. I don't want to go near the sundial ever again."

"I get it," I said. "Do you mind if I bring Bailey?"

"Not at all. I'll bring Chris."

We hung up and I sat back down on the lounge chair to bring Bailey up to speed.

The four of us met at The Old Stone Keep, ordered a pitcher of draft, and sat at one of the booths at the back. Sylvie listened to every detail of my story with fascination, nodding her head constantly, and I was relieved to feel as if I were not alone—that someone else had experienced many of the same sensations as well as the bafflement I was currently experiencing.

She confirmed that the dizzy spells, tingling fingertips, and pins and needles were all consistent with what she had experienced each time she woke up in a new reality. But she was amazed that I had gone back more than a century to another woman's lifetime, not my own.

I told her and Chris as much as I could, then I brought the conversation back around to the reason I had called her in the first place—to ask about the sailboat she had mentioned the last time we met. The one that had been washed up onto her lawn.

"Yes," she said, leaning back and fingering the handle of her beer mug. "That happened in the alternate reality where you had your cycling accident, after the hurricane hit. I don't think I mentioned this before, but I was living at the Fraser House, which, in that reality, belonged to me, not Angela. It wasn't a hotel. Anyway, everyone on the coast was advised to evacuate because of storm surges, so I spent the night in Portland with my grand-mother. When I came home, I was surprised to find a sailboat on my back lawn. It was quite a sight, as you can imagine, tossed up on the grass like a bathtub toy."

"Holy cow," Bailey said.

"What's interesting," Sylvie continued, "was that it knocked over the sundial, which we had to pick up and set back into po-sition. It was no easy task, mind you, because it's very heavy. Sometimes I wonder if I might never had made it back to this life if it had been smashed to bits." She shared a look with Chris.

I sat back, shaking my head in disbelief as I listened to her story. "So who owned the sailboat? Where did she come from?"

"There was no one onboard," Sylvie explained, "so we had to call the yacht club and report it. I told them the name of the boat and they tracked down the owners, who sent a crew to remove her from my lawn and return her to the club."

"Who owned her?" I asked a second time.

Sylvie let out a breath as she pinched the bridge of her nose, searching her memory for the details. "Let me see. It was an older couple from Chicago. They were very apologetic on the phone and told me they'd left Cape Elizabeth in a hurry to attend a fu-neral, and had left their boat moored outside their summer house at Kettle Cove. Obviously they had no idea there was a hurricane coming, or they would have taken her ashore."

"I feel like I need to track them down," I said. "Do you re-member their names?"

Sylvie strained to remember. "Peterson, I think? And I might be able to remember the name of the boat." She turned to Chris. "God, what was it?" She was quiet for a moment, then at last, she looked back at me. "It was *Evangeline*."

My lips parted. "Are you sure?"

"Yes," she replied. "I'm positive."

"Did you know that Captain Fraser's wife's name was Evangeline?"

"You're kidding," Chris said.

Sylvie's eyebrows drew together with shock and disbelief. "No, I didn't know that. Like I said, I only visited the inn that one time, and I don't think Angela ever mentioned Mrs. Fraser's first name. That's unbelievable. It can't be a coincidence."

I took a sip of beer. "I'm starting to wonder if there are no such things as coincidences, because this keeps getting weirder and weirder."

"I wonder if the boat even exists in this reality," Bailey put in. "Because like you said, so many things are completely different."

"Like Logan," I mentioned with regret and a feeling of sadness and longing I couldn't seem to escape.

We were all quiet for a moment.

"So where do we go from here?" Bailey asked me. "Obviously, we need to find out if that boat exists, because there has to be some connection. It's just too fluky."

"The Peterson's were members of the Portland Yacht Club," Sylvie told us. "That's a good place to start."

Bailey and I finished our drinks and I placed some cash on the table. "I hope you guys don't mind if we skip out. I want to drive over there now."

"Of course not," she replied as we slid out of the booth and reached for our sweaters and purses. "But please, will you let me know what you find out? Call me anytime. Here's my personal cell number." She jotted it down on a napkin and handed it to me.

I was pleased that she no longer considered me a threat to her marriage. She actually seemed eager to talk to me again.

"I will." I folded the napkin and slid it into the outside pocket of my purse. "And I can't thank you enough, Sylvie. Truly. Bye Chris."

With that, Bailey and I walked out and googled directions to the Portland Yacht Club.

W e arrived at the club fifteen minutes later, found a place to park, and discreetly wandered around the docks, making an effort to look as if we fit in, while searching the names on all the boats. There were none called *Evangeline*, so we decided to be bold and venture into the clubhouse to speak to the manager, who turned out to be a handsome middle-aged man with salt and pepper hair.

"I wonder if you could help us," I said, smiling warmly at him. "We're looking for some old family friends of ours who I think are members here. The Peterson's from Chicago? The last time we spoke, they had a boat called *Evangeline* and they invited us for a sail. I don't suppose you know if they're still members here?"

"The Petersons? Yes, they are, but they don't usually keep their boat here at the club when they're in town. They keep her moored at their summer house."

"Oh!" I replied, brightly. "Would you mind giving us their address? I'd love to pop by."

The manager regarded me warily. "I wish I could help you, but I can't give out that kind of information. I'm sure you understand."

I casually waved my hand about. "Of course. We'll just give them a call. I'm sure we can find their number. They're in Cape Elizabeth, aren't they? Kettle Cove?"

The manager shrugged apologetically.

"No problem," I said, letting him off the hook. "Thank you for your help."

By the time we drove back to Cape Elizabeth with Bailey behind the wheel, the sun was low in the sky and the wind had died down. The water was blissfully calm.

"I'm nervous about calling," I said after finding their number in an online search, which also listed their address—assuming it was the same Petersons who owned a sailboat called *Evangeline*. "Maybe we should just knock on their door."

"And say what?" Bailey asked. "Hi, my friend had a vision that your boat washed onto her lawn during the hurricane a year ago. Do you know why she might have envisioned that?"

"That does sound crazy," I said. "There's got to be a better way to handle this, because I honestly don't even know what we're searching for. I don't know what I'm hoping to discover."

"I wish I could help," Bailey replied, "but I don't know either. It sure is pretty out here, though."

We followed the twisty road along the coastline and admired the view of the water while the tide was out.

"What if you play the TV reporter card," Bailey suggested, "and say you're doing a story on something? I don't know what. You're better at this than I am."

"That's a possibility," I replied, trying to think of a reason why I would knock on someone's door to ask questions about their sailboat.

Just then, we saw the Peterson's home and slowed down as we drove by. It was a modest little cottage with gray cedar shakes and black trim, overlooking the beach, not far from a grassy park with benches. I admired the nautical lawn ornaments—the old wooden buoys, driftwood and an aged lobster trap. A white painted lifesaving ring hung on the gate.

"This is it," Bailey said, pulling over in the parking lot at the end of Kettle Cove Road.

"I noticed a car in the driveway," I said. "They must be home."

Bailey shifted the vehicle into park and shut off the engine. "So what do we do now?"

I thought about it for a moment, then unbuckled my seatbelt, opened the car door and got out. "I'm not sure yet, but you stay here. I'm going to go and knock, and if they answer, I'll probably make everything up as I go along."

"Hello," Mrs. Peterson said guardedly as she opened her door and greeted me on her front step.

She was a plump older woman with a dark brown bob and red plastic-rimmed glasses.

"Hi there," I replied in a friendly voice. "I hope I'm not interrupting your supper."

"No, we just finished. Stan is doing the dishes. What can I help you with?"

I swallowed hard and tried to sound sure of myself, when I was merely putting one foot in front of the other with no idea what I was about to step into.

"This may sound a bit strange," I said, "but I'm a reporter from a TV station in Seattle. My name is Katelyn Roberts and I'm doing a story on the poet, Henry Wadsworth-Longfellow. I couldn't help but notice when someone mentioned a sailboat in the area called *Evangeline*. I believe you might be the owners?"

"That's right," Mrs. Peterson said, sounding suddenly delighted.

"Would you mind if I asked you a few questions about your boat?"

"Not at all. Please come in. I'm Margie." She opened the door to invite me inside and called out to her husband. "Stan! There's a reporter here from Seattle who wants to talk to us about *Evangeline*."

Her husband appeared from the kitchen at the back, wiping his hands on a dishtowel. He looked to be in his late sixties, with thinning white hair and silver-rimmed glasses.

"Hi there." He strode toward me and tossed the dishtowel over his shoulder. "I'm Stan."

"I'm Katelyn." We shook hands. "It's nice to meet you."

They led me into their living room which boasted cottage-style white painted walls and a blue-and-white striped sofa and chair. I noticed a ship in a bottle positioned on the window sill.

"Please have a seat," Margie said. "Would you like a cup of coffee or anything?"

"No, thank you," I replied. "I don't want to take up too much of your time." I withdrew a notepad and pen from my bag. "It's so good of you to talk to me. Maybe you could tell me about your boat. How long have you had her?"

They glanced at each other, questioningly. "About thirty years," Stan replied. "We bought her brand new when I inherited this cottage from my parents, so that we'd have something to do with our children during the summers."

"How many children do you have?"

"Two boys."

"Are you from here originally?" I asked.

"I grew up here," Margie replied, "but Stan was born and raised in Chicago. We met in college, and now we travel back and forth."

I wrote a few things down, then looked up. "So you named your boat *Evangeline*. Did that have anything to do with Longfellow's poem?"

Margie blushed. "Not exactly," she confessed. "It was our son who suggested the name. He was only five when we bought her. We were trying to decide on a good name, and we told him it had to be a girl's name, because boats were usually named after girls, so he pulled that name out of a hat. Not literally, of course."

I wrote this down and looked up again. "Was he studying the poem at school?"

"I don't think so. He was only five." She glanced at her husband. "Of course we told him about the poem after that, but you know boys. He wasn't much interested in poetry. He just wanted to be captain of the boat. But he did once mention to me that he was going to marry a girl named Evangeline. I thought that was so cute."

I wrote that down as well. Not that I needed to. Everything she was saying seemed to be imprinting itself permanently on my brain.

"How old was he when he said that?" I asked, working hard to maintain a light and casual tone and not reveal that my heart was beginning to pummel my ribcage.

"It was around the same time, when we first got the boat."

I thought back to the research I'd done about reincarnation cases where very young children remembered their past lives, and with all the connections here, I felt compelled to probe a little further.

I cleared my throat. "And what's your son's name?"

"His name is Aaron and he's our eldest. He still sails the boat all the time. Our younger son is Jack, but he lives in New York."

My gaze shot up from my notebook. "Really. What does he do there?"

"He's a news director at CNN."

My head drew back in surprise. "No kidding. I just applied for a job there."

"I thought you worked for a station in Seattle," Stan said.

I set my pen down. "I do, but I've been there for more than ten years and I had my sights set on a promotion to lead anchor. Unfortunately they hired someone new from another station. It just made me feel like it was time for a change."

"Understandable," Stan said. Then he glanced at Margie. "Maybe we could call Jack tonight and put in a good word for her."

"For sure," Margie replied. "What an amazing coincidence. Or a lightning-strike of destiny."

"This week has been full of those," I mentioned under my breath as I glanced down at my notepad and looked over my notes, all the while struggling to stay on track with this so-called interview. "Let's go back to your other son, Aaron." I said, looking up. "Would I be able to talk to him as well?"

Margie and Stan looked at each other. "I suppose we could give him a call at work."

"Where does he work?" I picked up my pen again, poised to take a few more notes.

"He owns a boat-building company in Portland," Margie explained, eyes suddenly beaming. "He's *very* successful with it."

I swallowed with difficulty and struggled to find my voice. "He builds boats? That sounds interesting."

"Yes, we're very proud of him," Stan said. "He built that company from the ground up. Specializes in luxury yachts, but his real passion is for racing schooners. A number of his boats have done extremely well. We all hope that one of these days, one of them will win the America's Cup. That would be a proud moment." Stan stood up to fetch a framed photograph from the mantelpiece, which he brought over to me. He handed me the picture and pointed at it. "That's him right there, on one of his racing boats on the day they launched her."

Aaron was dressed in a navy windbreaker and cream-colored trousers, and sat casually on the helmsman's seat, behind the steering wheel of the boat. His hair was thick, dark and wavy, and the sun shone brightly on his smiling face.

As I gazed down at the photograph, I felt a sizzle of electricity in all my extremities, a sense of familiarity, as if we knew each other already. He wasn't a mirror image of Sebastian Fraser by any means, but there was something about him that seemed to reach out to me. I wanted to go and sit next to him in that picture.

At the same time, I was worried that I was imagining things, fantasizing that he might be my husband from another life.

"That's impressive," I replied, handing it back. "So he lives right here, in the area?" A frenzied flock of butterflies invaded my belly.

"Yes, in Portland."

"Is he married?" I blurted out, realizing at once how inappropriate that question was, when I was supposed to be conducting an interview about Henry Wadsworth-Longfellow.

"Not anymore," Stan replied matter-of-factly. "He's divorced."

"I see." I couldn't explain why I was so happy to hear that, when I knew how painful a divorce could be, under any circumstances.

Although I suppose, deep down, I knew exactly why I was entertaining such selfish thoughts—because I was letting my imagination run riot.

Could it be that Aaron Peterson was Captain Sebastian Fraser, reincarnated? A man who had loved his wife desperately enough to sail around the world in search of a time machine to bring her back from the dead? Could he also have followed her across the centuries to be with her again?

And was I the wife he had loved so devotedly and passionately?

All at once, my mind began to flounder. I didn't know what to make of all this, or what to do next. I felt anxious and jittery, as if I were going insane, losing touch with reality. I'd always considered myself to be a rational person, but none of this seemed the least bit real. How could it possibly be?

"I'm sorry," I said, flicking my pen, tapping it on the paper. "I don't know why I asked that question."

"Are you all right?" Margie asked. "Can I get you a glass of water or something?"

I lifted my gaze and fought to give them an easy smile. "No, I'm fine. I'm just processing everything. Thinking about my story. But I would love to meet Aaron if you wouldn't mind putting me in touch with him. I'm interested in his boat-building company. That sounds like another great story."

"I'm sure he'd love the publicity," Stan said to Margie.

She stood up and walked to the kitchen. "I'll give him a call right now."

When I returned to the parking lot a short while later, I found the rental car empty, and the doors locked. Glancing around, I spotted Bailey sitting on a bench in the park overlooking the water. I stepped onto the green grass and walked toward her.

"Hey," I said, taking a seat.

She turned to me. "How did it go? Did you learn anything?"

"Oh, yes," I replied as I set my purse down on the bench between us, "and I will never again question the magic of the universe."

Her eyebrows lifted. "Why? What happened?"

I leaned back and pointed at a few sailboats moored in the cove. "Do you see that boat right there? That's her. *Evangeline*."

Bailey faced the water. "The big one?"

"Yes. And get this. The Petersons didn't come up with the name. It was their son Aaron who came up with it. He was only five at the time, and he said he was going to marry a girl named Evangeline."

"Seriously?"

I nodded. "They also said that all he wanted was to be captain of the boat. Now he owns a boat-building company in Portland."

She inclined her head at me. "Isn't that where Captain Fraser's money came from? A shipbuilding company in Portland?"

"That's right. Kind of strange, isn't it?" I raised an eyebrow as I regarded her in the late-afternoon light.

"It could just be a coincidence," Bailey replied, as if she wanted to grab hold of my ankle and prevent me from lifting off the ground and floating up into a bunch of fluffy white clouds of fantasy.

"Of course it could," I replied, "and I'm trying to keep my head on straight about all this. But they showed me a picture of him, and maybe I was under the influence of everything they'd just told me, but he looked so familiar to me. Like we already knew each other, though I'm absolutely positive we've never met."

She turned toward me and touched my knee. "Please be careful, Katelyn. I don't want you to get your hopes up and be devastated if it doesn't pan out, and then spend the rest of your life alone, believing that he was your one and only true soulmate. He's likely just a guy who happens to share a few things in common with…" She stopped herself and looked out at the ocean again. "Oh, I don't know. It is mindboggling, all the links and connections. I had a hard time believing all of it when we first started, but now…" She met my gaze. "What are you going to do?"

I watched *Evangeline* bob gently on the wake of a passing fishing boat, then I fixed my eyes on the distant horizon. "I'm going to go and meet him right now."

"*Now?*"

"Yes." I rose from the bench and picked up my purse. "His mother just called him and arranged for me to meet him at his office. I'm going to interview him for a story about his racing schooners."

Bailey stood up as well. "It's a perfect cover, at least."

We started walking back to the car. "If you don't mind," I carefully said as we reached the vehicle and got inside. "This time, I'd like to go on my own. I can drop you off at the inn first, then I'll meet you back there later."

"Are you sure?" Bailey asked, sounding concerned as she buckled her seatbelt. "It might turn out to be a terrible disappointment. I can come if you want. I could wait in the car or do some shopping."

"I'll be fine." I inserted the key into the ignition and started the engine. "I really want to try and get a sense of who he is, just in case there's something there. And don't worry. I won't do anything stupid. And I'll call you as soon as I'm done."

I backed out of our parking space and drove onto the main road. "Oh," I added, "and there's one other thing I forgot to tell you. They actually have two sons, and the other one lives in New York. You'll never guess where he works."

She stared at me intensely. "No way."

"Yes. He's a news director at CNN."

Her eyes grew wide. "Did you tell them you just applied for a job there?"

"Of course. And they said they'd call him, too, and put in a good word for me."

Bailey faced forward again. "Well, if nothing else, maybe this whole bizarre escapade will result in you getting the job of your dreams."

"Maybe so," I replied. "But first things first. I need to go and meet that boat builder."

I sat on a comfortable black leather chair in the reception area of Voyager SeaCraft, flipping through a sailboat magazine while I waited for Aaron Peterson, Owner and Managing Director, to arrive from the factory.

The luxurious head office was located in one of the century-old brick buildings in downtown Portland. The reception room boasted oak doors, mahogany furniture, and a shiny modern chrome chandelier overhead. It wasn't at all what I'd expected. Although I don't know what I *had* expected, exactly, because everything seemed to be happening at lightning speed, and I was barely able to keep up with the twists and turns my life was taking from one moment to the next.

When I woke earlier that morning with tingling hands, I never imagined that, within hours, I would be tracking down a man who could very well be my beloved husband from another life. *Would he know it when he saw me? Would he recognize me?*

Stop it, Katelyn. You need to control your expectations or he'll think you're mad.

I set the magazine down, and my eyes fell upon the large antique desk where an attractive silver-haired receptionist sat. She was busy working on something at her computer.

Just then, the sound of a car door shutting outside caused me to sit up in my chair. The office seemed to go absolutely still and quiet as I waited. Then the front door swung open, and Aaron Peterson walked in.

"Sorry I'm late," he said to the receptionist as he passed by my chair and approached the desk.

He was casually dressed in jeans and a golf shirt. His dark hair appeared windblown. He had to be at least six-foot-two and was lean and fit like an athlete. He was likely in his late thirties. Perhaps forty—but, if so, a very young and fit-looking forty.

The receptionist paused her work and smiled up at him. "No trouble, Aaron. But Ms. Roberts is here, when you're ready."

He turned around and faced me, our eyes locked and held, and the whole world seemed to fall away beneath my feet.

It took me a moment to gather my composure as I rose.

"Hi there," he said, blue eyes glimmering with an infectious warmth and that arrestingly familiar quality I couldn't put my finger on, which made me feel almost dizzy with rapture. He approached me and held out his hand. "I'm Aaron. You must be Katelyn."

I placed my hand in his. "That's right." I felt an odd shudder in my chest, originating from the grip of his hand. It was as if all the cells in my body had awakened to the physical connection. "Thank you for seeing me on such short notice."

"My pleasure," he easily replied. "I had to come back to the office anyway. It worked out perfectly." He turned and opened a door in the back corner which I assumed led to his office. "Come on in."

In an effort to collect myself, I cleared my throat and took a deep breath before I followed him through the door into a massive open space with maple floors, white walls and enormous floor-to-ceiling windows that looked out over the harbor. There were a few large drafting tables in the center of the room and a whiteboard on one wall, and bean bag chairs in one corner. The side wall housed a large glass cabinet full of books and rolled documents.

"This is our design studio," he said, gesturing with a hand as he led me to another door at the side which took us into a smaller, carpeted office with filing cabinets and more large windows. There was an antique mahogany desk similar to the one out front.

"Have a seat," Aaron said, gesturing to one of the leather chairs facing the desk while he sat behind it.

Then we stared at each other for several seconds and I felt completely dumbstruck. He ran his fingers through his thick dark hair.

"I'm sorry," he said, his forehead crinkling with dismay. "You look very familiar to me. Have we met before?"

"I don't think so," I said, deriving immense pleasure from the question as I crossed one leg over the other and tugged my skirt a bit lower to cover my bare knee. "But you look familiar to me, too." We continued to regard each other wordlessly in the bright light streaming through the windows.

Feeling awkward, I resumed some light conversation. "This is quite a place you have here."

He seemed to shake himself out of his reverie before he spoke. "Obviously this isn't where we build the boats. The factory is outside the downtown core. But this is a good space to be creative."

"Creative..." I dug into my purse for my notepad and pen. "Do you mind if I take a few notes?"

"Not at all."

I launched into a series of questions about how he got into the business and how many boats he had built. He explained that he started racing dinghies during summers when he was a kid, and by the time he was sixteen, he began to purchase beat-up boats to repair and restore, then resold them for a profit. In his early twenties, he traveled to Europe to work in a number of international boatyards where he completed some apprenticeships.

When he returned home, he joined a boatbuilding firm in Connecticut and was quickly promoted from shipwright to head foreman. Then he took out a bank loan to start his own company and built his first racing skiff. The boat did well in competitions, and soon he had contracts to build others, and the company grew from there—one boat at a time.

"How many employees do you have?"

"Here in Portland," he replied, "twenty. But our Southampton facility employs forty-seven, and our factory in Norway employs..." He paused. "Sixty-two, I think."

I looked up. "You have facilities in the UK and Norway?"

He nodded.

"How many boats have you built?"

He sat back and thought about it. "I used to be able to keep track, but now everything moves so quickly. I'd have to check the files and do a count, but I would estimate around six hundred and fifty."

I wrote furiously, trying to get everything down. Meanwhile I wasn't even sure what I was going to do with this information, since I was a television reporter and I hadn't arrived with a cameraman. I was out of my wheelhouse, so to speak. Perhaps this could work out as a freelance magazine article.

"That's impressive." I looked up to find him staring at me again, with intensity and fascination.

My cheeks flushed with heat. Lowering my gaze, I set my pen down and swallowed hard.

"I'm sorry," he said. "I can't stop staring at you. I'm sure I must know you from somewhere. Even your voice sounds familiar."

I wet my lips and chose my words carefully. "Maybe we knew each other in a past life."

He chuckled softly and nodded. I lowered my gaze again, shy all of a sudden, my heartbeat quickening. He truly was an impossibly attractive man by any standards, whether we knew each other in a former life, or not.

I knew he was divorced, but he couldn't possibly be single. Surely some woman had swooped in and snapped him up by now.

Picking up my pen again, I asked him a few more questions about his company and the success of his boats in the racing circuit. He gave me a quick rundown and promised to email me a document that showed the racing stats of all the boats he'd ever built.

Then I heard the receptionist's heels clicking across the hardwood floor in the design studio. She knocked lightly on Aaron's open door before she peeked in. "Sorry to disturb you, but it's after five," she said. "Do you need me for anything else before I go?"

"No, Martha. Go on home. I'll lock up."

She smiled at him. "Great. I'll see you tomorrow."

I waited until the sound of her heels disappeared into the carpeted reception area, then I met Aaron's gaze again.

Still, he was watching me with those intense blue eyes that caused a ruckus of exhilaration in my core. Honestly, I felt as if this were the most thrilling experience of my life, as if my whole body was coming alive with sensation and awareness.

"I missed lunch," he said. "Are you hungry? Maybe we could grab a bite while we continue with this. Unless you already have all you need."

Feeling flustered and goosebumpy all over, I closed my notepad. "Hardly. And yes, I'm starving."

The lines on either side of his mouth deepened as he smiled. "Good. There's a decent restaurant within walking distance of here, if that sounds all right to you?"

"Sounds great."

He stood up and grabbed his jacket.

I texted Bailey from the restaurant to tell her I wouldn't be home for a while, and managed to enjoy my dinner with Aaron without falling into an internal debate with myself about whether or not we had been formerly married, each reincarnated from an earlier century—which still seemed implausible and fantastical to me, despite all the coincidences.

We ordered a bottle of wine and talked about all sorts of normal things, mostly to do with his company as I continued to conduct my interview. Soon, we progressed smoothly and naturally into more personal subjects, and he asked about my life in Seattle.

"I see that you're not wearing a ring," he said. "You're not married?"

The question left me feeling positively overjoyed—to the point where I found it difficult to sit still—because I was flattered and thrilled that he was taking an interest in my personal circumstances.

I wiped the corner of my mouth with my napkin and set it back down on my lap. "I was, for seven years, but now I'm divorced."

"Sorry to hear that," he said. "Any kids?"

"Sadly, no—which was part of the problem," I explained. "I was ready to start a family and I wanted a child, very much, but Mark wasn't interested. It caused some tension in our relationship, which I guess is what drove him away, straight into the arms of a younger version of me. A woman who wasn't pushing him to slow down and have kids. She was only twenty-one. And he married her last year."

Aaron shook his head. "If he wasn't ready to have a child with you after seven years, he probably won't ever be."

I agreed. "What about you? Are you married?"

I didn't want to mention that I already knew the answer to that question because I'd brazenly asked his parents a few hours earlier.

Aaron finished his meal and set down his fork. "I'm divorced as well. The simple explanation for that is that we got married too young. We really rushed into it. But nothing's ever simple when it comes to a breakup."

"That's true. Any children?" I asked, taking a sip of my wine.

"Two girls." He reached into his pocket for his cell phone and searched for some pictures. "Elisa is fifteen and Mary is sixteen." He held his phone out to show me a number of photos. "They're terrific sailors."

"I can see that," I replied, looking at all the action shots of the girls in brightly colored team uniforms on racing boats.

Aaron put his phone away. "It was rough at first," he explained, "when I first realized it was over, because the girls were very young. But so were we. We were only twenty-two when we tied the knot and we had Mary right away."

"What happened, if you don't mind me asking?"

Aaron leaned forward. I looked down at his strong, sun-bronzed hands on the table and wanted overwhelmingly to reach out and touch them. To hold on to them. As if, by touching him, I could learn, through some sort of soulful transference, everything there was to know about him. About the life he had lived which I had not been a part of. I wanted to know *everything*.

"Remember when I told you I spent time in Europe, working at different boatyards?" he asked. "Well, Eve and the girls came with me. Elisa was barely eighteen months, but Eve hated it over there and she wanted to come home and live closer to her mother. I asked her to stick it out for one more year so I could finish my apprenticeship, but she was impatient and we were arguing all the time. We weren't on the same page about anything. She was miserable, so she packed up and left on her own. Took the girls with her. Looking back on it, I probably should have put her and the girls first and given up the apprenticeship, but I honestly thought she'd just go home and wait for me. But she found someone else—who happened to be her first love and high school sweetheart. They're married now."

"That must have been very difficult," I said, my eyebrows pulling together with compassion.

"It was," he continued, "because she broke our marriage vows and I saw it as a betrayal. I remember thinking…" He paused. "Why can't people just *resist* the desire to stray? Wait for the urge to pass. Love the one they're with."

I felt a shock of response and absolute understanding in my heart, for I'd been through the same thing with Mark—and

Sebastian—and still felt the wounds of those betrayals. "I felt the exact same way when Mark cheated on me."

Aaron nodded. "I didn't know how I would ever trust anyone again," he continued. "I haven't yet. Not really." He tried to shrug it off. "But enough years have passed and I've accepted that Eve was always meant to be with Corey, and she and I were never really in tune with each other. I think when we married each other, we were searching for something we could never find in each other. But things are good now. I've moved on and we're friends. There are no hard feelings anymore. I put that away because of the girls. Now I see them whenever I want and it's easy. I get along great with Corey. He's a good guy."

"That's wonderful," I said. "You're lucky to have that."

Aaron reached for his wine. "I am, but this isn't exactly the life I imagined for myself."

"In what way?"

"Don't get me wrong," he said. "I love my work. That's what keeps me going every day, but I always thought I'd be coming home to a wife and a house full of kids by now. *Lots* of kids."

"How many?" I asked with a laugh.

He considered it for a moment. "I don't know. Like…*five.*"

An image of the old photograph in the front hall of the Fraser House Inn flashed like an exploding light bulb in my mind. Sebastian and Evangeline had had five children. *What was happening here? Was this real—the magic that the rational part of my brain continued to resist?*

Feeling flustered, my cheeks aflame, I tucked a lock of hair behind my ear. Then I gestured toward Aaron with my hand. "You already have two. Only three more to go."

He chuckled softly. "Yeah. No problem. Just a little catching up to do."

He gazed at me with unwavering intensity, and my heart began to pound at a frantic pace because he was so breathtakingly gorgeous. I almost couldn't bear it. I was practically trembling inside. Never in my life had I felt such an intense attraction to a man, not even with Mark in the early days of our relationship.

Yet, everything about this was completely different, with more than just one layer. It was overpoweringly physical, because I couldn't keep myself from imagining what it would feel like to be kissed by those lips and touched by those hands. But there was so much more to it than that. I wanted to know everything there was to know about each moment of Aaron's life leading up to this one. I felt as if I'd missed out, not knowing him before now. I felt deprived and cheated out of something.

Those beautiful lips parted, as if he were about to say something important, but then he let out a breath and sat back, abruptly, in his chair. For a long moment he regarded me with something that resembled frustration, then his expression slowly revealed a hint of amusement. He dropped his gaze, chuckled to himself and shook his head.

"What is it?" I asked.

His blue eyes lifted, and he looked so vulnerable all of a sudden, and yet happy at the same time. His expression was friendly and open. I melted right there on the spot.

"I'm sorry," he said, "but I'm finding it hard to think. My brain's not working properly. You are just so darn pretty."

My insides exploded with excitement, and I felt as if I were free-falling from a high place, with no fear of when or where I might land. A smile spread across my face and I held nothing back.

"Are you seeing anyone?" I asked. "Dating anyone...I mean?"

"No," he replied. "Are you?"

"No."

He continued to stare at me from across the table, then gave me a mischievous, knowing smile. "Then I think we need to go sailing."

I laughed, and so did he. It felt like an inside joke.

"I know some terminology like port and starboard," I said, "but I don't know how to sail. I've always wanted to learn though."

He spread his arms wide. "Then I must be your guy."

I continued to smile at him, until I felt like a quivering mass of total happiness. "Yes, I think you must be."

"Are you free tonight?" Aaron asked.

"It just so happens I am."

"Then I should get the bill."

He signaled to the waitress and paid the bill, while I sat wondering, with painful dread, how I was going to step on a plane in less than forty-eight hours and return to Seattle, when all I wanted to do was stay here in Portland and continue to explore what was happening with this man, who was quickly setting my heart on fire.

Forty-five

W̶e returned to Aaron's office, where my rental car was parked, and he told me to meet him in an hour in the parking lot at Kettle Cove in Cape Elizabeth, near his parents' summer cottage, and to bring a warm jacket. From there, we would take a small tender out to *Evangeline*.

With little time to spare, I drove back to the inn and told Bailey everything about my interview with Aaron over dinner, and asked if she'd be okay alone that evening.

"Of course," she said while I freshened up in the bathroom and changed into some warmer clothes for the moonlight sail. "And I can't believe it. He's single and gorgeous and taking you sailing tonight. It's all so perfect."

I peeked my head out. "Don't say that. I'm afraid you'll jinx it."

She rolled her eyes playfully. "Of course you *would* be superstitious. But really, Katelyn, it's pretty amazing."

"I know, I know." What else was there to say? Except that it wasn't going to be quite so perfect when I was boarding a plane and flying back to the West Coast in less than forty-eight hours.

A short while later, Bailey drove me to the parking lot at Kettle Cove where Aaron was waiting for me. I introduced them and they shook hands, chatted for a few minutes, then Bailey made her excuses and promised to see me back at the inn later that evening.

As soon as she was gone, I faced Aaron in the twilight's glow. He had changed into an off-white fisherman's knit sweater and faded blue jeans with deck shoes. A large gym bag was slung over his shoulder, and he looked more muscular than I remembered at dinner. My heart fluttered at the sight of him.

"Are you ready?" he asked, and I felt as if I'd been ready for this all my life.

Yet, I couldn't shake the instinctive urge to protect my heart, because we'd only just met and all of this was almost too overwhelming. I thought of Bailey's warnings earlier that day: *Please be careful, Katelyn. I don't want you to get your hopes up and be devastated if it doesn't pan out.*

I didn't want that either, so I resolved to take this slow and at least pause before I leapt in with both feet.

⸺ↄ⸺

As soon as we climbed aboard *Evangeline* and left the rowboat tied at the mooring, Aaron switched on the cabin lights and gave me a tour below deck. He showed me the galley and dining area, which included cushioned benches around a saloon table. There was also a navigation area, two double cabins aft, and another cozy V-berth forward.

We then returned to the top deck where he gave me a quick lesson about boat safety, showed me the lifesaving rings and took me back down to show me the fire extinguisher and how to use the radio.

By then it was fully dark, so he turned on the masthead light and running lights, then set to work, moving about from the cockpit to the foredeck to unfurl the mainsail and jib, while I sat on the back bench watching him move with speed and agility, as if it were all second nature to him. Soon, he was hoisting the mainsail, which helped me to understand why he was so fit and muscular.

A cool breeze came out of nowhere and snapped the canvas tight. His hair blew about, and he looked up at the sail, then down at the water as if he were assessing the strength and direction of the waves.

"It's a good night for a sail," he said with an irresistible smile that sent a surge of heat and excitement into my blood. He moved along the starboard side and hopped down into the cockpit beside me.

A few minutes later we were free of the mooring and heading out to the sparkling black waters beneath the incandescent light of the moon. Aaron asked me to take hold of the wheel while he raised the jib. As I felt the resistance of the rudder beneath my grip, I was filled with curiosity and a desire to learn the workings of the boat, to become familiar with all the different lines, how they fed into the blocks and cleats, and to understand how to trim the sails to change direction.

For the next hour, Aaron showed me when and how to tack, although it was a relaxed lesson as the wind was gentle, the water was fairly calm, and we were in no particular hurry to set any records or reach any preset destination.

Later, on our way back, we relaxed on the clean white seat behind the wheel, where he talked passionately about his childhood aboard this boat and how it had turned him into the man he was today.

"My father and I learned together," he said. "We spent a lot of hours out here on the water, sailing and fishing and swimming.

It was good for me because I learned what I was capable of when I was given the responsibility, at a very young age, to command a vessel like this." He looked up at the starlit sky, then smiled at me. "Maybe that's what planted the entrepreneurial spirit in me, because there's such a sense of freedom and control when you're at the helm, aiming your bow into the crashing breakers, timing the swells and feeling like you know exactly what you're doing. You make your own decisions and you live by them."

We both looked up at the night sky and I felt positively mesmerized by the beauty of it all—the miracle of this world we lived in and the vastness of the universe. But especially the fact that I had somehow been drawn to this place on the other side of the country from where I grew up—by a vision—which ultimately led me to meet this man. I still wasn't sure if there was such a thing as destiny, but if there was, this had to be it.

Aaron's voice was quiet as he rested his arm along the back of the seat behind me, and stroked my shoulder with his thumb. "And when you find a safe little cove somewhere," he said, "and the water is calm, and you lower your anchor to dive off the stern, it's like living in a dream."

"That's beautiful." I looked down from the white sails in the light of the moon to find Aaron watching me.

"Thanks for coming out with me tonight," he said, his voice husky and low. "I haven't enjoyed a sail like this since…I can't remember when. I've been working too much lately."

"I don't know why you enjoyed it so much," I said with a laugh, retreating into humor when I was feeling afraid on the inside—afraid that I was making too much of this. "I wasn't much help to you. I probably slowed you down."

He toyed with a lock of my hair, tucking it behind my ear. I felt a pleasant shiver of desire all over, like an electric current across my skin, and drew in a quick breath as he leaned closer and pressed his lips to mine.

Around us, the wind held steady and the ocean rushed, fast and foaming, past the hull. I wanted to wrap my arms around Aaron, pull him close and never let go.

As he deepened the kiss, a wave of euphoria ripped through me, for the touch of his lips was so achingly familiar. It was like coming home after a long journey to foreign places. There was a glorious lushness to the moment, and I felt content and completely alive.

When we drew apart, I was in a daze, drowsy with a sense of awe and wonder. The world had never seemed more beautiful to me.

"What is it about you?" he whispered as he stroked my cheek with his thumb.

"I don't know what's happening," I replied, "but I feel it, too." I was breathless. Excited. Confident in this explosive mutual attraction. I took hold of his hand and he threaded his fingers through mine. "I'm so glad I met you today," I whispered.

"So am I," he replied. "How long will you be in Portland?"

"I fly out the day after tomorrow."

He shut his eyes and touched his forehead to mine. "No, please, you have to stay longer."

"I'm supposed to be back at work on Monday."

"Can you ask for more time off? I really want to get to know you better."

"I want that, too."

He looked up quickly and scanned the surrounding area, as if to make sure we weren't about to sail into a reef or another oncoming boat, then he kissed me again, and my body erupted in a storm of pleasure and wanting. In that instant, I wanted to quit my job and never go back. Even if it meant losing everything. At least I wouldn't have to walk away from his kiss.

"I suppose I could ask for a few more days," I said breathlessly.

He dragged his lips across my cheek and down to my neck where he laid a trail of soft, intoxicating kisses on my shoulder.

"I don't owe them anything," I continued. "They just passed me up for a promotion I'd been working toward, for years."

He drew back slightly. "Really. What was it?"

I felt suddenly embarrassed for having brought it up, because I didn't want to put a damper on the evening. "It was just the anchor desk on the evening news," I explained, trying to make light of it.

"*Just* the anchor desk? That sounds big."

Unable to hide my disappointment, I let out a breath. "It was, to me."

"What happened?"

I shrugged. "I don't know. My boss had been telling me for years that I was the top choice when our long-time anchor retired, but at the last minute, they brought in someone new from another station. I haven't felt particularly loyal to the station since then."

"I don't blame you," he said. "Are you going to stay on there?"

I spoke with a more positive tone. "As it happens, I've already applied for another job—at CNN in New York. Your mother mentioned that your brother works there and she was kind enough to say she'd give him a call and put in a good word for me, so we'll see."

Aaron's expression stilled and grew serious. He sat back slightly and said nothing. Then he slowly stood up, moved to the wheel, and leaned away from me to check our direction on the compass.

"Would you mind taking the wheel?" he asked without looking at me. "It's time to tack."

"Sure." I rose to my feet and took hold.

"When I tell you to, turn the boat hard over toward the wind like we did before. In that direction." He pointed. "Don't stop turning until I say, and don't forget to duck when I yell 'tacking' because that's when the boom swings across."

"I promise, I'll duck."

He left me there while he quickly adjusted the sails. A moment later, we were on a new direct path toward the mooring at Kettle Cove.

I remained at the wheel while Aaron left me alone and went below for a few minutes. When he came back up, he took over. "Thanks, you can have a seat for now."

I moved to the bench, feeling certain that something had gone wrong. The magic had disappeared and he seemed focused only on returning to the cove.

"Is something the matter?" I asked after a few more minutes of silence. "Did I say something I shouldn't have?"

He inhaled deeply, then shook his head and finally looked down at me. "No, it's fine. I apologize. It's not you. It's just that…" He looked out at the water again. "You mentioned my brother, and we don't get along too well."

"I see." I thought about Aaron's stories about his childhood and all the sailing he had done with his father, and realized that he had never once mentioned his brother. "You haven't talked about him."

"No. We haven't spoken in a long time. Years."

This surprised me, because everything about Aaron struck me as serene and sensitive. He didn't seem like the type of man who would hold a grudge against his brother or enjoy conflict. But how well did I really know him? He was a bachelor, after all—a very handsome, rich, eligible one who should have been snapped up by now. Why hadn't he been? Was he unwilling or unable to sustain a long-term relationship?

I felt a shiver of unease suddenly as I watched him steer the boat, and was reminded of Bailey's warnings, and how I had resolved to be careful with my heart, because this man was *not* my deeply devoted husband who could not bear the loss of me. I was not Evangeline. He was not Captain Sebastian Fraser. Not in *this* lifetime. He was Aaron Peterson. A complete stranger before today.

"What happened between you and your brother, if you don't mind me asking?"

Aaron remained at the helm, staring straight ahead. "It wasn't just one thing. It was an entire childhood of disagreements and fistfights and competition."

"Competition?"

He glanced briefly at me. "Over everything, pretty much. I was the oldest and maybe he always felt like second fiddle or something. I don't know what started it, but he seemed jealous of anything I had, and we just…never seemed to like each other very much. Different personalities, I guess."

"How did you parents handle it?" I asked.

"Not very well. When we were small, they used to punish us for fighting and they'd force us to apologize to each other. Then they gave up eventually and put us in separate rooms so they wouldn't have to deal with it on a daily basis. When we were teenagers, my dad spent more time with me while my mother always favored Jack. That's why I'm closer to my father than to my mother. But as soon as I was old enough to move out, I came here and Jack stayed in Chicago, until he got the job in New York."

Aaron looked down at me. "So what will you do if you get the job?"

The wind felt stronger and colder all of a sudden, and I folded my arms across my chest to keep warm. "I don't know. It depends on what they're offering, and what the job's going to be like. It's not an anchor position, but all I want is a fresh start somewhere so I can work my way up."

Aaron nodded and made an effort to sound supportive. "That sounds like a good plan."

When we drew nearer to Kettle Cove, he dropped the sails and used the motor to bring us back to the mooring. We didn't talk much while he secured the boat. He told me he didn't need any help, so I went below to check my phone for texts.

There was only one, from Bailey: *How's it going?*

I quickly texted her back: *Just okay. We're back now but we're still on the boat. I'll tell you about it when I see you.*

Aaron came down the companionway and looked at me. "I'm sorry about all that," he said. "I didn't mean to be rude."

"You weren't," I replied, even though I had felt—quite deeply—the obvious chill of his withdrawal, and I still felt uncomfortable.

He studied my expression and glanced down at my phone, which I slipped into my jacket pocket. "I was just texting Bailey," I said, not knowing why I felt the need to explain myself.

"That's good," he said. "Now that we're back, would you like a glass of wine?"

I glanced at the open hatch door and rubbed my hands together. They felt numb from the cold. "I should probably get back soon."

His shoulders fell, and he took a few steps closer. "Please, don't go like this. Let me make it up to you. We can stay down here where it's warmer and sit at the table."

Recognizing a genuine look of regret in his eyes, I made an effort to let go of my unease. "All right. I guess it's not that late." I texted Bailey with the change in plans and smiled at Aaron as I hit the send button.

"Good." He moved to a storage compartment and retrieved a bottle of red wine, opened it and stood at the galley counter to fill two clear plastic tumblers.

I slid onto the cushioned bench behind the table and waited for him to join me. He set the glasses down, and we clinked them together and shared a look of apology.

"I'm really sorry," he said again. "Even after all these years, from miles away, my brother still brings out the worst in me."

I wasn't sure what to say, but I felt some relief when Aaron reached for my hand and held it. I felt the natural intimacy between us begin to return.

"You just caught me off guard, that's all," he continued to explain. "I really like you, Katelyn, and when I imagined my mother setting you up with my brother—even though it was just for a job interview—my back went up."

"It shouldn't bother you," I said. "Haven't you been able to tell how much I've been enjoying myself tonight? With *you*?"

He looked down at our joined hands on the table. "Yeah, but I wouldn't put it past Jack to make a move on you, just to spite me."

"Would he really do that?" I asked. "After all these years? You're not kids anymore. Maybe he's matured."

Aaron picked up his glass and raised an eyebrow. "Maybe," he said skeptically.

"You don't think so."

He shook his head. "When we were in high school and I was a senior, I asked a junior out, because she seemed interested in me. When Jack found out, he accused me of dating her just to agitate him, because unbeknownst to me, he'd been in love with her since the fifth grade. Or so he claimed. Of course I didn't know this because we weren't close, and I genuinely liked the girl, so I didn't back off. I dated her for a year and Jack never forgave me. Then, when I started seeing Eve, he came here to stay at the summer house for a few weeks, and behind my back, he asked her out and didn't say very good things about me. He caused all sorts of problems." Aaron took another drink of his wine. "Eve and I broke up over it until she figured out that Jack was just trying to get back at me. When we got back together, I proposed."

"Do you think, maybe, that's why you rushed into marrying her when you were so young? To make sure Jack wouldn't steal her away?"

Aaron ran his fingers across my hand and squeezed it gently. "That might have had something to do with it."

I felt warmer all of a sudden, pleased that Aaron was at least opening up to me. "Competition between brothers," I lightly said. "I'm sure you two are not the first."

I raised my plastic tumbler and finished my wine. Aaron reached for the bottle and gave me a refill.

"So now you know the whole story," he said with an intimate and almost seductive look that made me feel shivery and happy inside.

Leaning closer, I touched my lips to his. He immediately took my face in his warm hands and deepened the kiss. The lush, heated pressure of his mouth caused a burst of sensation over every inch of my body and I felt an urge to squirm closer against him.

Soon we were making out like a couple of teenagers on the cushioned seat, and it was starting to get a little out of hand, so I placed my open hand on his chest and pushed him back slightly. "Easy, sailor. Let's not go *too* crazy on the first date."

He chuckled softly, closed his eyes and touched his forehead to mine. "Sorry," he whispered. "I'm not usually this impatient, but from the first second I saw you today, sitting by the window with the light in your hair, I was a goner."

I felt a warm glow inside me.

"I wanted you, too," I replied, and it was the truth. Whether we were soulmates, or whether this was just plain old-fashioned love at first sight, I had no idea. But whatever it was, it was powerfully hot, and wonderfully irresistible.

And I knew one thing for sure. I wouldn't be flying back to Seattle just yet. Bailey would simply have to go home without me.

Over the next few days—after Bailey flew home and I made arrangements to stay at the inn for another full week—my life began to feel like a fairy tale.

The magic began the night Bailey left, when Aaron offered to cook me dinner at his condo, which turned out to be a luxurious, modern penthouse overlooking Portland Harbor. Based on the building amenities and high-end appliances and décor, I guessed it must have had a market value of well over a million dollars.

We sat on his balcony where he barbequed two perfect steaks, which he served with sautéed mushrooms, roasted potatoes, boiled beets, and a delicious green salad. For dessert he brought out a tub of chocolate chip ice cream, which we ate straight out of the container. We had dinner out the next night and went sailing again. This time he let me do more things on my own. He was an excellent teacher.

The following night, we went to the movies and drew straws over which film to see. By the time he drove me back to Cape Elizabeth and pulled up the long tree-lined lane to the Fraser House Inn, it was almost midnight. Knowing what I knew about the history of the house—and the possibility that he had been its owner in another lifetime—I was curious to find out if he might recognize anything about it, or feel something extraordinary as it came into view.

I watched him carefully in that moment, but saw no indication of any past life memories or a sense of déjà vu. He simply pulled to a halt on the gravel lot, shut off the engine, and took hold of my hand.

"I had a great time tonight," he said.

"Me, too," I replied. Then all too quickly, I asked, "I know it's late, but would you like to come in and have a drink? Have you ever been inside this house before?"

He sat forward slightly, seeming almost amused by my enthusiasm. "I actually looked at it when it was on the market a number of years ago, but I decided not to offer on it."

"Why not?"

He shrugged casually. "I don't know. I decided it was too big for just one person, and I couldn't really afford it anyway. Not back then." He reached to unbuckle his seatbelt. "And yes, I'd love to come in."

We got out of the car and I found myself watching him discreetly, but intently, as we climbed the stairs to the veranda and approached the front door. I used my key to let us in, as Angela always locked the front door after 10:00 p.m.

I expected it to be quiet as we stepped into the entrance hall, but I heard the hum of conversation in the library, followed by laughter. "The owners sometimes like to get a card game going," I explained to Aaron.

Just then, Angela appeared out of the library to greet us. I introduced her to Aaron and they shook hands.

"Would you like to join us for the next round?" she asked. "We're playing crazy eights."

I shared a look with Aaron, and answered for both of us. "I think we'll just take it easy tonight, and have a drink in the front parlor, if you don't mind."

"Of course. What can I get you?"

Aaron ordered a cognac and I asked for Baileys on ice. While she went to get our drinks, I took Aaron by the hand to show him around, even though he said he'd been there before.

I led him into the dining room. "It's beautiful, isn't it?" I said.

"Yes," he replied from the doorway, taking in the portraits on the walls, the fine china in the cabinet, the antique furniture.

Still seeing no signs of recognition in his expression, I led him to the photograph of the Fraser family in the front hall. "This is Captain Fraser and his wife, Evangeline," I said, still holding Aaron's hand. "She had the same name as your boat."

Aaron bent forward to look more closely at all the faces, and I found myself on edge with a racing pulse and butterflies in my belly. But after a moment, Aaron simply straightened and said, "Interesting."

Angela appeared out of the back kitchen with our drinks on a small silver tray, and passed by us to set them down in the front parlor.

"There's a large portrait of the captain's wife over the fireplace in my room," I added as we sat down on one of the upholstered sofas. I signed for the drinks and Angela left us to return to the card game. "Bailey seemed to think Mrs. Fraser looked like me." I picked up my drink and watched Aaron carefully.

He picked up his drink as well, and said nothing.

His lack of a response left me feeling disheartened, even though rationally, I knew I couldn't expect him to consciously remember something from a former life, if that's what it was, which it probably wasn't. Nevertheless, I pressed on.

"I could show it to you," I suggested. "Would you like to see it? We could take our drinks."

"Sure."

Gathering up my purse, I led the way up the wide, carpeted staircase. When we reached the top, I dug into my purse for my key as we moved down the hall.

"Here we are," I cheerfully said, and unlocked the door.

My belly began to flutter nervously as I walked in and gestured toward the gilt-framed portrait over the mantel. "There she is. What do you think?"

Aaron moved to stand before the fireplace and looked up at it, quite thoroughly, for a long, drawn-out moment. My heart raced with anticipation.

"She definitely is beautiful," he said at last, still looking up at her. I wondered what he was thinking and feeling. *Anything?*

At last, he turned to face me. "And she *does* look like you. Her hair is the same color, and there's something similar in her eyes. She has the same spark you do."

"I have a spark?" I asked with a grin.

"Oh, yes." His gaze roamed over my face, and I could barely breathe, as the space between us electrified. "It must be strange sleeping in here," he said, "looking up at your own doppelganger."

"A little," I replied, pondering his choice of words.

He sipped his drink, still watching me over the rim of the glass, and I wanted overwhelmingly to tell him everything—that I believed Evangeline and I shared the same soul, and that he was quite possibly in possession of the soul of Captain Fraser, her beloved husband. I wanted to step into Aaron's arms and tell him how much I'd missed him, and let him know how grateful I was that we had found each other again.

But of course, I didn't say any of that, because a part of me—the stubborn rational part—still felt like it was all a bunch of mumbo jumbo, and I was afraid he would think I was a delusional freak. Maybe I was.

Besides all that, I was still hesitant about leaping into this very new relationship, and simply handing over my heart. I wanted to see and hear it from him first. I'd been burned before, and it wasn't easy for me to trust what was happening here, or to trust *him*. In this life, we barely knew each other, and the fact of the matter was, there were permanent scars on my heart and soul.

While I was mulling over that idea, my cell phone chimed in my purse, and I jumped. "Who's texting me at midnight?" I said, feeling compelled to check, just in case it was something important.

Aaron stood patiently while I swiped the screen and read the text, which had come from an unknown number.

Hi Katelyn. This is Jack Peterson. I work at CNN in New York and I just sent you an email. I wanted to let you know because I understand you're on vacation in Maine and I wasn't sure if you'd be checking your messages. Looking forward to hearing from you.

My whole body tensed and I blinked a few times, thrilled that I'd gotten a response from CNN, but feeling unsure, under the circumstances, about how to handle this.

"Is everything okay?" Aaron asked.

All I could do was nod and read the text a second time. Finally I looked up. "It's from your brother," I immediately confessed. "He said he just sent me an email. They must have looked at my resume."

Aaron's eyebrows pulled together as he watched me. He finished his drink and set the empty glass down on the desk by the door. "He's certainly working late."

"Yes," I replied, as I tapped the screen to access my emails. Sure enough, something had come in from Jack's account at CNN five minutes earlier. "I'm just going to read the email," I explained, glancing briefly at Aaron.

"Should I leave?" he asked.

"No," I quickly replied. "Please stay. But close the door."

He moved to close it while I read the email. "He says they watched my sample tapes," I explained, "and they were impressed with my resume, and they want me to come to New York for an interview right away. Tomorrow, if possible."

I glanced up again. Aaron made no comment, but he was watching me like a hawk, his eyes intense and contemplative as he searched my expression.

"You're not happy about this," I said.

He raised his hands, as if in surrender. "It's your life and your career. What I told you the other night should have no bearing on this."

"So you think I should go."

He inclined his head at me. "It's a great opportunity, and I don't want to hold you back, Katelyn. We only just met."

I should have been pleased that he wasn't trying to make me feel as if I were being disloyal somehow, but the reference to how briefly we'd known each other felt like a punch to the gut. To me, it seemed as if we'd known each other forever, but I had to be careful about over-romanticizing what was happening between us. Perhaps he was just a good-looking guy I'd gone out with a couple of times. There was no commitment. There had been no promises, nor was there any proof that he was my one true soulmate who had followed me across time.

And yet...

I lowered the phone to my side. "I don't want this to get in the way of what might be happening here," I said. "I mean, I don't want to presume anything, but I don't want to say good-bye to you either."

Without warning, he strode forward, gathered me into his arms and pressed his lips firmly to mine. The kiss was fierce and passionate, and I felt the heady sensation of his hands roving up and down my back. I met his mouth with willing, open abandon and was so happy—so immensely relieved—that he still wanted this. Whatever *this* was.

Slowly withdrawing from the kiss, he held me close in his arms and spoke in a quiet, husky voice that sent shivers of desire down my spine.

"I have no intention of saying good-bye to you. Just please promise me…" He paused. "Don't listen to him, okay? Go for the interview and take the job if that's what you need to do, but remember that I'm still here, wanting to be with you." He closed his eyes and shook his head. "Ah, hell. What I really want to do is beg you to forget about CNN. Really, it's not that great. And New York is…It's fast and loud and you'll hear sirens all day."

I couldn't help but laugh softly. "For the record," I assured him, "I have no interest in your brother. I like what's happening right here, and I want to continue this."

He pulled me even closer, almost jerking me up against him. I couldn't lie—his physical vigor was a definite turn on. "Then don't go. Turn down the offer."

"They haven't offered me anything yet."

"Then why not just leave it at that?" He spoke with a touch of humor, trying not be possessive like some sort of brutish Neanderthal, but I could sense that he truly *did* want me to decline the request for an interview and never meet his brother.

Part of me was tempted to do exactly that, because all that mattered to me in this moment was the beautiful man standing before me, holding me in his arms, arousing my passions—because he made me feel as if I were exactly where I was meant to be.

At the same time, I could not abandon my common sense as a woman of the twenty-first century. I could not possibly throw away a fabulous career opportunity on the whim of an infatuation that may or may not turn out to be something more. I'd been a television journalist all my adult life. It had been my dream since I was a small girl, and I truly believed it was my calling. Professionally, at least.

"I have to go to New York," I whispered. "Just to see."

For a long moment, Aaron gazed down at my lips without speaking a word, then he released me from the embrace and stepped back. "I understand."

He kissed me on the cheek, then turned and started for the door.

"Wait. Are you leaving?" I asked, feeling a terrible pang of dread and regret. What if everything fell apart between us because of this one decision?

I tried to tell myself that if this single event was enough to put an end to our brief romantic acquaintance, then it was *not* meant to be after all.

"Yes, I'm going now," he said with his hand on the door knob. "But I'm assuming you'll call me or text me from New York to let me know how the interview goes."

"Of course I will," I replied, feeling almost dazed with frustrated desire as he opened the door to leave.

"And I hope you'll come back, Katelyn, because I suspect I'll want to be kissing you again, as soon as possible."

"I want that too," I replied with a smile.

He walked out into the hall. "Goodnight. Sleep well."

I could barely breathe as I watched the door close behind him. Then I looked up at the portrait of Evangeline and tried to trust whatever was meant to be.

CHAPTER

Forty-seven

S ince it was only a five-hour drive to New York City from Cape Elizabeth, I decided to rise early, take the rental car, and stay in a hotel after the interview, which was scheduled for 4:00 p.m.

I was lucky enough to find a charming 1920s-era hotel, located on the edge of New York's Theater District, four blocks from Times Square. I booked it online before I left and texted Aaron to let him know where I would be staying, and told him I'd head back to Cape Elizabeth the next morning.

The drive to New York was smooth and uneventful, and I arrived in time to check in, take a much-needed power nap, then grab a shower and make myself presentable.

It took some effort not to become nervous during the cab ride from the hotel to the Time Warner Center, but I kept my cool and found my way to the CNN newsroom, where I was greeted by an older woman named Jean who gave me a quick tour, then escorted me to a small private office where the interview was to take place.

To my surprise, Aaron's brother Jack was not present in the room when I walked in, nor did he pop his head in to say hello. The interview was conducted by two other news directors—one male and one female.

In point of fact, I was relieved Jack wasn't there, because I didn't want Jack and Aaron's rivalry to affect anything about the interview which, in the end, went extremely well. I felt confident as I walked out of the building onto Columbus Circle, and stopped on the crowded sidewalk to do a little dance, which attracted some attention.

Feeling spirited and overly energetic—and despite the fact that I was wearing heels—I decided to walk back to my hotel rather than flag down a cab, because the weather was fine, and I needed to work off some of my excitement.

The first thing I did was call Bailey. Naturally, she was thrilled to hear how well the interview went, and she asked me to let her know as soon as I heard back from them. Then she asked about Aaron.

"He's been amazing," I replied, "and I think I might really be falling for him, but he doesn't remember anything about Evangeline or a past life—if there's anything to remember. Last night I invited him into the inn and showed him the picture of Captain Fraser and his family in the entrance hall, and then the portrait of Evangeline in my room, but it didn't seem to spark anything or ring any bells. Maybe all of this is just in my imagination."

Bailey paused. "Either way, it doesn't matter. If you're into him and he's into you, the present is what matters."

After I hung up, I sent a text to Aaron: *Hey there. I just finished the interview. It went really well. I think I have a good chance. And in case you're wondering, Jack wasn't there. I didn't even meet him.*

Aaron immediately texted me back. *Congrats! I'm not surprised it went well. You're a rock star. I'll call you later when I get home. Dealing with a minor company crisis right now.*

I paused at a stop light and typed my reply. *Okay. Good luck. Talk later.*

The light turned green and I moved with the crowd across the busy intersection. As soon as I stepped onto the curb, my phone buzzed again. I pulled it out and swiped the screen.

It was a text. This time, it was from Aaron's brother, Jack, and my belly did a nervous flip.

Hi Katelyn. Congratulations. I just heard that you knocked their socks off. Sorry I couldn't be there but I would still like to meet you. There's something I think we need to talk about. Can we meet for a drink?

My belly exploded immediately into an even bigger firestorm of butterflies—not just because of the positive feedback about the interview, but because Jack wanted to talk to me about something. What could it be?

I didn't answer right away, because I wasn't sure what to say. What if he knew about my relationship with Aaron and he simply wanted to compete?

Needing a moment to process this, I walked the length of another block and stopped at the next light, then read the text again.

Jack was a producer at CNN where I was hoping to get hired. I'd be crazy to say no. But what about Aaron's warnings?

Thinking long and hard about my options, I decided, in the end, that I couldn't possibly refuse Jack's invitation—and not just because of the potential job offer.

There's something I think we need to talk about.

My curiosity got the better of me. I wanted desperately to know what that "something" was.

ᴐᴄ᷾᷾ᴏᴊᴐ

Jack suggested we meet half an hour later at the Shake Shack in Madison Square Park, so I hailed a cab because I didn't think I could make it on foot in the heels I was wearing—at least not without the resulting torture of chafing and blisters.

How will I find you? I texted when I accepted his invitation.

I'll find you, he replied. *I know what you look like, but just so you know what to look for, I'll be wearing a red T-shirt and a navy New York Yankees baseball cap. But don't worry. I have a feeling you'll recognize me.*

My breath caught in my chest at the suggestion that I might recognize him, for his parents hadn't shown me any pictures. All I'd seen was a picture of Aaron.

The rush hour traffic was slow and congested on Broadway, but the cab driver managed to get me to the park early, so I got out and wandered leisurely toward the Shake Shack. When I reached the outdoor restaurant, I searched all the tables where tourists and New Yorkers sat in the shade eating burgers and fries, and kept my eyes peeled for a man in a red T-shirt and navy baseball cap. I stopped for a moment to look more carefully about, but saw no one who fit that description.

Mindful of the fact that I had arrived early, I continued along the stone path to explore the park and admire the fountains and statues.

Eventually, I reached the opposite end and turned around to head back toward the Shake Shack, where I paused to shade my eyes from the early evening sun and search again for a man in a red T-shirt.

Then I spotted him. He was of medium height with a muscular build, wearing loose-fitting, faded blue jeans. He walked slowly, head down while reading his phone. His face was shielded by the brim of his ball cap.

My heart began to pound—not because he was a news director at CNN who might be able to help me get a job. No…it was something else. Something very familiar about the way he moved.

He paused on the path and finally lowered his phone to look up.

Suddenly, my own phone buzzed and I stopped to dig it out of my purse. I quickly swiped the screen and read a new text.

Hi, are you here? It was Jack.

I texted him back: *Yes. I'm standing behind the Shake Shack. I see you.*

I pressed send and watched him from afar. He checked his phone again, then raised his eyes and looked directly at me.

My whole body exploded with chaos and commotion. I couldn't seem to move, because I was certain I *did* recognize him, and the shock of it was almost debilitating.

He raised a hand to wave at me. I waved back and started walking toward him.

"Katelyn," Jack said confidently, sauntering closer. I took in his friendly expression and tousled golden hair beneath the hat, and the smoky blue of his eyes.

I held out my hand to shake his. "Hi Jack. It's nice to meet you."

He regarded me with a look of intense fascination, as if he were searching my face for some sign or clue about something.

I felt the same urge—to seek answers. To know who he was. To connect the past with the present.

But was he truly who I thought he was? Or was I just imagining the likeness?

Surely, there could be no mistaking it, and it wasn't simply a physical resemblance. Yes, there was a similarity in the distinctive facial features, the casual swagger, and the short, strapping build, but there was also an intuitive recognition on my part. A knowledge of the heart. It took me straight back to 1878, when I had felt such an immediate, relaxed affection for the kind and caring Mr. Williams, who had been such a good friend to me when I needed one.

Or rather, he had been a friend to Evangeline.

I could barely process it. I was in shock—not just because I recognized this man from Evangeline's life, but because I believed he recognized me as well. At least I thought he might…

"Are you hungry?" Jack asked, "or would you like to walk for a bit?"

"Let's walk," I replied, turning to go deeper into the park.

We strolled side by side for what felt like endless moments of intense wonder. He glanced at me a few times, and we met each other's gazes with a touch of unease, as if we were both afraid to enter into a conversation. Was it because he wanted to ask if I had lived in another century, or was he simply shy?

"Thank you for meeting me," he said.

"Thank you for inviting me." The awkward silence stretched on for a few more seconds.

"This may sound strange," Jack said at last, "but I kind of feel like we already know each other."

Clearly, he was feeling me out. I wanted to do the same. "Yes."

He cleared his throat. "How's your memory for people you might have known before? Like…a really long time ago."

"It's excellent," I replied, looking up at him sharply. "I'm quite sure I remember more than the average person."

Jack stopped and faced me on the path. Others in the park had to file past us, but I didn't care if we were in the way.

Jack continued to scrutinize me, as if he were waiting for me to say something, but I didn't know what to say. My brain had gone numb, trying to comprehend what was happening here. Was I dreaming?

"It's really nice to see you, Katelyn," he said meaningfully. "I've been waiting a long time."

"But you don't even know me," I replied, testing him.

He seemed to understand exactly what I was up to. "No, I suppose I don't. But I think we were friends…*before*. Do you know what I'm referring to?"

I was careful with my reply. "I think maybe I do."

There was a long pause. "You can tell me what you're thinking," he said. "I'll understand. I'm probably the only person in the world who can."

In the end, I couldn't fight his persistence. I had no choice but to surrender. "I do think I know what you're referring to."

As I said the words out loud, my heart exploded with panic, because I didn't know where this would lead, or what I was supposed to do with this information.

We started walking again.

"Did you recognize me from the video samples I sent?" I asked.

He nodded. "I thought it might be you when my mother called and told me about a red-haired female reporter who was curious about our boat, *Evangeline*. She told me all the questions you asked, and that you had applied for a job here. I thought maybe you'd been searching for me, so I immediately dug out the recordings you submitted. You look almost exactly the same. I couldn't believe what I was seeing."

"You look the same as well," I said, "and I'm still recovering from the shock of meeting you just now."

"So you really do remember…"

I nodded.

We walked a few more paces in silence. I found myself still a little afraid to speak openly about what was happening here.

"How long have you known about this?" I asked.

"As long as I can remember," he replied. "I always knew I'd lived another life."

There it was, at last, spoken in plain terms.

"When I was young," he continued, "I mostly remembered things from my childhood in the past, but everyone told me I just had a vivid imagination. I believed it at the time, because I didn't know any better. As I got older, memories of that same age in Mr. Williams's life would come to me. I didn't have a clear picture of you in my mind until I was in my early twenties, which is when Evangeline and Laurence Williams met at the lighthouse."

I stopped again and faced him. "I met your brother, Aaron, in Portland, and he said you don't get along very well. I've been thinking that he might be someone I know as well. Someone we both know."

I still couldn't seem to bring myself to spell it out in words—that I was Evangeline Fraser, Jack was Mr. Williams, and Aaron could possibly be my husband, Sebastian.

Jack didn't answer the question. He simply started walking again, very slowly, encouraging me to follow. "Let's back things up a bit," he said. "How long have you known about this? When did the memories start?"

"It's kind of a long, convoluted story," I told him. "It started with a vision I had during an accident a year ago, which led me out here to the East Coast. Maybe it was a coincidence, but I booked a room at the Fraser House Inn. I found it online."

"Trust me, there are no coincidences," he said.

This time, I couldn't argue.

"I'm not sure what brought it on," I continued to explain, "but when I went to sleep one night at the inn, under the portrait of Evangeline, everything came back to me. Well, not everything. Only certain sections leading up to the morning I almost got swept off the rocks at the lighthouse—the morning I went to you after I found out about my husband's infidelity. Do you remember that?"

"Yes," he replied. "I remember every word we spoke that morning, and how Sebastian showed up and dragged me out of my house by my shirt collar."

The fact that Jack could recount specific details about a situation I had seen in a dream left me feeling shaken and even more riddled with confusion and awe over the fact that all this might truly be real.

"There's a sundial on the lawn that I think might have had something to do with it," I added.

"Really," Jack replied with interest. "I've been to the Fraser House a number of times, just to help myself remember things, and I've seen that sundial. What makes you think that?"

For some reason, I wasn't ready to tell him *everything*, and I was sorry I had brought it up. Sylvie would kill me if she knew.

"Oh, I don't know," I replied, waving a hand dismissively. "Maybe it just sparked a memory of something. I saw a picture of Evangeline and Sebastian, much later in life, standing next to it. But I don't remember that picture being taken. As I said, I only remember things up to what happened at the lighthouse that morning, when you and Sebastian fought."

He nodded. "I know the picture you're talking about. I researched their lives extensively." He glanced at me again. "So you don't remember anything after what happened that morning?"

"No. That's when I woke up and the dream ended. I don't know much about what happened to *you* after that, either. There's only one single picture of you in a book at the Portland Head Light Museum. No other information."

He quietly explained. "I left Cape Elizabeth after you had your third child, and I moved to New York to work as a bricklayer, constructing buildings. Some of them are still standing. I go look at them sometimes, and it still feels surreal."

"I'm sure it does. This feels surreal to me, too. Did you and I ever see each other again?"

"No," he replied. "I knew you would never want to leave your children, so I stayed away. I did my best to move on."

"And did you?"

He let out a small, bitter laugh. "Not very successfully. I eventually married, but we were only happy for a short while. Money was tight and there were mouths to feed."

"I'm sorry to hear that," I replied. "Are you married now?"

Aaron hadn't mentioned whether or not Jack had a wife, but I wasn't sure he would have, because he didn't seem to enjoy talking about his brother.

"No," Jack replied. "I haven't found the right woman, I guess. I've been waiting for all the puzzle pieces to slide into place." He gazed at me in that moment, with a hint of melancholy, along with that warm, comfortable familiarity that I remembered so well.

He had once told me he loved me. I had a strong feeling there was still hope in his heart.

This was too much to take in. Suddenly I felt as if I were drowning in a sea of questions about destiny and fate and what I was meant for, and who I was meant to be with—if anyone. I thought of Mark as well, and the loneliness I had felt in our marriage, even before he left me for Mariah. Bailey had always said he wasn't "the one." Maybe she'd been right. Maybe what I had been searching for was the forever kind of love, and I'd wanted it so badly, that for a while I'd convinced myself that Mark was the true mate of my soul.

But did I know any better now? No—I still felt completely unsure of this life and who I was meant to love.

"What about your brother, Aaron?" I asked for the second time. "Is he who I think he is? Is he Sebastian?"

Jack turned to me. "Yes, but he's completely clueless about it, at least consciously. All he knows is that I have no fondness for him, and he hates me equally in return, but he has no idea why. Not *really*."

"Were you ever tempted to tell him?" I asked. "To talk to him about it?"

"I did," Jack explained. "When we were young, I told him we had been enemies once, in another life, but he told me I was crazy and made me feel like an idiot. I stopped confiding in him after that. I never spoke of it again. And we continued to fight over everything. Even from a very young age, we were never very good at sharing."

Obviously the animosity between them was rooted very deep, even to this day. I couldn't imagine what it must have been like growing up in their home.

"I don't know what to make of this," I said, still struggling to find my equilibrium, "or what to do with this information."

Jack stopped on the path and touched my arm. "I know it's a lot. But take your time, Katelyn. I'm here for you, for whatever you need—always."

My insides trembled as every single cell in my body darted about in a state of disorientation. I still couldn't believe this was real, and that here was someone who understood what I was going through. Someone who was the same as me, because he remembered a past life.

Nevertheless, I couldn't fail to remember Aaron's warnings about his brother.

Aaron's handsome face flashed in my mind just then. I was whisked back to how it felt to be kissed by him—how the whole world had fallen away beneath my feet. I felt horribly disloyal to him suddenly. And confused.

I started to walk again, slowly. "I should tell you that I've been seeing Aaron this week, and he's expecting me back tomorrow. He's waiting for me."

Jack walked on in stoic silence. "Are you in love with him?" he asked, point blank.

The directness of the question hit me hard, like a sudden gust of wind. "I don't know. We only just met."

And I'd been guarding my heart very carefully.

Jack inhaled deeply, as if steeling himself for whatever might lay ahead. "Please consider staying in New York an extra day. We have a lot of catching up to do, Katelyn, and I'm sure you have more questions."

I stopped on the path. "Yes, I do."

He regarded me intently in the fading light. "Then let's go get some supper. I promise I'll tell you everything you want to know."

ᶜᶜᵔᵔᵔᵔ

We took a cab back to my hotel so that I could change into something more casual—a pair of skinny jeans, ballerina flats and a tank top and sweater—while Jack waited in the lobby.

We then went for dinner at a little Italian restaurant a few blocks away, and drank a bottle of wine while we talked keenly and openly for hours, about our experiences with past life memories and how they had affected our lives in the present. At times, Jack, like me, had suffered from anxiety and feelings of loss and confusion, when he was unable to understand where those feelings were coming from. Then a year would pass, and he would remember something new, and everything would become clearer.

He told me about some of the books he had read on the subject, and how it was possible that we'd all lived not just one, but a number of different past lives. I asked if he remembered any others, but he did not, and he had no interest in submitting himself to hypnosis and past life regression techniques.

"I'm okay, dealing with this on my own," he explained. "I know all I need to know."

It struck me, as Jack walked me back to my hotel, that with Aaron, I had shared none of my suspicions about a past life. Bailey, my best friend, was the only person I had fully confided in. What did that say about my feelings toward Aaron and Jack, or Evangeline's true feelings toward Mr. Williams and her husband? Had she always felt more comfortable sharing her private thoughts with Mr. Williams? I pondered those questions beneath the flashing lights of Time Square as Jack took my hand and shouldered his way through the throngs of people ahead of us.

At the same time, I couldn't let myself forget what Aaron had warned me about—that Jack was not to be trusted. Meanwhile, something in me *had* trusted him enough to spill all of my secrets and fears onto the table between us over dinner that night.

It had been that way between Evangeline and Mr. Williams as well. He was the person she had gone to more than once, when she needed friendship, comfort or advice.

My phone buzzed in the front pocket of my jeans just then, and I pulled it out. While Jack walked ahead, I checked it for messages.

It was Aaron, calling me. It was the second time he had called in the past hour, and again, I ignored it and slipped the phone back into my pocket, because I wasn't ready to talk to him just yet. I didn't know what I would say, or what I felt.

When Jack and I reached my hotel, he walked me into the lobby.

"Thank you for everything," I said as I let go of his hand.

"It was my pleasure," he replied. "And please don't go back to Maine yet. I have to go to work tomorrow, but I'll try to find out what I can about the job offer and let you know. And I'd love to spend more time with you. Can I cook you dinner tomorrow night? I still feel like there's so much we need to learn about each other. And I have some books you might be interested in. You're welcome to borrow them."

"I need to think about it," I found myself saying, realizing that if I decided to stay, I would have to call Aaron and tell him

I wouldn't be back the next day, after all. And if I did that, what else would I tell him?

I said goodnight to Jack and walked to the elevator. As soon as I was back in my room, I called Bailey and told her everything about my meeting with Jack. She could hardly believe it.

"He asked me to stay another day," I said, "and I told him I'd think about it. Meanwhile Aaron's been calling me, and he expects me back tomorrow. I haven't answered his calls. I don't know what to tell him, or what I should be doing. They're both amazing men and I don't want to mess this up."

"What's your gut telling you?" she asked.

"I have no idea." I sat down on the edge of the bed and thought about it for a moment. "Although, I must say, I'm not as physically attracted to Jack as I am to Aaron. The first moment I laid eyes on Aaron, I wanted to jump his bones right there on his desk. But I feel really, really comfortable with Jack, like I could open up to him about anything. He's just so down to earth and normal, while Aaron is kind of…" I paused. "Larger than life."

"But you believe he's your husband from another century," Bailey reminded me.

"Yes, but what if he was never truly 'the one'? I don't remember anything about our lives after that morning at the lighthouse. What if I only stayed with Sebastian because of my children? And to honor my marriage vows? What if I was always secretly in love with Mr. Williams, and he was always the one I was meant to be with? What if that's what this is all about? To right a wrong. To give Evangeline and Mr. Williams the chance to be together. The chance they never had."

Bailey considered that. "I think you need to stay another day in New York and see how you feel about Jack. Besides, he works at CNN. That kind of smacks of fate, don't you think?"

I sighed with resignation, because I was thinking the same thing, yet I didn't know how I was going to tell Aaron I wouldn't be coming back to Cape Elizabeth just yet.

Heaven help me, I didn't want to lose him. Not now, when I was still so unsure.

After I ended the call with Bailey, I sat for a moment and considered my options. I could always text Aaron and lie—tell him I'd gone to a show that night and had turned off my phone, and that I needed to stay an extra day for a follow-up interview at CNN.

But no. If I was going to end up with Aaron, the last thing I wanted to do was begin our relationship with a lie. So, in the end, I decided to come clean, dial his number, and tell him the truth.

At least some of it.

"You had dinner with Jack," Aaron said, after I rambled my way through an explanation about why I hadn't answered his calls all evening. His voice was cool, aloof. "I thought you said you didn't meet him today."

"I didn't," I replied. "Not at the news station, but then he texted me later and asked to meet me, and it wouldn't have been smart to say no."

"Because of the job," Aaron said, as if he needed a firm confirmation as to why I would accept an invitation to dinner from the brother he had explicitly warned me against.

"That's right," I said.

There was a long pause. "What did you talk about?"

It hardly seemed like the right moment to tell Aaron that I believed I was reincarnated and that I had known him, and his brother, in a past life, and that's obviously why they hated each other in this one—because they had fought over me before. Based on how he had responded to Jack's revelation all those years ago, I wasn't confident he would respond well to mine either.

Would I *ever* tell him about it? I wondered uneasily. And could I be happy with someone who didn't know everything about me? Wouldn't that be like living a lie?

"Work, mostly," I replied. "The whole news industry. There's a lot going on these days. It's not what it used to be."

It wasn't a complete lie. Jack and I had spent time discussing that.

Again, Aaron was quiet, and I had the sense he was pacing around his condo, not wanting to reveal how agitated he was.

"So you're not going to come back tomorrow," he said. "Is that because you're planning to see Jack again?"

I knew I had to answer the question truthfully, but I couldn't seem to find the right words.

"Please don't," he firmly said. "Don't see him again. Just come home."

I found it odd that Aaron would use the word "home," when I didn't have a home in Maine. I was only visiting from Seattle, and there was no commitment between us. No promises. We weren't together like that.

Not that I didn't want something more solid. I did. Even now, when I was so utterly and totally confused about what was happening here, I wanted that.

The prospect of losing Aaron stirred something in me. A sense of longing. I felt desire in my bloodstream—the desire to return to him, touch him and hold him tight, to give myself over to him completely and never let go, despite the fact that we knew so little about each other.

Surely *that* meant something, didn't it? That I was feeling desire in this moment? Or was it just a physical response to the sound of his voice and the memory of what a good kisser he was?

At the same time, I didn't want to be pressured right now. I didn't want to be given an ultimatum. "I don't know," I said. "I need time to think about this."

He was quiet for a long moment. "You didn't just talk about the news industry, did you," he said in a low voice.

Suddenly, I had no trouble finding the right words to reply. "No."

A prolonged silence caused my stomach to clench tight with apprehension. I waited with bated breath for Aaron to say something, but there was only silence on the other end.

"Hello?" I said. "Hello?"

Still…no reply.

"Aaron? Are you there?"

But the call went dead. He'd hung up on me.

I did not try to call Aaron back that night, because I still didn't know what I wanted, and I didn't wish to be forced into making a decision. Nor did I feel that I was in any position to explain the complexities of the situation to him. He could never understand. I wasn't sure I understood everything myself.

What I needed was a little time and space to figure this out, and if Aaron wasn't willing to give me that, then maybe he wasn't the right man for me after all.

What I wanted—what I'd *always* wanted—was someone who understood me completely and would love me forever. A man I understood and loved equally in return. A relationship with mutual trust.

My thoughts flitted back to what Jack had said to me that final morning in the lighthouse keeper's cottage—or rather what Mr. Williams had said to Evangeline when she was devastated over her husband's infidelity.

I want you to know that I meant what I said. I do love you, Evangeline, and I always will. I will be right here waiting, if you ever need me.

Feeling a reassuring sense of peace wash over me, I picked up my phone again and texted Jack.

Thank you again for a great night. I'm going to stick around for another day. Let me know what time I should come by tomorrow.

He responded immediately: *Thank goodness. How about 6?*

I agreed and he texted me his address, which was not far from Madison Square Park, where we had met that afternoon.

Afterward, I stayed up watching CNN for a while, then I finally fell into a deep and dreamless slumber.

⤳

The following day, I did what any normal twenty-first-century woman, with time to kill, would do in New York City. I went shopping in the morning, then I walked around Central Park at lunch time. I spent the afternoon at the Metropolitan Museum of Art, where I bought a unique piece of jewelry—a reproduction of a first-century Roman ring that I couldn't resist.

I wore the ring to Jack's place for our dinner date, along with a black floral sundress I'd purchased that morning at Saks Fifth Avenue, which I wore with a crimson sweater that matched the tiny flowers in the dress, and my black ballerina flats.

When I arrived at Jack's apartment on the third floor of a century-old building, he opened the door and surprised me by kissing me on the cheek.

"Welcome," he said. "Come in."

He stepped back and invited me inside. It was a modest one-bedroom apartment with plenty of light and a view of the street below. A full wall of bookcases was jammed with hardcovers and paperbacks, as well as a shelf of vinyl record albums. The dark-brown leather sofa looked comfortable and well-worn.

"This is cozy." I glanced toward the small white kitchen where a pot was simmering on the stove.

"I hope you like chili," Jack said. "You're not a vegetarian are you? I probably should have asked."

"No, I eat everything."

"Good," he replied. "Please, make yourself at home. Take a look around. Can I get you a glass of wine?"

"That would be nice, thanks." While he went into the kitchen to pour me a glass, I set my purse down on a chair, then sauntered toward the bookcase. Curious about what he liked to read, I discovered that he had very eclectic tastes. There was everything from Tom Clancy novels to biographies of historical figures, Garfield comics and non-fiction books about world politics and economics. I reached the record albums and pulled one out.

"I see you like Van Morrison," I said, finding three more of his classic albums. I slid them back into place and pulled out the Beatles' *White Album*, and next, a Nina Simone record.

"You should stop there," Jack said from the kitchen as he poured the wine, "before you come to *Barry Manilow's Greatest Hits* and you change your opinion of me."

I laughed. "I love Barry Manilow." I glanced around and spotted a turntable and full stereo system that looked like it had been purchased in the eighties. "We should put it on."

Jack approached me and held out a glass of wine. "Whatever your heart desires."

I took the wine from him, and he located the album in his collection, right away. He removed the vinyl record from the sleeve and placed it on the turntable, switched it on, and carefully set the needle down on the first track, "Mandy."

"Ah," I said with a sigh. "That takes me back. My mother used to play this album all the time when I was a kid."

We chatted about our childhoods and how different everything was from today, basically because of the explosion of digital music.

"You were smart to keep your turntable," I said. "Most people got rid of them when they switched to CDs."

"What can I say?" Jack replied as he returned to the kitchen. "I have an appreciation for antiques."

While he put a salad together, I turned my attention back to the books and found several titles about heaven, reincarnation, and near-death experiences. "*The Illustrated Tibetan Book of the Dead*," I said as I pulled the book out and flipped through it. "This sounds a bit creepy."

"It's not at all," Jack replied, reaching for a knife to chop a tomato. "You can borrow it if you like."

"Maybe." I slid it back into place, and ran my finger along some of the other spines. I then came to a book entitled *Only Love is Real—A Story of Soulmates Reunited*. I pulled it out to discover that it was written by a psychiatrist named Brian Weiss, M.D., who appeared to be an expert on the subject of past lives and regressions through hypnosis.

While Jack worked in the kitchen, I quietly moved to the sofa and sat down to read for a minute or two.

Chapter one began with a quote from Kahlil Gibran, and the words "There is someone special for everyone." I continued to read, and came to the following passage:

> He takes your hand for the first time, and the memory of his touch transcends time and sends a jolt through every atom of your being. She looks into your eyes, and you see a soul companion across centuries. Your stomach turns upside down. Your arms are gooseflesh. Everything outside this moment loses its importance.

He may not recognize you, even though you have finally met again, even though you know him. You can feel the bond. You can see the potential, the future. But he does not. His fears, his intellect, his problems keep a veil over his heart's eyes. He does not let you help him sweep the veil aside. You mourn and grieve, and he moves on. Destiny can be so delicate.

I felt shivers along my spine as I read those words and thought of how Aaron had hung up on me the night before, angry about my decision to remain in New York and communicate with his estranged brother. All the hair follicles beneath my skin tingled, and I found myself covered in goose bumps.

You mourn and grieve, and he moves on…

My stomach muscles clenched tight with a feeling of dread—a fear of inescapable heartbreak. Was that what destiny had in store for me? Mourning and grieving?

But of course, there was no veil over Jack's eyes. He knew exactly who I was, and what we were to each other. There was some comfort in that.

Obviously, Dr. Weiss knew a thing or two about the experiences of people like me. I wished I could read the rest of the book that very night, along with every other book Weiss had written on the subject.

"Could I borrow this one?" I asked Jack, holding it up.

"Of course," he replied, as he continued to work on the salad.

I picked up my wine and read the next chapter.

After Jack and I ate dinner at the small round table in his kitchen, we sat down on the sofa to listen to more music and resume our conversation about the past.

Maybe I drank too much wine, but I soon found myself confessing my truest, innermost feelings, even though it probably wasn't exactly what Jack wanted to hear.

"I know that Aaron doesn't believe in any of this." I said. "But that breaks my heart—because if he *was* my husband once and we shared a life together, I feel like he should know. Like I have a duty to convince him. Make him believe it. Help him to remember."

Jack shook his head. "He doesn't want to believe it. And besides that…" He paused. "I don't understand why you care so much, considering what he did to you. Back then, I mean. He cheated on you. He slept with another woman."

The reminder caused an immediate aching sensation in my heart, and I buried my forehead in my hand. "I don't understand it either. I can't explain."

"I think it's his surface charm that trips you up," Jack said. "And his money—the success and the giant penthouse apartment. That's what it was back then, too—when he had the fancy coach and servants and silk top hats. I always knew there was no way I could compete, because I was just a lowly lighthouse keeper in a threadbare jacket. But don't be distracted by all that. Think about how he cheated on you."

I closed my eyes and tipped my head back. "*Argh.* Maybe I'm doomed to keep coming back over and over to repeat the same mistakes, because my husband in this life cheated on me, too. He was handsome and successful. Is that my problem? Am I that blind and shallow that I can't see what's beneath the surface?"

Jack knew all about Mark. I had shared my story with him at dinner the night before.

Jack reached for my hand. "Maybe this is your chance to turn that around and learn the lessons that you're meant to learn." He gazed intently at me. "Not all men are cheaters, Katelyn. I certainly would never do that to you. I'm not built that way."

I squeezed his hand in return. "I know. You're a good man. A true friend."

His eyes roamed over my face and settled on my lips, and I had the feeling he was going to lean closer and kiss me. I felt a rush of nervous butterflies suddenly, because I wasn't sure what it would feel like to kiss Jack. I wasn't even sure I wanted it to happen, because after the time I'd spent with Aaron over the past week, I was far too confused and disoriented to start kissing other men. Even if it was someone I cared for deeply.

A knock sounded at the door, and Jack's shoulders slumped with frustration. I chuckled softly. "As luck would have it."

Although a part of me was relieved.

Jack rose from the sofa and opened the door without checking the security peep hole. I couldn't see who was outside in the hall, but when I heard the tone in Jack's voice, I knew.

"What the hell are you doing here?" he asked.

Who else could it be, but Aaron?

He wasn't going to be pleased to find me with Jack. But he must have known I would be here. It's probably why he had come.

Jack tried to shut the door, but Aaron blocked it with his foot and forced it open. He walked into the apartment while Jack backed up and shook his head with disgust.

"Come on in then," Jack said, irritably, his tone dripping with sarcasm.

I rose to my feet. A part of me wanted to say, "This isn't what it looks like." But I didn't say that. Instead, I said something equally lame. "Aaron. What are you doing here?"

"I drove all this way to see you," he replied, "because I don't want you to be with him." He gestured toward Jack, who scoffed and walked to the kitchen to get a beer out of the fridge. "Come with me now. We'll go somewhere and talk."

Jack returned to the living room. "She's not going anywhere with you. And you should leave."

Aaron pointed a finger at him. "You had no right to move in on her like this, Jack. She's mine."

"I'm *not* yours!" I shouted. "I'm not anyone's."

Jack set the beer bottle down on the counter, and with that masculine swagger—which seemed dangerous all of a sudden—he approached Aaron. "I told you to go."

Aaron turned to me. "Come with me."

I glanced uneasily at Jack, who gave me a pleading look, as if to say, "You're not going to do this *again*, are you?"

My whole body tensed. I didn't know what to do. Part of me wanted to go with Aaron and clear the air, but I didn't know how to, unless I told him everything—that I thought I was reincarnated from a past life where he was my husband. But that sounded crazy, even to my own ears. I couldn't possibly say those things to someone who didn't understand. Not yet, when we were still just getting to know each other.

Maybe Jack recognized my desire to make things right with Aaron, because his cheeks flushed red with anger. He spoke to Aaron. "I told you to leave, but Katelyn will be staying here."

Aaron shook his head. "She can make up her own mind." He turned to me. "Katelyn…"

Jack scoffed. "Is it your mission in life to take everything I want?"

By now I was speechless, watching them argue. I began to wonder if the root of this rivalry went even further back in time, long before my existence as Evangeline.

"I told you, she's mine," Aaron said.

I gasped as Jack shoved Aaron. Aaron fell backwards onto the desk by the door and knocked a stainless steel water bottle to the floor with a noisy clatter.

Aaron immediately came hurling back toward his brother, tackling him like a linebacker. The loud, crashing sound caused me to jump back in fright.

"Stop it!" I shouted, lunging forward, wanting to pull Aaron off of Jack, but before I could get close enough, Jack slammed Aaron into the kitchen cupboards.

"Jack! Stop it!" I grabbed hold of Jack's arm to prevent him from going after Aaron again.

Aaron glared with malice at his brother. "You had no right," he said. "Not then and not now. She was *my* wife."

I blinked a few times in shock, and turned to look up at Jack, who frowned at Aaron.

"What did you just say?" Jack asked.

Aaron ran his tongue over a bloody gash on his upper lip. "I said, she was *my* wife, and I loved her. No matter what you think, I made her happy."

I stared in a daze at Aaron, who said this as he hugged his ribs from the impact against the cupboards.

"You knew," Jack said with disgust. "You remember everything?"

"Why didn't you say something?" I asked Aaron. "I didn't know if it was you."

"I didn't know it was you either," he replied. "Not for sure. I didn't want you to think I was crazy."

Exhaling sharply with disbelief, I simply stared. "I wouldn't have thought that."

"But I didn't know. I couldn't risk it. At least not so soon."

"Wait a second," Jack said, striding forward. "How long have you known about this? Because I tried to talk to you about it when we were kids, and you told me I was crazy then. You made me feel like a fool, so I never told anyone else. Not until now."

"I *did* think you were crazy," Aaron replied, "because I didn't know any of this until much later. When I was a kid, I just thought I had an overactive imagination. I only figured it out after Eve left me and I came back to Cape Elizabeth. That's when I started having recurring dreams I couldn't explain." He turned to me. "It was after I went to see the Fraser Mansion, when I wanted to buy it." Aaron went into the kitchen, ran the water, and rinsed his knuckles.

Jack exhaled heavily and sank onto the sofa, raked his fingers through his hair.

"It doesn't change anything," Aaron said as he moved into the living room. "I came here for *you*, Katelyn, and I want you to come home with me."

"Why?"

"Because you're meant to be with me, not him."

I shook my head. "I don't know what I'm meant for, and I'm starting to wonder if you both want me to choose you, just so that you can triumph over the other. Is that what this is about?"

Aaron and Jack regarded me with concern.

"No," Jack said. "I've always loved you, Katelyn. You know that. But *he* cheated on you, and once a cheater, always a cheater."

Aaron turned to him. "That's not true."

I hurried to grab my purse. "I'm sorry, but I have to go."

"Wait." Aaron followed me out the door, down the hall, all the way to the stairwell.

"Please don't follow me," I said, my shoes clicking hastily down the steps. "I need time. Don't call me. Just please, leave me alone."

Thankfully he did not argue. I reached the bottom floor of the apartment building, ran outside and flagged down a cab.

Only then, when I shut the car door and the driver pulled away from the curb, did I realize how badly my hands were shaking. Tears filled my eyes. I turned on the seat to look back at the apartment building, and wondered what Jack and Aaron were doing in that moment.

I hoped they weren't killing each other.

C H A P T E R

Fifty-three

Jack and Aaron both texted me and called a number of times that night, but I didn't answer my phone. I did, however, text each back to ask that they give me time and space to process all of this.

I called Bailey of course and told her everything. The only advice she could offer was for me to sleep on it and review everything with fresh eyes in the morning.

Eventually, my phone stopped buzzing, and I fell asleep with the television on.

I slept in the following morning, and was hesitant to check my phone when I woke, because I wasn't ready to make any decisions yet. Part of me just wanted to walk away from all this and never see either Jack or Aaron again. So I slid my phone under the pillow while I took a shower, and left it there when I went downstairs for breakfast.

After devouring a full plate of eggs, bacon and toast, and two cups of coffee, I felt more myself and was ready to return to my room and turn on my phone.

To my surprise, there were no messages from either Aaron or Jack, but there was an email from one of the CNN news directors who had interviewed me at the station. I clicked on it, and held my breath.

Dear Ms. Roberts,
   Thank you for your interest in the news reporting position at CNN, but we regret to inform you...

I read the rest of the email which assured me that they had been very impressed with my reporting experience and my performance during the interview, but unfortunately, another candidate was more suited to the position. They did want to keep my resume on file, however, in case any other positions became available in the near future.

Flopping onto the bed, I blinked up at the ceiling and rested my hand over the sickening knot of disappointment that was forming in my belly. Rejection was never easy.

So much for fate and destiny.

Suddenly an image of Aaron and Jack tackling each other in Jack's apartment flooded my mind, and I wondered again if their issues weren't really about me. Perhaps I was just another toy, another girl, they needed to fight over.

Finally, I sat up on the edge of the bed and decided to text Jack: *Hi. I just heard from the news director. I didn't get the job. They chose someone else.*

He texted me right back: *Seriously? I thought you were going to get it. They loved you. It must have been really close. I'm at work now. I'll try to find out what happened.*

Thanks, I replied. *But you don't have to.*

I waited for another text to come in from him. It seemed to take longer. At last, my phone buzzed.

Please don't leave New York. I want to be with you. Aaron's gone. Are you free tonight?

I set my phone down and wiped a hand over my face. It was barely 10:00 a.m., but the noise outside the window—the constant roar of the traffic and horns honking—was touching a nerve. I couldn't think. I couldn't make sense of my life. All I wanted to do was go home to Seattle and sleep in my own bed again, and talk to Bailey.

I sat up and texted him back: *I'm sorry, but I need to take a break from all this. Please give me the space I need. I know you'll understand, because you've always understood me. Thank you for everything. You are a good friend.*

I pressed send, and his only reply was three little heart icons in a row.

I flew home to Seattle that night.

Three months later

⸎

As soon as the cab dropped me off and I walked through the front door of the Fraser House Inn, I felt as if I had arrived home from a long journey. I set my suitcase down and looked around at the familiar wood paneling and wallpaper, the enormous chandelier overhead. Then I breathed in the invigorating scent of fresh flowers in a vase on the entrance table.

Sounds of laughter from the library reached my ears, and I smiled.

Angela came hurrying out. "Katelyn! You're here at last. Welcome. It's so good to see you again." She embraced me like an old friend, and said, "Congratulations on the new job. I was thrilled when I heard it would be you. I'm so happy for you, and for the *Portland Evening News*. We couldn't ask for anyone better."

"Thanks, Angela," I replied, as I picked up my suitcase again and followed her to the reception desk in the front parlor. "It happened pretty fast. I'm still pinching myself."

Barely two weeks earlier, I'd heard about the long-time news anchor taking an early retirement because he'd won the lottery. It was all over the Internet, so on a whim I'd sent in my resume and audition tapes. Now, here I was.

"And thanks for putting me up until I find a place to live," I said as I dug into my purse for my wallet and pulled out my credit card. I heard more laughter from the library. "It sounds like you're enjoying one of your famous card games."

Angela laughed. "Yes, and we're into the Rusty Nails, too. Care to join us?"

"Not tonight," I replied. "It was a long flight from Seattle. Maybe tomorrow, though."

"Of course." She checked me in and handed me my key, then showed me to the same room I'd stayed in the last time, with the portrait of Evangeline over the fireplace.

As soon as Angela left me alone and closed the door behind her, I looked up at the portrait and said, "Hey there, gorgeous. You must be surprised to see me back here so soon."

She gave no reply—she simply stared at me with those penetrating eyes—so I turned and strode to the window, flicked the latch and opened it so I could listen to the sound of the waves crashing onto the rocky beach beyond the edge of the lawn.

It was late November, and there was a biting chill in the air. I smelled snow and spotted a few flakes floating down from the dark, cloudy night sky. Feeling a shiver in my bones, I shut the window again and began to unpack my suitcase.

My first day as lead anchor of the *Portland Evening News* couldn't have gone better, considering how nervous I was. No one seemed to notice, however, because when we finished the broadcast and were off the air, the production crew cheered, whistled and applauded.

I couldn't help but blush and let my face fall forward onto the news desk. Everyone laughed, and patted me on the back. I knew in that moment that I was in the right place—that I had found my calling, and I was among friends.

Be that as it may, I still didn't have it all figured out yet, and I knew there were matters in my life not yet resolved.

At least I knew exactly what those things were, for I'd taken plenty of time to work through it in my mind—and in my heart—over the past few months.

When I walked out of the news station and breathed in the distinctive scents of the East Coast and Portland in particular, I closed my eyes and reveled in its exquisiteness. It was a surprisingly warm and mild night for so late in November. It made me feel as if I had come home, and this was where I was truly meant to be.

I reached for my phone and scrolled through my contacts, then tapped the number I was searching for.

It was time to send a text.

*H*i. Long time no see. I'm back in Portland. Got a new job. Sorry for the radio silence over the past few months, but thank you for giving me the space I needed. Would you be free for a drink sometime?

Of course it was entirely possible that Aaron would never reply, that he had given up on me after all this time, and was annoyed with me for refusing to discuss any of it, even on the phone. Or perhaps he had met someone else.

I need time. That's what I had told him in a brief email from the airport in New York the night I flew back to Seattle. *I need to figure out who I'm supposed to be in this life. Not in any other life, because the past isn't important. What matters is the here and now and the people we've become, today.*

He had responded with a lengthy email that I didn't read until I got off the flight on the other side of the country, took my phone off airplane mode, and stood at the baggage carousel reading my messages.

Dear Katelyn,

I understand what you need to do, but I can't leave you alone to choose your future without at least explaining myself and telling you what I believe you need to know.

I'm sorry for not being honest with you right away about what I knew of our history together. I'm still kicking myself for not recognizing the fact that you knew who I was. I should have seen it in your eyes and accepted that fate had brought us together again. But sometimes the physical world and the things we experience can get in the way of what we should be able to see with our hearts. I believe my marriage knocked me around a bit, planted doubts in me about my ability to know what—and who—was right for me. And when you went to New York and told me that you were with Jack, I couldn't help but fear that a part of you had never truly forgiven me for what happened in that other life, and that you always wished you had left me for Laurence Williams. Maybe you always wondered "what if?"

Or maybe, because I knew about what happened in your marriage to Mark, I was afraid you would equate me to him and never be able to trust me. I wanted a chance to earn your trust and your love again, with no past mistakes to color our future. I suppose I wanted a fresh start.

I also need you to know that I spoke to Jack for a long time after you left, and he told me that you remembered nothing from our life together beyond that day at the lighthouse, when you were angry with me for what I did. You had every right to be angry, but please know how deeply I regretted that foolish, terrible mistake. I had to live with that regret the rest of my life, and it haunted me until I drew my last breath, knowing how I had hurt you and how close I came to losing you.

But somehow, you were able to forgive me, and it was your love and trust that turned me into a better

*man. A wiser man. I said these words to you once, and
I will say them again: Regret is a powerful teacher.*

*If we come into each life with the purpose of learn-
ing something, then my lesson is complete. I will never
again betray your trust or anyone else's, and if you come
back to me, I will spend the rest of my days proving myself
worthy. I will never leave you. I will never hurt you. I
will continue to love you forever, until the end of time.*

Aaron

I had read that email in the airport three months ago and burst
into tears. My bag must have gone around the carousel a number
of times because when I looked up, I found myself standing alone
with no other passengers about. The carousel had shut down, and
I was in a daze.

Now, here I stood again, back in Maine where I first met
Captain Sebastian Fraser, and my friend, the lighthouse keeper,
Laurence Williams.

Suddenly, my phone buzzed and a text came in. I sucked in a
breath and felt a smile spread across my face. It was Aaron.

*Welcome back. You were terrific on TV tonight. Yes to a drink.
Are you free right now?*

I continued to smile as I texted him back with lightning-fast
thumbs: *Free as a bird. Can you meet me at The Old Stone Keep? I
could be there in ten minutes.*

I started walking toward my rental car. My phone buzzed
before I got there.

Sounds good. I can't wait to see you.

My heart exploded with excitement and anticipation as I
crossed the parking lot.

In that moment, it began to rain. I stopped to look up at the cloudy night sky and felt the sensation of cool raindrops touching my cheeks. Then suddenly my heart was transported back to that moment on the old road in Cape Elizabeth, when Captain Fraser stepped out of his coach to save me from the storm, and there was no escaping what I felt.

I knew in that moment, over a century ago, what I knew now with all of my heart. The veil had been lifted, and Aaron Peterson was the only man for me.

Ten minutes later, when I walked into the pub and saw him rise to his feet from the booth at the back—so handsome, it hurt just to look at him—I stopped in my tracks, laid a hand over my heart, and fell in love all over again.

It took me a moment to gather my composure and rein in my happiness. Then slowly, buoyantly, I walked toward him, and he did not hesitate before he swept me, weightless, into his arms and held me.

Epilogue

I was once the sort of person who didn't believe in miracles—or if I did believe in the possibility of such magic in our world, I didn't believe anything like that would ever happen to *me*. Like most people, I had watched movies about heaven that claimed to be true, or I read news items or books about real-life impossible events happening to regular everyday people, but always, on some level, in my mind, it felt like fiction.

But on the day I flew over the handlebars of my bicycle on a mountaintop in Seattle, fearing I was about to die, I experienced something miraculous, which I now understand was an awakening to my higher self and my higher purpose. What I envisioned on that mountaintop was not my future or my past. It was a recognition of a wise soul who wished to guide me to love in this lifetime—to an incredible love that came in the form of my husband Aaron, and in the form of our son, Logan, who is now three years old and eagerly awaiting the arrival of his younger sister, due to arrive any day now. I cannot wait for my labor to begin, so that I can hold her in my arms at last, as I held Logan on the day of his birth, when everything finally became clear, and the last piece of the puzzle fell into place.

Logan had been the wise soul who reached out to me from beyond and guided me to higher knowledge and truer love.

Today, as I look back over the challenges and obstacles I encountered on my journey toward this bliss, I understand that my rational mind—the part of me that required physical proof that Aaron and I were meant to be together, or the practical side of me that once thought Mark was the one—had gotten in my way. Looking for the logic had stopped me from following my intuition and my heart.

The same thing got in Aaron's way in the early days of our reunion, but today, all doubts and fears are gone. I feel a tremendous inner peace in regard to the choices I have made, and the limitless future before us. I love Aaron and our two children with all my heart and soul. I also know that this love is eternal, and when we must step apart at the end of our lives, we will eventually come together again, somehow, in heaven or in another life.

As for Jack, I worry that he, Aaron, and I are doomed to continue repeating this cycle—that I will meet Jack again, and I will always choose Aaron, and Jack will never be able to forgive. He will distance himself from us to escape the frustration and anguish, and to wallow in the anger he feels toward his brother.

Neither I nor Aaron have heard from Jack since the day Logan was born, when Jack sent me flowers in the hospital to congratulate me. He signed the card "With love," and later I heard from Aaron's mother, Margie, that Jack had decided to leave the country and work abroad as a foreign correspondent for CNN.

I hope, in the end, that he finds the happiness and bliss he so deeply deserves. When that happens, I suspect he will have an amazing story to tell—a story about miracles and magic, because he was always, at heart, a loving, extraordinary soul.

As for Aaron and me, we wake up each morning feeling incredibly blessed by the bounty in our lives. We enjoy our work, we adore our beautiful son Logan, and we look forward to our daughter's arrival.

I keep in touch with Bailey—who I am convinced is a soul-sister I've known forever. I am certain we will always be friends. And there are others in my life who have come and gone, having made their mark on me in some way, or taught me something about myself, about love, God, or life. They are never forgotten.

We are all still learning about ourselves and what is possible in this awe-inspiring world. The journey continues, and I will treasure every moment, forever and always, and I hope you will, too.

Dear Reader,

Thank you for taking the time to read *THE COLOR OF FOREVER*. I hope you enjoyed Katelyn's story and will look for the next book in the series: Jack's story, *THE COLOR OF A PROMISE*.

If this is your first time reading a book in my *Color of Heaven Series*, I encourage you to start at the beginning with the first novel, *THE COLOR OF HEAVEN*. There are many books available in the series, and they all address the theme of real-life magic and everyday miracles, big and small. Read on for a complete list and descriptions of the other books.

In case you are wondering, each novel stands alone, so you can enjoy any of the books without reading the previous title. But if you choose to read them in order, you may enjoy how each book leads into the next and how certain characters, like Jack in this novel, reappear later to have their stories told.

If you enjoyed the historical section of this book, you might also enjoy my historical romances, most of which take place in the late-Victorian period. But I warn you—unlike my *Color of Heaven Series*, my historical romances have explicit love scenes, so if that is not your cup of tea…

Before we part ways, I'll invite you to visit my website at www.juliannemaclean.com to learn more about my books and writing life, and while you're there please sign up for my email newsletter so I can keep you informed about when a new *Color of Heaven* novel is released. You can also follow me on Facebook and Twitter.

As always, happy reading!
Julianne

The COLOR *of* HEAVEN

Book One

A deeply emotional tale about Sophie Duncan, a successful columnist whose world falls apart after her daughter's unexpected illness and her husband's shocking affair. When it seems nothing else could possibly go wrong, her car skids off an icy road and plunges into a frozen lake. There, in the cold dark depths of the water, a profound and extraordinary experience unlocks the surprising secrets from Sophie's past, and teaches her what it means to truly live...and love.

Full of surprising twists and turns and a near-death experience that will leave you breathless, this story is not to be missed.

"A gripping, emotional tale you'll want to read in one sitting." – *New York Times* bestselling author, Julia London

"Brilliantly poignant mainstream tale." – 4 ½ starred review, *Romantic Times*

The COLOR *of* DESTINY

Book Two

Eighteen years ago a teenage pregnancy changed Kate Worthington's life forever. Faced with many difficult decisions, she chose to follow her heart and embrace an uncertain future with the father of her baby – her devoted first love.

At the same time, in another part of the world, sixteen-year-old Ryan Hamilton makes his own share of mistakes, but learns important lessons along the way. Twenty years later, Kate's and Ryan's paths cross in a way they could never expect, which makes them question the possibility of destiny. Even when all seems hopeless, could it be that everything happens for a reason, and we end up exactly where we are meant to be?

The COLOR *of* HOPE

Book Three

Diana Moore has led a charmed life. She is the daughter of a wealthy senator and lives a glamorous city life, confident that her handsome live-in boyfriend Rick is about to propose. But everything is turned upside down when she learns of a mysterious woman who works nearby – a woman who is her identical mirror image.

Diana is compelled to discover the truth about this woman's identity, but the truth leads her down a path of secrets, betrayals, and shocking discoveries about her past. These discoveries follow her like a shadow.

Then she meets Dr. Jacob Peterson—a brilliant cardiac surgeon with an uncanny ability to heal those who are broken. With his help, Diana embarks upon a journey to restore her belief in the human spirit, and recover a sense of hope - that happiness, and love, may still be within reach for those willing to believe in second chances.

The COLOR *of*
A DREAM

Book Four

Nadia Carmichael has had a lifelong run of bad luck. It begins on the day she is born, when she is separated from her identical twin sister and put up for adoption. Twenty-seven years later, not long after she is finally reunited with her twin and is expecting her first child, Nadia falls victim to a mysterious virus and requires a heart transplant.

Now recovering from the surgery with a new heart, Nadia is haunted by a recurring dream that sets her on a path to discover the identity of her donor. Her efforts are thwarted, however, when the father of her baby returns to sue for custody of their child. It's not until Nadia learns of his estranged brother Jesse that she begins to explore the true nature of her dreams, and discover what her new heart truly needs and desires…

The COLOR *of* A MEMORY

Book Five

Audrey Fitzgerald believed she was married to the perfect man - a heroic firefighter who saved lives, even beyond his own death. But a year later she meets a mysterious woman who has some unexplained connection to her husband….

Soon Audrey discovers that her husband was keeping secrets and she is compelled to dig into his past. Little does she know… this journey of self-discovery will lead her down a path to a new and different future - a future she never could have imagined.

The COLOR *of* LOVE

Book Six

Carla Matthews is a single mother struggling to make ends meet and give her daughter Kaleigh a decent upbringing. When Kaleigh's absent father Seth—a famous alpine climber who never wanted to be tied down—begs for a second chance at fatherhood, Carla is hesitant because she doesn't want to pin her hopes on a man who is always seeking another mountain to scale. A man who was never willing to stay put in one place and raise a family.

But when Seth's plane goes missing after a crash landing in the harsh Canadian wilderness, Carla must wait for news…Is he dead or alive? Will the wreckage ever be found?

One year later, after having given up all hope, Carla receives a phone call that shocks her to her core. A man has been found, half-dead, floating on an iceberg in the North Atlantic, uttering her name. Is this Seth? And is it possible that he will come home to her and Kaleigh at last, and be the man she always dreamed he would be?

The COLOR *of* THE SEASON

Book Seven

Boston cop, Josh Wallace, is having the worst day of his life. First, he's dumped by the woman he was about to propose to, then everything goes downhill from there when he is shot in the line of duty. While recovering in the hospital, he can't seem to forget the woman he wanted to marry, nor can he make sense of the vivid images that flashed before his eyes when he was wounded on the job. Soon, everything he once believed about his life begins to shift when he meets Leah James, an enigmatic resident doctor who somehow holds the key to both his past and his future…

The COLOR *of* JOY

Book Eight

After rushing to the hospital for the birth of their third child, Riley and Lois James anticipate one of the most joyful days of their lives. But things take a dark turn when their newborn daughter vanishes from the hospital. Is this payback for something in Riley's troubled past? Or is it something even more mysterious?

As the search intensifies and the police close in, strange and unbelievable clues about the whereabouts of the newborn begin to emerge, and Riley soon finds himself at the center of a surprising turn of events that will challenge everything he once believed about life, love, and the existence of miracles.

The COLOR *of* TIME

Book Nine

They say it's impossible to change the past…

Since her magical summer romance at the age of sixteen, Sylvie Nichols has never been able to forget her first love. Years later, when she returns to the seaside town where she lost her heart to Ethan Foster, she is determined to lay the past to rest once and for all. But letting go becomes a challenge when Sylvie finds herself transported back to that long ago summer of love…and the turbulent events that followed. Soon, past and present begin to collide in strange and mystifying ways, and Sylvie can't help but wonder if a true belief in miracles is powerful enough to change both her past and her future….

"The Color of Time is an emotionally charged, riveting exploration of how our lives may change within the scope of a single event. And sometimes what we want isn't always what we need. Fabulous, thought-provoking read."

—Tanya Anne Crosby,
New York Times bestselling author

"I never know what to say about a Julianne MacLean book, except to say YOU HAVE TO READ IT. I always find myself very introspective after reading one of her books and The Color of Time was no exception…In the end, Sylvie's story ends up the way it was meant to be, but she and the reader take a wonderful, heartbreaking, mysterious path to get there. It's so difficult to discuss much about this book without divulging spoilers, so I'll just reiterate what I said at the beginning. YOU HAVE TO READ THIS BOOK."

—AllRomanceReader.ca

The COLOR *of* FOREVER

Book Ten

Recently divorced television reporter Katelyn Roberts has stopped believing in relationships that last forever, until a near-death experience during a cycling accident changes everything. When she miraculously survives unscathed, a deeply-buried memory leads her to the quaint, seaside town of Cape Elizabeth, Maine.

There, on the rugged, windswept coast of the Atlantic, she finds herself caught up in the secrets of a historic inn that somehow calls to her from the past. Is it possible that the key to her true destiny lies beneath all that she knows, as she explores the grand mansion and its property? Or that the great love she's always dreamed about is hidden in the alcoves of its past?

Praise for Julianne MacLean's
Historical Romances

"MacLean's compelling writing turns this simple, classic love story into a richly emotional romance, and by combining engaging characters with a unique, vividly detailed setting, she has created an exceptional tale for readers who hunger for something a bit different in their historical romances."

—BOOKLIST

"You can always count on Julianne MacLean to deliver ravishing romance that will keep you turning pages until the wee hours of the morning."

—Teresa Medeiros

"Julianne MacLean's writing is smart, thrilling, and sizzles with sensuality."

—Elizabeth Hoyt

"Scottish romance at its finest, with characters to cheer for, a lush love story, and rousing adventure. I was captivated from the very first page. When it comes to exciting Highland romance, Julianne MacLean delivers."

—Laura Lee Guhrke

"She is just an all-around wonderful writer, and I look forward to reading everything she writes."

About the Author

Julianne MacLean is a *USA Today* bestselling author of over twenty historical romances, including The Highlander Series with St. Martin's Press and her popular American Heiress Series with Avon/Harper Collins. She also writes contemporary mainstream fiction, and THE COLOR OF HEAVEN was a *USA Today* bestseller. She is a three-time RITA finalist, and has won numerous awards, including the Booksellers' Best Award, the Book Buyer's Best Award, and a Reviewers' Choice Award from Romantic Times for Best Regency Historical of 2005. She lives in Nova Scotia with her husband and daughter, and is a dedicated member of Romance Writers of Atlantic Canada. Please visit Julianne's website at www.juliannemaclean.com for more information and to subscribe to her mailing list to stay informed about upcoming releases.

OTHER BOOKS BY
JULIANNE MACLEAN

The American Heiress Series:
To Marry the Duke
An Affair Most Wicked
My Own Private Hero
Love According to Lily
Portrait of a Lover
Surrender to a Scoundrel

The Pembroke Palace Series:
In My Wildest Fantasies
The Mistress Diaries
When a Stranger Loves Me
Married By Midnight
A Kiss Before the Wedding - A Pembroke Palace Short Story
Seduced at Sunset

The Highlander Series:
The Rebel – A Highland Short Story
Captured by the Highlander
Claimed by the Highlander
Seduced by the Highlander
Return of the Highlander
Taken by the Highlander

The Royal Trilogy:
Be My Prince
Princess in Love
The Prince's Bride

Western and Colonial Historical Romances:
Prairie Bride
The Marshal and Mrs. O'Malley
Adam's Promise

Time Travel Romance
Taken by the Cowboy

Contemporary Fiction:
The Color of Heaven
The Color of Destiny
The Color of Hope
The Color of a Dream
The Color of a Memory
The Color of Love
The Color of the Season
The Color of Joy
The Color of Time
The Color of Forever
The Color of a Promise
The Color of a Christmas Miracle

Made in the USA
Middletown, DE
12 October 2018